BODY COUNT

FBI-K9 Series - Book 2

JODI BURNETT

 Created with Vellum

To all my fellow writers who teach me, challenge me, and insist I keep getting those words down.

Prologue

✥

The skin on Susan's neck and shoulders bunched sending a cold tremor through her body. Night sounds filled the surrounding forest. A silent presence lurked in the darkness beyond her view, outside the glow of campfire light—something perceived, yet unseen.

"Did you guys hear that?" Kiera Johnson, a twenty-two-year-old yoga instructor, sat up with a start. Her long, multi-colored, streaked blonde hair swung over her shoulder as she peered into the blackness.

All six women in the group quieted and listened to the chirps, clicks, and distant hoots in the dark woods surrounding them.

Susan stared at the impenetrable velvet that enveloped their circle of light like a blackout curtain and shivered. "I only hear crickets and an occasional owl." She strained her ears and wondered if she should share the sense of being watched she'd felt on and off all day with the others.

The uncomfortable inkling impressed itself upon her a

few hours after their small troupe separated from the larger women's conference for a white-water rafting excursion down the Arkansas River.

"I'll be glad to get back to the convention tomorrow, but spending the night up here under the stars for one night suits me. Noises and all." Audrey, a pixie sized fireball stood and stretched. "Riding the rapids today was a blast."

Susan had always wanted to try river rafting. The experience was thrilling and definitely team building, but now she felt vulnerable in the deep Rocky Mountain woods with only five other women. Something eerie prowled the outskirts of their camp in the dark, she felt it. Her mind shot back to the memory of her near kidnapping by a serial killer in the grocery store parking-lot six months ago. Susan had her pepper-spray then and escaped capture, but the fear never fully went away. *I'm probably just overreacting because of that experience.* She rubbed her arms to warm up and also in an attempt to rub away her anxiety.

Heat from the campfire warmed the soles of her hiking boots as she propped her feet up on the stones circling the undulating flames. Susan, and those she shared the glow with, were there together for a Women Entrepreneurs Strength Building Conference.

Audrey sat next to her and poked at the fire with a long stick. "What business did you say you were in?"

Susan continued to rub the chill from her arms. "I'm a nutritionist by trade. I want to build an online presence and counsel people, one-on-one, regarding their dietary choices and health goals."

"You want to? Is this a new business venture?"

"Yeah." Susan laughed softly. "Instead of waiting until I was successful enough to quit my day job at a long-term-care facility, I quit and dove headfirst into running my own business. Now, if I'm being honest, I'd have to admit I'm in way over my head. It's much harder to get clients than I expected."

Audrey raised her auburn brows. "Well, I guess you'll sink or swim. You can always get another nutritionist job if you have to. I think it's awesome that you just went for it." She held her hand up for a high-five. "Way to go."

The evening's beer-brats and baked bean supper sat contentedly in Susan's belly. She sipped a decent Cabernet with dark cherry undertones out of a tin cup and listened to the others share their specific challenges as women who owned their own businesses. The ladies gathered around the fire represented organizations of all kinds. It both comforted and encouraged Susan to spend the long weekend with these smart and ambitious business owners.

Nancy Kaufman, a freelance bookkeeper, crossed and uncrossed her arms. She glanced over both of her shoulders intermittently. "I don't like it. What if something comes into our camp? Like a bear?"

"As long as we clean up our trash and store our food properly, we'll be fine. Bears would rather leave people alone." Nora James, their stout, out-doorsey rafting guide, poked the fire with a stick. "I'm sure what you're hearing is nothing more than exhaustion allowing your imagination to go wild."

Susan acknowledged the truth of Nora's statement in the weariness of her bones. "You're probably right. After spending the day rafting the river, the sun and water are now demanding their tariff." Sleepiness plucked at her eyes, and Susan yawned. It took extreme effort to move her fatigued limbs.

Prue Wilkens, owner of a women's boutique, stood and

stretched. "I for one am worn out after all the sun and fighting the rapids. I'm turning in." She clicked on a flashlight and made her way to a tent pitched about thirty feet away from the campfire. Unzipping the door, she slid through the nylon opening and morphed instantly into a two-dimensional silhouette that shimmied on the side of the shelter.

A whirring noise sounded from just beyond the camp. "Seriously, guys. You heard that, right?" Kiera shifted closer to the fire.

"Most likely an owl." Nora peered into the star filled sky. "They're silent on approach. You can't hear their wings until after they fly by. Kind of like a Stealth Bomber. Have any of you ever seen one of those at an air show?"

Several heads shook no.

Susan nodded. "I saw them do a fly-by in formation, once. They're pretty awesome, and you're right. I didn't hear them coming, but they blew my eardrums out once they passed by."

"What do we do if it *is* a bear, Nora?" Nancy stood and turned her back to the fire, rubbing away the goose-bumps on her arms. "How do we protect ourselves?"

"Great question and now's the perfect time to talk about it." She angled toward the tents. "Can you hear me in there, Prue?"

"Loud and clear."

"Okay, first of all, you ladies may have noticed that I bagged all our food and garbage then hung it in that tree with a couple of ropes." Nora gestured to three large canvas bags hanging about fifteen feet off the ground. "We equipped all the tents with a flashlight and bear spray. Don't sleep in the clothes you cooked or ate in and do not take any food into your tents. If a bear, or any wildlife enters the camp, make lots of noise. That alone usually scares them away."

Susan thought about her eerie sensation of being watched. Perhaps it was a wild animal that had been stalking them. Either way, she was certain that whatever caused her internal alert system to go off was real. She wished she'd brought a weapon. Lowering her feet from the ring of rocks, Susan folded her legs into a crisscross position.

"It sure is beautiful up here—hard to believe there could be anything dangerous around." Audrey, placed a few more pieces of wood on the fire. "I'm surprised it's not developed yet. Who owns this land?"

Susan winked at her, happy to move away from the topic of bears. "Planning on moving from selling real-estate to development?"

"You never know. I could probably make a fortune if I did." Audrey waggled her red brows.

Nora carried a bucket of water she had filled earlier from the river toward the flames. "Not out here, you won't. We're deep in the middle of tens of thousands of acres of BLM country. The government owns this property, and it isn't for sale. At least not for anytime in the near future."

"BLM?" Kiera stretched and then bent over in a forward fold with her hands flat on the ground.

"Bureau of Land Management." Nora set the bucket down. "Everyone ready to hit the hay?"

Audrey stood and shook out her limbs. "I guess it's that time."

"Yep, I'm turning in." Susan untwisted her legs and

pushed herself to her feet. "Anything we can do to help out here, Nora?"

"Nope—just dowsing the fire to make sure it's out. Then I'm hitting the rack too."

As soon as Susan stepped away from the flames, she was cold. She'd always enjoyed camping as a girl in scouts, but she hated when it came time to get into a freezing sleeping-bag.

"I'll be up early tomorrow, if anyone wants to join me for morning yoga." Kiera stretched, with her hands above her head, and then leaned to her side. "We'll welcome the sun."

"Sounds good." Susan clicked on her mag-light. "I'll meet you out here at dawn. Are you ready to go to the tent, Nancy?"

Nancy latched onto Susan's arm, and Keira skipped to catch up with them. "Can I walk with you? Prue took our flashlight already."

They made their way to the tents. After saying good-night, Susan and Nancy ducked inside theirs. Susan shook off her jeans, rubbing her hands up and down her legs for friction. "It's so cold."

"I didn't think it could be this cold in the middle of June." Nancy wriggled into her sleeping bag with all of her clothes on.

"Some years it can even snow up here in the summer." Susan changed into thermal underwear, rushing to pull clothing on between the freezing air and her bare skin. She slid into her sub-zero mummy bag and clicked off the light. In a few short minutes, she was toasty warm.

"Susan? Do you think there are bears out there? Are you scared?" Nancy's voice quavered.

Something was out there, but not wanting to make

things worse for Nancy, Susan kept her sensations to herself. "No. I mean, I'm sure there's wildlife, but nothing that wants to harm us. Don't worry. Get some sleep. Morning will be here soon and with it, the warmth of the sun."

The wind blustered through the night. At one point, something knocked into the camp supplies out by the firepit. Susan slept fitfully and heard Nancy tossing and turning as well. But at dawn, the sun rose with a golden charm and defrosted the early hours. No bears, no mountain lions, no specters—or whatever Susan imagined was watching them—had attacked during the long night. When Susan and Nancy emerged from their tent, Prue was already up percolating coffee in a pot over the fire.

Susan drew a deep satisfying breath in through her nose. "One of the most magnificent scents in the world is fresh coffee brewing on a crisp, cool morning in the mountains." Susan approached the flames and held her hands out to the warmth. "Good morning, Prue. Thanks for getting the heat going."

"Morning." Prue handed both Susan and Nancy tin cups. "I thought maybe Nora would have started things, but she's not up yet and I didn't want to wait."

"I, for one, am glad you didn't." Susan pulled her sleeve down over her hand to protect her skin from the heat and reached for the coffeepot. She filled Nancy's cup and then her own. Susan normally preferred herbal tea to start her day, but the scent of coffee was too enticing in the coolness of the morning.

Keira and Audrey emerged from their tents. Keira's fresh-faced appearance was the same day and night, but Audrey—who leaned more toward full-on battle makeup and professionally blown-out hair—appeared a little rough around the edges.

"Coffee?" Audrey stumbled in the direction of the fire ring.

Prue wrapped a cloth over the handle of the pot and poured her a cup. "Keira?"

"No thanks. I'll have tea after my yoga practice. Anyone want to join me?"

Susan raised her mug. "I will, as soon as I finish this." She sipped the steaming rich brew.

Prue nudged Nancy. "Help me pull those bags down from the tree. Then you, Audrey and I can get breakfast going while those two do their sun-salutations."

Glancing around the camp, Audrey asked, "Where's Nora?"

"Isn't she still in your tent?" Susan cocked her head.

Audrey shrugged. "No. She got up before dawn and went out to start the fire."

Prue and Nancy carried the sacks to the firepit. Nancy dropped her bag and said, "No she didn't. Prue started the fire. I haven't seen Nora."

Susan set her cup on a stump. "Maybe she went down to the river to get water or check on the raft?" She peered into the surrounding trees. The camp looked completely different in the morning with the bright sun glinting through the tall pines. It was peaceful and comforting after her fretful night. No ghosts or goblins in sight.

"Probably." Prue rummaged in the food and dish bags. "Let's get breakfast going."

Susan chose to eat over practicing yoga, so Keira meditated on her own until the cured scent of bacon sizzling over the flames drew everyone to the fire ring. As Susan sipped from her steaming cup, the prickly sense of being spied upon returned, pervading her awareness. She glanced furtively around, but seeing nothing, she helped Prue scramble the eggs. She fried them with hash browns, all while keeping one eye on the pan and the other on the edge of the forest.

"Nora should be back by now. Do you think we should check on her?" Nancy paced, tapping the rim of her coffee cup with nervous fingers.

Susan handed the spatula to Audrey. "Will you watch the food? I'll go down to the river and look for her."

"I'll come with you." Prue set a stack of plates down next to the cooking station.

Keira picked up two collapsible water jugs and passed one to Nancy. "We can fill these up while we're down there."

"Be right back," Susan called over her shoulder to Audrey as she led the way down the path to the water. Sun dappled the narrow trail through the canopy of aspen and pines, and a chipmunk skittered in front of them, ducking inside his hiding place in a gray rock outcropping. Fresh air invigorated her as Susan edged down the steep track to the river. The ground leveled out at the muddy bank where they had secured their float the day before.

Susan stopped abruptly, and Nancy bumped into her from behind. "Hey. Where's the raft? Isn't this where we left it?" A cold tremor ricocheted through her body. Prue, Nancy, and Keira gathered around her and they all stood staring at the matted grasses where they had tied the craft after yesterday's excursion.

"Could it have blown into the river with last night's wind?" Prue stepped to the edge of the water and looked up and down the rapids.

"I don't think so. Nora lashed it to that tree." Susan

pointed at a rope knotted around a thick pine trunk. "Look, it's been cut."

"Did Nora leave us here?" Nancy crossed her arms over her middle. "Maybe it's a team building challenge?"

"I doubt it." Susan inspected the rope. "I don't think she'd leave the group here on purpose. Maybe she was cutting the raft loose, and the wind caught it, knocking her into the river?"

"Let's see if we can find her." Prue jogged down the path along the bank and called over her shoulder. "She might need our help."

Susan followed, but drew up short as they rounded the next bend. Her stomach hardened into a tight fist. The bright yellow float, turned upside-down at the edge of the water, was caught on a broken branch and bobbed up and down with the current. A booted foot peeked out from under the side of the craft.

"Nora!" Susan ran past Prue and sprinted to the float. Prue was at her heels and together they lifted the heavy raft, turning it right-side up and shoving it over. Underneath, Nora floated face-down in the water. Her short hair swam with the ripples of the water, rinsing tendrils of blood away from an injury on the side of her head.

From her spot on the trail Nancy screamed, and Keira took the woman in her arms, tucking her head into her shoulder. Susan leapt into the river and struggled to turn Nora over. Prue helped her and together they pulled Nora up onto the dry bank.

Susan's fingers sought a pulse and not finding one, she immediately started chest compressions. Nora's blank, open eyes registered no life. Susan told herself not to panic, but her body refused to heed her order. Sharp nerves jabbed her scalp and torso.

"Oh, my God! She's dead!" Nancy cried.

Susan shuddered at what she knew to be the truth.

Kiera's wide-eyed gaze sought Susan. "She could have been down here since dawn needing our help."

"We didn't know. Couldn't have known." Prue's eye darted around the scene as though trying to make sense of it all. "She shouldn't have come down here by herself. Isn't that one of the big rules of being in the wilderness?" She covered her face with her hands. "Oh, God! What are we going to do?"

Susan continued the chest compressions until she exhausted herself, but to no avail. Finally, she sat back. "Does anyone have a phone?"

Keira took a deep breath. "No, remember they had us all turn them in at registration?"

"Surely, Nora had a way to contact the retreat center. What if someone got hurt and needed help?" Prue squatted and patted Nora's pockets. She pulled out a water-logged Samsung and held it up, dripping. "Damn."

"Okay. Well, let's get the raft up out of the river and secure it to a tree. We'll have to work together to lift Nora inside the craft." Susan left Nora's body and grasped onto a handle on the side of the boat.

Nancy's tear-filled voice bounced off the trees. "We can't be on the river without a guide."

Susan straightened and pressed her hands to her hips. "Look Nancy, we don't have a choice. We have no means of contacting anyone and no other option than to try to find our way to the main group. You need to buck up and help us with this raft."

Nancy sniffled, but together they tied the float, with Nora aboard, to a thick tree and hiked back up to the camp to tell Audrey what happened.

"Audrey?" Susan called out when they returned to their firepit. "Audrey!"

There was no answer. Eggs and hash browns were burnt to ash in the frying pan on the fire. Susan's gaze moved from the eggs to where the bacon had been cooking. Congealing fat smeared the pan, but all the meat was gone.

Prue strode to the row of tents and opened the flap to Audrey and Nora's tent. She stuck her face inside and then withdrew. She shook her head. "No one."

Susan's pulse rate spiked. "Audrey!" She yelled into the wilderness. She turned around, taking in the details of the camp. "Maybe she tried to follow us and got lost? We should have never left her here alone."

Nancy wilted to the ground in tears, mumbling incomprehensible syllables. Kiera huddled over her like a mother hen. Susan met Prue's gaze. "Let's check to see if there's anything missing."

Prue leaned into her and whispered, "I'm scared, Susan."

Susan clenched her teeth together and drew a deep breath in through her nose. "I am too, but we must stay focused, find Audrey, and figure out how to make it out of here."

Prue pulled a tent stake from the ground. "Should we break down the tents?"

"No, the conference organizers can return for this stuff later. Right now, we just need to get down the river and back to civilization." Susan crossed the camp to Kiera and Nancy and knelt down. "Come on, you two. Pack only what is essential. As soon as we find Audrey, we're getting out of here."

On their way to the tents, Kiera kept her arm around

Nancy, holding her tight. Prue rifled through the food bag and filled her backpack with protein bars, fruit, and nuts for their trip. Susan poured water over the ashes smoldering in the fire-pit.

Unzipping the fly to their tent, Nancy pulled back the flap, and shattered the morning with her scream.

Chapter One

❧❧❧

Burke Cameron opened the door of his silver Tacoma truck for Susan after he parked in the parking lot at Shanahan's Steakhouse in Greenwood Village. He was clean cut in his white button-down and navy blazer. His blonde hair, parted on the side and neatly combed over, held a slight glint of red. Susan met his sky-blue eyes as he helped her out of her seat.

"Thanks." She smiled and took his hand. When she stood, Susan breathed in his subtle aftershave, fresh, cool, and straightforward.

Burke pressed his warm, solid palm into the small of her back as he directed her toward the doors of the restaurant. "I hope you don't mind having dinner with my friends on our first official date?"

"Not at all." Susan smiled up at him.

"When Rick called, he said they had some news to celebrate."

"It really is fine. I've been looking forward to meeting them anyway after the whole serial killer situation." Susan thought back to the night when the FBI caught the crazed murderer who had at one point tried to kidnap her from the grocery store parking lot. "I'm thankful that none of you were hurt worse than you were during that investigation. How is Kendra doing?"

Burke nodded. "She's lucky to be alive." He paused before opening the door to touch her jaw with his fingertips. "So are you." He grasped the brass handle and pulled. "Kendra's tough. I think she's already shaken the incident off and is ready to catch the next criminal."

A tremor coursed across Susan's shoulders. "I'm just glad the FBI caught that guy and that he's behind bars now. The whole scenario was terrifying."

Susan stepped inside the restaurant and hesitated while her vision adjusted to the dark atmosphere. Soft piano music played under the murmured words of multiple conversations. Following the hostess, they passed by a wall-sized wine cooler and a round, glassed in bar. The woman led them to a table in the back of a dining room boasting an artsy chandelier crafted from gold and orange glass balls. A strikingly handsome man with jet-black hair and obsidian eyes stood as they approached.

He offered his hand to Burke, and they shook before he turned his gaze to her. "You must be Susan. Burke can't seem to stop talking about you." He flashed a brilliant smile at her. "I'm Rick Sanchez." Turning to his date he touched her shoulder. "This is Kendra Dean. I'm sure Burke told you we all work together."

Susan slid into the booth across from Burke's friends and smiled at the pretty, no nonsense, brunette. "It's nice to meet you both. I've heard a lot about you, too, and I'm not intimidated—at all—to be having dinner with three FBI agents." Susan laughed.

Kendra grinned. "Burke, everything you've been

gushing about is true. You'll have to work at keeping things closer to the vest if you hope to be a decent agent. But, I have to admit, you're right, Susan *is* beautiful." She snickered, and heat bloomed on Burke's fair-skinned neck.

Taking pity on him, Susan countered. "Burke told me what he could about the night Abbot Lee abducted you, Kendra. You must have been terrified. I know how scared I was when he tried to take me."

The humor left Kendra's warm brown eyes, and she swallowed. "It was scary, that's for sure, but I have a great team and they came to my rescue." She reached for Rick's arm and his hand covered hers. They shared a look before he leaned over and kissed her cheek, whispering something into her ear. Kendra responded with a soft, adoring smile. Susan felt as though she intruded on a private moment and envied their obvious affection.

She glanced at Burke and saw that he too watched them with a wistful expression. He noticed her gaze and winked at her.

Rick sat forward. "We invited you to dinner tonight because we're celebrating."

Burke cocked his head in question, but Susan thought she knew—if the look on Kendra's face meant what she figured it did.

Kendra thrust her left hand across the table at him. A flash of glittering white-light sparkled from her finger. "We're engaged!"

Burke reached for her fingers as a genuine smile warmed his face. "That's great you guys. Congratulations." He lifted his chin toward Rick. "You're a lucky man, Sanchez. You better take good care of her, or you'll have to deal with me."

"No worries there." Rick's black eyes glittered.

"What a lovely ring." Susan leaned over for a better view. "It suits you, I think." She peered at the sparkling gem.

A bright smile lit Kendra's features as she displayed her new engagement solitaire.

Their server arrived and Susan asked for the Ahi, the others wanted steak. Burke ordered a bottle of champagne, and they toasted the future while waiting for their meals to arrive. The fish practically melted on her tongue and she closed her eyes in pleasure as she savored the rich flavor of tuna enhanced by the heat of a spicy wasabi sauce. The food choice was only one of several indicators that Susan differed completely from the others at the table.

The most obvious, of course, was that all three of the other diners were FBI agents, whereas Susan was employed by a retirement home as a nutritionist. Then, there was the concealed carry issue. Burke, Rick, and Kendra all carried pistols strapped to their bodies underneath their dark blazers. Guns made Susan nervous. She had worn a flirty, floral dress that could never hide something cold and hard like a handgun. The people sitting across from her were serious, professionals. Susan worked with the elderly, many of whom were gradually losing their cognitive processes and it was necessary to maintain a good sense of humor. Though she felt rather out of her element with these new acquaintances, still she was truly enjoying the dinner and the company.

"Tell me what it's like being an FBI agent. Are you constantly scared?"

The men glanced at her sideways, but Kendra gave her a warm smile. "No. The truth is, as with most law enforcement work, we spend most of our time doing paperwork, or talking to witnesses, and running down leads. I have it a little better than these guys, because I get to spend the majority of my time with my new K9 partner, Annie. She's a chocolate lab, who has a great nose for sniffing."

"Burke told me what happened to your bloodhound. I was sorry to hear about that. How's he doing?"

Kendra's eyes suddenly glistened with tears, but she laughed. "Baxter's loving retirement. Losing a leg hasn't deterred him from enjoying life. Now all he does is eat, play, and sleep."

"Sounds like the title of a book," Burke teased.

"Right?" Kendra grinned at him. "But we'd have to include something about love. He's absolutely smitten with Annie."

"Eat, Play, Love?" Susan laughed. "Well, that's a good thing. Poor guy." Susan swallowed and picked at some lettuce with the tines of her fork. The table grew quiet as the diners enjoyed their food. After swallowing a bite of Ahi, Susan looked around at her new friends and asked "How long did it take you guys to get comfortable with carrying guns all the time?"

"I suppose we each got used to it when we were in the service." Burke reached for her hand and she welcomed the touch. "Rick and I were both in the Marine Corps. Kendra worked with military K9s in the Army."

"Oh." Susan sipped the Sauvignon Blanc she ordered with her meal, wondering if she had anything at all in common with them. "I bet you all agree with stricter gun laws, though, since you have to face the bad guys on a daily basis."

Three sets of eyes stared at her from under three scrunched brows. *That was obviously the wrong thing to say to this crowd.*

Kendra tilted her head to the side and deftly changed the subject. "Burke tells us you're a nutritionist?"

The last thing Susan wanted to do was explain her dreary job in the nursing home kitchen, but she was thankful for the escape Kendra offered her. "Yes. But I'm hoping to launch an online business and offer personal diet and health counseling."

"Wow. I'm always impressed by people who are brave enough to start their own business. How will you go about it?" Kendra seemed genuinely interested, and Susan was grateful to her for drawing her in and helping her feel more comfortable.

"I've been blogging about nutrition and healthy lifestyles for a couple of years now, and I have a pretty decent following. I'll start with them and offer one-on-one personal nutritional counseling." She sipped her wine.

Kendra nodded. "That sounds interesting. Do you think you'll be able to make a living at it?"

"I do—eventually. Though my mother isn't so sure." Susan grimaced. "She says I'm crazy—that it's too big of a risk."

Burke raised a bite of perfectly cooked steak to his mouth, but hesitated. "Maybe she thinks you might want to have a family one day and knows how hard that would be while trying to run a business?"

Both women's brows shot up, and Kendra's lips flattened into a flat line. Rick's eyes rounded, and he shook his head at Burke. "That's dangerous territory, man." He joked to ease the sudden ire at the table.

Susan tucked Burke's comment away for the time being. Her mother had never said anything like that, so she wondered where Burke was coming from. Did *he* believe she wasn't capable of running a business and having a family too?

Choosing to ignore Burke, Kendra continued. "I'm sure you've looked into all the details. I think you should go for it. It might be awhile before you're able to support yourself completely, but that's kind of the beauty of it. You can learn the ropes as you go, while keeping your current job. Besides, risk is good for us. You should do something every day that scares you at least a little."

The side of Rick's mouth hitched up into a half smile. "To be honest, Susan, I'm not sure you should take advice from this one." He tilted his head toward Kendra. "She thrives on risk and finds trouble around every corner."

Kendra poked him in the ribs with her elbow. "I do not. Besides, I may have found my share of trouble, but if that didn't happen, we wouldn't be sitting here together."

"I'd like to think we'd have figured things out without your life being in the balance." Rick leaned toward Kendra and brushed a kiss across her cheek. She responded with a soft curve of her lips.

Susan's heart glowed with a romantic warmth as she watched Rick and Kendra. "My adventure won't be anything as dramatic as yours, Kendra. Nobody's life will be in danger if I start my own business. The worst that could happen is my bank account might get a little tight."

Kendra flashed her a smile filled with encouragement. "Then I say, do it!"

Burke raised his glass. "Here, here!" He lifted Susan's hand to his lips, kissing the back of it. He gave her fingers a squeeze. "We'll help anyway we can." He turned to Rick and Kendra. "Won't we, guys?"

Rick grinned. "Sure. Your first client should be Burke. He eats fast-food for lunch almost every day."

"Shut-up." Burke laughed. "Who's the Chick-fil-A king at this table?"

"Don't leave Kendra out of this." Rick sat back and put his arm around his fiancée. "She has a wicked ice-cream addiction."

Susan beamed at her new friends. "Sounds like I have my work cut out for me already."

BURKE FINISHED HIS STEAK, SAVORING THE FINAL BITE with its peppery-garlic rub. It seemed to him that they'd all made it through any potential social landmines and were all laughing and relaxing, so he took the opportunity to slip his arm casually around Susan's shoulders. Without missing a beat, she leaned into him and edged closer in the booth. He sensed that Susan's initial tension had dissipated, and he'd have to thank Kendra later for smoothing the way.

They'd ordered red and white wine for the table, and as they sipped, jokes and stories were told over their glasses until the bottles were dry. Burke did his best to prevent the conversation from gravitating purely to tales of FBI cases, but it was hard when that was the lifestyle three of them lived. Still, Susan held her own and asked interesting questions.

Kendra waved to the server. "Can we see your dessert menu, please?"

Rick pulled her close. "What did I tell you? She has a sweet tooth."

"An occasional treat is good for the soul." Susan winked at Kendra.

"Is the operative word 'occasional'? Because, there is

nothing occasional about it," Rick teased.

Kendra held her arms up and shrugged. "Guilty. I'm not even going to try to come up with an excuse."

They lingered over fancy desserts of salted caramel crème brûlée and warm s'more brownies with coffee and an herbal tea for Susan, relaxing as though no one wanted the evening to end.

When they finally left, the night air flirted with a bitter chill and they rushed to their cars. After saying their goodbyes, Burke helped Susan into his truck.

"I hope you had a nice time tonight," he said, as he got behind the wheel.

Susan buckled her belt and smoothed the skirt of her dress over her lap. "I did. Your friends are fun. I can see why you like them."

A final knot released in Burke's shoulders. He'd cleared the first hurdle. Susan was adorable and full of energy. She was kind and funny. Burke had high hopes that their new relationship might build into something lasting. He wanted a family—kids, a dog, the picket fence. All of it. And he could picture it all with Susan, but for now, he would play it cool. He'd already seen that their worldviews were on opposite sides of the track, and he wasn't completely sure they could overcome that.

"You look deep in thought, though." Susan brushed her fingers across his shoulder. "Did *you* have a good time?"

Burke turned to gaze into her Prussian blue eyes and smiled. The urge to keep the truck in park and kiss her until dawn filled his mind, but he pushed the ignition button. "I had a great time. I hope you'll let me take you out again? Maybe our next date could be just the two of us?" When she smiled, he noticed the faint sprinkle of freckles dusting the bridge of her nose and cheeks and it charmed him.

"I would love that. Let's make it soon." With her spunky short hair-style and the sparkle in her eyes, she looked like a willowy pixie or woodland sprite, except for her height. She fit perfectly under his arm which meant she was around five foot, six or seven—too tall for a faerie.

His gaze drifted back to her mouth. "What kinds of things do you do for fun?"

"I'm game for any kind of adventure. I like to be active, so hiking, biking, I don't know. What do you like to do?"

"What do you think about camping?"

Her eyebrows quirked. "For a date?"

Burke chuckled. "No, sorry. I just meant, is it something you enjoy? It sounds like you enjoy being outdoors."

Her laugh circled him, and he settled into it. "Yes, I love camping. In fact, I've signed up for a conference for women entrepreneurs in June. Mostly the event takes place in a big mountain lodge, but I've also signed up for a team building excursion. A small group of us are going white-water rafting and camping overnight."

"Wow. Have you ever been?" Burke started his truck and pulled out of the parking lot.

"Rafting? No, but I think it looks like a blast."

"It's fun. Good for you." Burke merged onto the highway. "A women entrepreneur's conference, huh? So are you really planning to start your own business?"

"You sound skeptical. Don't you believe I can do it?"

Burke glanced at her and shook his head. "I don't doubt you can do it. I'm just wondering what your long-term goals are? In your life, I mean." Susan considered him for an extended moment and Burke wondered if he'd said something wrong, again.

"Owning a business *is* a long-term goal, don't you think?" Her tone seemed friendly on top, but there was a tenor underneath that sent a warning jolt to Burke's gut.

"Yes, of course, but I mean personal goals. Business is a professional venture."

She bit gently on her lower lip, her gaze not wavering from his face. "Does this have something to do with your question earlier about if I wanted a family?"

Burke swallowed. In for a penny, in for a pound. He plunged ahead. "Yeah, I guess that's what I'm asking. Do you?"

She narrowed her eyes slightly. "Yes, I do—someday. But, right now, that's not in the cards, so I'm focusing on other goals."

A smile burst across his face before he could temper it.

"How about you?" She turned in her seat, facing him.

"I do. I'd love to have a bunch of kids and a dog. The whole thing."

Susan laughed. "I meant, what do you like to do? But I can see where your mind is. Do you plan on having a mother for these imaginary future children of yours?"

Burke's neck heated, and his collar seemed to shrink a size. "Yeah, of course." He cleared his throat. "I like to play sports. I'm in a men's softball league, and I golf. Sometimes I go camping and fishing, and occasionally hunting when I can get away."

"Those all sound like things you could teach your future kids someday. Except maybe the hunting."

He fumbled with loosening his tie and undoing the top button of his shirt one-handed. He was an idiot. Why was he talking about wanting a family on their first date? She must think he's nuts. "That's the plan."

"Hey." Susan pressed his knee with her fingers and gave

it a gentle squeeze. "I'm just teasing you. It's a wonderful dream. Truly." She pulled her hand back into her own lap, and Burke missed the warmth on his leg. "How would that work, though? You, being an FBI agent *and* a dad? Yours is a dangerous job, isn't it?"

"It can be, but so is being a soldier, a cop, or a fireman. Men in all those careers have families. They make it work. Besides, it's a solid government job. One that still has benefits and a retirement."

"Hmm. Women work in those jobs too, I suppose. Like Kendra, for example. Do you think she and Rick will have kids?"

He smiled at the thought. "I'd be surprised if they didn't."

"Even though they're both in the FBI?"

He glanced at her to read her face. "I guess. I don't know. What are you getting at?"

"Just that Rick didn't seem like the kind of man who would expect his wife to quit her job to stay home with a family."

"Kendra wouldn't quit even if he wanted her to."

"That's my take on her too. Even though her work is dangerous."

"Are you trying to make a point?" Burke took the off-ramp that led to Susan's neighborhood.

"I'm just saying that working, or owning a business, doesn't preclude wanting to have a family."

Burke didn't respond immediately. He knew she was right, but when he dreamed of his own family, it looked like the one he was raised in. His mom was always home. He'd had a happy, stable childhood. It's what he wanted for his own kids. "Of course it doesn't. I don't think that. I just grew up in an old-fashioned family and it was good."

"My mother always worked, and I turned out okay, I think."

"You definitely did." Burke gave her an appreciative grin. "Was your dad around?"

"He's an attorney in Charleston. He was physically around, but never present, if you know what I mean."

"I'm sorry." He glanced at her and offered an apologetic smile. "What did your mom do?"

"She ran charities. It wasn't a paying job, but she worked harder than anyone I've ever known. Typical southern society kind of thing."

Burke pulled into Susan's apartment complex. "I liked your mom when I met her. That was the day I interviewed you about your attack. She's protective of you."

"That's an understatement. It felt like just the two of us for so many years, so I get it. She's extremely supportive of my business plan, by the way."

Burke parked in the lot. "No siblings, then?"

"Nope. You?"

"I have both a brother and a sister. Both younger."

"I bet you were a wonderful big brother. I always wanted one of those."

Burke walked Susan to her apartment door. When she opened her purse to look for her keys, he touched her chin and tipped her face up to his. "Tonight was fun."

"It was." She stared into his eyes.

Burke drew the moment out, letting the anticipation build before he lowered his mouth to hers. His heart pounded, but he held himself in check. He brushed his hand across her jaw and wove his fingers through her hair, drawing her into a deeper kiss. She slid her arms around his back and pressed into him. Burke breathed in her spicy deep floral scent. He'd have to step away soon if he was going to do it at all, so he shifted his weight to his heels.

"I'll call you in the morning," Burke murmured into her ear. "We can plan our next date." He pulled back.

Susan's eyes went from dreamy to confused and she cocked her head. Fortunately, a smile followed. "You really are a boy scout, aren't you?"

"Guilty." He wouldn't hold on to that image if he stood here much longer. He gripped his car keys with a jangle.

"I remember telling you I might have to try to change that." Her pert nose wrinkled when she laughed.

Unable to resist, he kissed the tip of it, then pressed his lips to her forehead. "I look forward to that."

Susan studied him and then stood on her toes to kiss his cheek. "I accept the challenge. I'll talk to you tomorrow." She unlocked her door and stepped inside.

Burke shoved his hands in his pockets and gazed at her. "Lock up." His voice was husky.

She gave him a smart grin. "What'll you do if I don't?"

"I'm afraid you'd win the 'destroy the boy scout challenge' without having to try."

Chapter Two

B urke was fifteen minutes late to work the next morning when he stepped off the elevator in the blue-glass, Denver FBI building and hustled toward his desk. Rick nodded at him from his office as Burke passed by.

"Hey, Cameron." As usual referring to each other by their last name when they were at work. "Late night?"

Burke turned back and leaned against Rick's door jamb. "Not too bad. Did you and Kendra have fun?"

"Yeah, and for what it's worth, we both really liked Susan."

Burke couldn't suppress his grin. "Yeah, she's amazing."

Rick chuckled. "In fact, she's meeting Kendra for lunch today. I think Kendra is giving her a tour of the K9 facility beforehand."

"Nice. Hopefully, Ken will build me up."

"You never know what women talk about." Rick chuffed. "So, obviously you two are going to see each other again?"

Burke grinned. "That's the plan, but we see a lot of things very differently, so we'll see how it goes."

"I gathered some of that last night with the gun laws comment."

"Exactly."

"Hell, you don't have to figure everything all out at once, do you?"

"No." Burke rubbed his chin. "Good point." *But I don't want to get in too deep if it isn't going anywhere.*

"On that note, if you want Susan to hang around, don't tell her you want to keep your future wife unemployed, barefoot, and pregnant."

"I didn't say that."

"You may as well have. Kendra bent my ear all the way back to her place about the *your wife could stay home with the kids* comment," Rick teased.

"There's nothing wrong with that." Burke crossed his arms.

"Not if the wife *wants* to stay home. Look, I know where you're coming from, but it's a whole new world out there, man."

"It's not that I don't think women are capable of whatever they want to do. Look at Kendra for example. She's one of the best agents we have, and she's way smarter than me. It's just I've always pictured my own family like the one I grew up in. It was a good way to grow up."

"I get you. But maybe you should wait to have those kinds of conversations until *well* after your first date." Rick smirked.

"No sense wasting time dating women who don't want the same things as I do. I'm not twenty anymore." Burke wanted to find a woman he loved, who he could raise a family with, and grow old with. Was that idea too old-fashioned?

"True, but you could scare any woman away with talk like that so soon." Rick laughed. "Now, get out of here. I've got a briefing on drugs and human trafficking at nine-thirty in the conference room."

Burke walked down the aisle to his cubicle. The office admin, Lucinda, glided toward him.

"Good morning, Burke." She purred, batting black eyelashes that were so thick and heavy he wondered how she held her eyes open. As she passed, Burke was enveloped in a cloud of spicy perfume. Lucinda was certainly sexy with her long blonde hair and even longer legs accentuated by sky-high heels, but he'd never gone for the dramatic, overly made-up type. He thought of Susan's natural beauty, her sunny energy, and his blood warmed.

"Morning." He nodded at Lucinda and turned into his space, avoiding any conversation. Burke had promised to call Susan this morning, and it looked like he might be tied up with some new cases involving the increase in human trafficking the rest of the day. He tapped her contact number on his phone.

Susan answered on the third ring.

"Hey, beautiful. What are you up to?"

"Hi. Just getting to work. You?"

"Looks like I'm in for a hectic day, so I wanted to call early to see if we could make plans to go out again."

Susan's tone broadened, and Burke could tell she smiled when she responded. "Great. When?"

"How about tomorrow? Do you have Saturdays off?"

"I do. What do you have in mind?"

"It's a surprise. I'll pick you up at two o'clock, if that works?"

"Sure. Now you have me curious. What should I wear?"

He laughed. "Wear something casual—comfortable." Burke leaned back in his chair and tapped a pen on the side of his desk. "I heard you were meeting Kendra for lunch today?"

"Well, I think it will end up being more like happy hour. I won't get out of here until three at the earliest. Kendra's going to show me around her work, and I get to meet some of the FBI dogs."

"Sounds like fun."

"Right? Well, I'd better get to work. I have hungry octogenarians to feed." Her giggle found its way inside his heart and he briefly closed his eyes, his mouth settling into a wide smile.

"Sounds good. I'll see you tomorrow, then."

Burke had just enough time to make a couple of reservations and shake off his dizzying sense of infatuation before he was due at the briefing.

SUSAN ARRIVED AT THE FBI K9 FACILITY AT THREE. SHE checked in at the reception desk and waited in the small anteroom for Kendra.

"Hi, Susan. Come on back." Kendra held the door for her. "Perfect timing. I just finished working with Annie. She's out in the turn-out yard now."

"How's the training going?"

Kendra's face brightened as she walked with Susan down a long, tiled hall. "Annie has a lot of natural talent and she loves to work. But she also loves to play. For her, it will be about disciplining her to know which behavior is appropriate when. She'll get there. She's still young."

"How's Baxter? Do you bring him in to work with you?"

A shadow moved through Kendra's eyes, and Susan regretted saying anything.

"No, he stays home. It would be too hard on him to sit on the sidelines when his friends are training." She bit her lower lip. "It would be hard on me too. So..."

"I'm sorry. I didn't mean to bring up a painful topic."

Kendra shook her head. "Not at all. It's an obvious question." She pushed the release bar on the door at the end of the hallway, and bright sunshine filled the space. "Let's go out and meet the crew."

Susan stepped outside into a wide alley of pea gravel that housed kennel runs on either side. The pens were vacant, and she assumed the dogs were all at work or in training. "Does Annie have her own kennel for when she's here?"

"She does, but mostly I keep her with me. Her training benefits from constant attention for now." Kendra pointed to a run on the end. "This is her space when she needs one." Kendra led the way out to a grassy area the size of half a football field. Four men and their K9 partners ran through different obstacle courses.

"This looks like a playground for dogs." Susan watched a German Shepherd leap over a six-foot fence. "Wow! I didn't know dogs could jump so high."

"Those dogs are practicing agility, balance, and strength." Kendra pointed to the end of the field where several old cars were parked. "That's where we begin practical training for searching out drugs, explosives, and so on."

"What else?"

"We train our sniffer dogs to use their senses to detect lots of substances such as explosives, illegal drugs, wildlife scat, currency, blood, and contraband electronics such as illicit mobile phones. Sniffers track people too, but in those cases they follow a specific scent we give them. Currently, we're working with these dogs to alert us to people who might be hiding inside of trunks or trucks, without having a prior scent to track."

"Wow. So, are people hiding in those cars?"

"No, the dogs are sniffing out drugs hidden in doors or the lining of seats, stuff like that. This is just a convenient place to practice. Our best training happens out in the real world, every day."

A deep voice sounded from behind Susan. "Often times we'll use abandoned buildings in the city. We hide drug scented towel rolls and then ask the dogs to search."

Susan spun around and came face to face with a chiseled chin and sea-green eyes. She sucked in a breath.

The man thrust out his hand. "I'm Clay Jennings. I work with Kendra." After shaking hers, Clay's fingers dropped to the top of a black head next to his thigh. "This is my partner, Gunner."

"I'm Susan Bell, nice to meet you." She took in the man's short military haircut and muscled bearing before shifting her gaze to the dog. "Hi Gunner." She started to bend but then glanced up at Clay. "Is it all right to pet him? He looks pretty fierce."

"As long as you don't try to attack me, you'll be okay." His dashing smile seemed incongruent with his rock-hard features, but when he offered it, Susan noticed he was engagingly handsome.

"I promise not to." Susan reached down to let Gunner sniff her hand before she stroked his silky ears. "What kind of dog is he? He looks sort of like a German Shepherd, but not."

"Gunner's a Belgian Malinois. They're smaller and lighter than shepherds which comes in handy in the field. They're especially suited to this type of work."

"Does he sniff things out, like Annie?"

"He can, but he's more of an attack and apprehend K9."

Kendra shaded her eyes as she looked up at Clay. "Speaking of that, how's the new dog coming?"

"Ranger? He'll be great. His nose reminds me of Baxter's."

"Seriously? That's saying a lot." Kendra raised her brows.

"It's true." Clay spoke a quiet guttural command and Gunner laid down. "He's got great potential to work as a biter and a sniffer. Perfect combination for the upswing in human trafficking that we're seeing."

"That's awesome. When do I get to meet him?" Kendra asked.

"Whenever. He's out there training now." Clay pointed out a dog who was a solid black version of Gunner.

"He's beautiful. No need to interrupt his workout though. Let's go get Annie." Kendra led the way and Clay walked next to Susan. Gunner glued himself to his handler's left side.

Clay inclined his head. "So, Susan, how do you and Kendra know each other?"

"We met through the serial killer case a couple of months ago." Susan didn't mention Burke and received a speculative glance from Kendra. *She must think Burke and I are exclusive.*

"Really? How were you involved in that?" They

approached the chain-link fence of the play area where Annie was, and Clay leaned his forearms against the top rail.

"The killer, Abbot Lee, tried to kidnap me from a parking lot, but I was lucky and got away."

Clay shifted his weight to one arm and twisted to face her. "That was you?" He flashed her a knee-melting smile. "Sounded to me like you gave him hell. Way to go."

Susan's cheeks heated. "Thanks, but honestly, I was scared to death."

"No doubt. You'll have to tell me the whole story sometime."

"Sure."

Kendra cleared her throat. "Come on, Susan. Let's put Annie up and get that drink." She opened the gate and waited for Susan to follow. The women walked down the length of the fence before Kendra called to her dog. Annie stopped mid-run and perked her head up, her ears squared to frame her face. The second she saw Kendra she bolted toward her.

"Hey, Susan," Kendra knelt down and clipped a leash to Annie's collar. "Be careful with Clay. He's kind of a flirt."

"He seems like a nice guy."

"He is, but I think he might be interested in you."

A trill of nerves flitted through Susan's belly. "Really?"

Kendra narrowed her eyes. "Yeah." She cocked her head to the side. "But what about Burke?"

"Well, they're both knock-outs."

"But..."

"But, what? Burke and I don't have any kind of understanding. We've only been out one time and that was on a double date with you and Rick. I'm sure Burke dates other women."

Kendra patted Annie's head and stood. She peered up at Susan. "If it were the other way around and it was Clay you were saying dated other women, I wouldn't bat an eye. He's a big flirt—but Burke is different."

"How do you mean?"

"Clay goes out all the time, plays the field—so to speak. Burke is much more selective. He doesn't date lightly."

Susan sighed. "I got that impression, and to be honest, it makes me a little uncomfortable. I mean I *really* like Burke, but I'm not ready to be super serious with anyone right now. I want to focus my energy on my business."

Kendra's eyes narrowed a fraction. "Burke is a good friend of mine, so I'm asking you to be straight with him. If you are going to date other guys, you need to tell him that."

"I will, I—,"

Clay interrupted them as he jogged up. "Hey, Dean, did you see that attack? The dog that just took Murphy down? That was Ranger. He's a natural. He loves the attack." The green and gold flecks in his eyes sparkled in the sun.

Kendra sought out the dog Clay was excited about. She saw the handler praising him. "Wow. Good job, Ranger! If he has as good a nose as you say, he will be invaluable to the team."

"He does." Clay touched the small of Susan's back, turning her in the right direction and pointed at Ranger. "What do you think?"

"Honestly, he looks terrifying."

"He is—if you're the bad guy." Clay grinned. "Listen, I've got to go, but I'd still like to hear your story some-time. I'll give you a call." He winked and jogged off toward the attack training, Gunner kept the perfect pace at his side.

"Told you." Kendra stood next to Susan and crossed her arms as they watched Clay run back to the training area. He moved like an oversized panther across the field.

Susan pushed a strand of hair behind her ear. "He didn't mean it. He doesn't even have my number."

Kendra raised an eyebrow at her. "He's an FBI agent, Susan. He can find your number in five minutes."

Chapter Three

Two-o'clock on Saturday afternoon took forever to arrive. Burke carried three, locked black cases to the back seat of his truck. On his way to the driver's door, he buffed a smudge on the paint. He hoped Susan would have fun on the date he had planned. He honestly wasn't sure she would, but no matter what, one thing was certain. They would find out a lot more about each other's worldviews.

Burke knocked at Susan's apartment. Nerves bounced around in his gut reminding him of his first date in high school, which hadn't gone well. Maybe he'd *always* been too focused—too driven. The girl complained that he never could "chill out". Susan's bright eyes smiled up at him from her doorway and interrupted his memories.

"Hey, Are you ready to go?"

"I think so. Am I wearing the right thing?" Susan spun around, a bundle of energy bouncing in Converse tennis shoes and displaying her long legs under a short khaki skirt. Her light blue and white layered t-shirts showed off her curves. "Where are you taking me?"

Burke indulged in a brief fantasy of staying at her place, but shook his head. "You're perfect, and you'll find out when we get there." He grinned and led the way to his truck.

When they pulled into the parking lot of the local shooting range, Susan's body tensed. "A gun club? Seriously?" Her eyes flashed and met his. "I thought I made it pretty clear how I feel about guns, the other night?"

"You made your perception about guns clear, but have you ever fired one?"

"No." Her tone was sharp, and she crossed her arms over her chest.

"Before you make up your mind, try it. If after fifteen minutes, you hate it, we'll leave and go somewhere else. Deal?"

Susan glared at him, but he saw a flicker of humor in her eyes. "All right. I guess. I always say I'm willing to experience new things, but you should know my negative opinion about guns is permanently set in stone."

BURKE HELD THE DOOR OPEN FOR HER AS SUSAN STEPPED inside and gawked at the various firearms displayed on the walls and in glass display cases. "I never knew there were so many different types of guns." Looking uncomfortable and intimidated, she kept close to Burke.

He gave her an encouraging smile. "Come on, we need to sign in." Burke led her to the back of the building, to a counter where an older man was ready to check them in.

"Hey, Burke. Bring a guest?"

"Tommy, this is my friend Susan. It's her first time at a gun club. First time shooting too, in fact."

"Nice. Well, you've got a great teacher in Burke, ma'am."

Susan nodded, staring wide eyed at the number of weapons surrounding her.

Tommy tapped on the computer keyboard. "Need to rent anything today?"

"I've got pretty much everything we need, except ear protection for Susan."

"Gotcha." His fingers flew. Tommy reached under the counter and pulled out a form. He set the paper and a pen on the counter. "Alright, ma'am. If you'll just sign this waiver, we can get you started."

Susan lifted the pen and ran the tip lightly across the words as she read them. She looked up at Burke. "This is dangerous. It says I might get hurt—even shot!" The paper shook slightly as she held it up for Burke to see.

He smiled at her. "You're not going to get hurt. This is like any other waiver you have to sign anytime you do something fun. I promise you'll be safe."

"We've never had anyone get hurt here before, ma'am. Burke's right. It's just a liability thing the corporate lawyers make us have. You know."

Susan glanced at Tommy, then cocked her head and stared at Burke. "I think this is a little more than that."

"It'll be fine. Come on, you said you like to try new things."

"Okay, but you promised we could leave if I don't like it." Susan scratched her signature across the line.

Tommy placed the waiver in a stack behind the counter. "Okay, I've put you in Bay One. The lanes are mostly open today, so pick whichever one you want."

"Great, thanks." Burke handed Tommy his credit card,

and Tommy gave Susan a set of pink-camo hearing protectors.

Burke opened the bay door for Susan and chose a lane in the middle. He removed his guns from their cases and laid them on a carpeted shelf between them and the targets, pointing their muzzles down range. He explained the parts of each firearm as he prepped it and then reviewed the safety instructions once again.

"What's that weird smell?" Susan's eyes were as big as racquetballs, she looked terrified.

"That's spent gunpowder."

She rubbed her arms to warm them from the breeze that fanned in from behind them. "Why do they keep it so chilly in here?"

"The fans force the breeze to move down range. It helps prevent us from breathing in any lead lingering in the air after firing." Burke wore a t-shirt under a black button down. He slipped off his outer layer and draped it around her shoulders. "I should have told you to bring a sweater. Sorry."

"Thanks. That's much better. But won't you get cold?"

"Nah."

Susan's eyes darted around the space. She jumped at the spit of the guns going off in the lanes near theirs.

"Hey, don't worry. None of these firearms can do anything without one of us engaging them. Before I load them, I want you to hold each one. Get a feel for their weight, look down the sight. Remember, never point the gun at anything you don't want to shoot, even if you believe it to be unloaded. In this case, the only direction you point the barrel is down range."

"I'm frightened."

Burke rested his hand on her shoulder. "Okay. What are you feeling scared of, exactly?"

"Guns are dangerous."

"Not when you learn to handle them correctly, and that's what we're doing today. Are you worried that you'll get hurt?"

"No, I just feel nervous. I don't think I'm going to like this, Burke." Her fingers trembled as she reached to touch the ridged barrel of his SIG P320.

"I'm impressed that you're at least willing to give this a try." He covered her hand with his and held it against the cold metal barrel of the SIG. "This is the gun I carry with me every day." Burke stood close behind her brushing her back with his chest. He ran a hand down her other wrist and curled her fingers around the pistol grip. She drew in a sharp breath and he waited for her to release the air before he moved on.

He demonstrated holding the pistol. "Keep your finger out of the trigger housing until you are ready to fire. Point at the target, notice the weight in your hand. How does it feel?" He released her.

"It's heavier than I thought, but it's also not as scary as I expected."

Burke chuckled. "Good." He pointed out the safety switch, the front sight, the trigger, and the slot the magazine would go in when they were ready. Picking up the magazine, he instructed Susan how to load it and snap it into the gun. He double checked her ear and eye protection.

"I'll shoot three rounds first, so you'll know what to expect. Then when you're ready, you can give it a try."

"Okay."

Burke selected round splatter targets so it was easy to

see where the bullets hit, and he didn't want to upset her with a target shaped like a man. He fired, one, two, three. All hit in the center circle.

"Wow. You're a good shot." Susan stared down the lane at the fluorescent green spots.

"Now it's your turn. Ready?"

"I guess. I still feel nervous."

"It's okay, I'm right here. I promise I won't let anything go wrong."

Susan nodded and accepted the gun from Burke. Step by step she followed the instructions he gave her. "Grip the handle with your right hand. Your left-hand cups the bottom of the grip only to stabilize your shooting hand."

Susan nodded and straightened her right elbow as she aimed. Burke placed his hands on her hips and squared them to the target. "For now, stand with your feet parallel. Later we can try other positions to see what you find more comfortable." He left his hands where they were, enjoying her soft curves. "Don't hold your breath. Remember the acronym, BRASS—breathe, relax, aim, stop your breath, squeeze. In other words, when you're ready to shoot, let out half your air, then hold it to fire."

She took a deep breath and aimed the pistol at the target. With her next inhale, she slid her finger onto the trigger, releasing half her breath before she pulled. Her bullet struck somewhere in the wall above the target, and she glanced at Burke with huge eyes.

He grinned, pleased to see her original fear dissipating.

Round two. Susan went through the steps again.

"This time lock your elbow out, focus on the front sight, and don't anticipate the kick."

Susan nodded and drew her breath. The second bullet hit the target paper at the top left corner, but still rewarded her with a bright green splatter mark. She bounced on her toes, and Burke was quick to slip the gun from her grip so she could celebrate safely. The delight in her eyes was that of a small child on her birthday.

Burke laughed. "Great job."

"Did you see? I hit it!"

"Nice!" He gave her shoulders a celebratory squeeze with his free arm.

"I still get one more turn, right?"

"You bet you do. This time, consider where your last shot landed and adjust your aim. Keep breathing. You've got this."

Susan faced the target once again, raised the firearm with more confidence, and aimed. She slowly let out her breath and squeezed the trigger. This time her round hit the edge of the outer circle. Her smile spanned her face as she set the safety and gently laid the gun down on the mat. Then she spun around, hopping up and down.

"I did it! Did you see that? I did it!"

"You certainly did. I think you might be a natural." Burke pulled her into his arms, and Susan reached both her hands up to his cheeks, pulling him down to kiss him. Heat spiraled out from his core through his limbs.

"This is really fun, Burke. I admit, I had no idea. Thanks for bringing me."

"You're welcome. I'm glad you're enjoying yourself." He tapped the end of her nose.

"But, it still doesn't mean I believe everyone should be running around with guns. My opinion hasn't changed about that."

"Of course not. I don't think that either, Susan, but unfortunately, stricter gun laws won't keep firearms out of the hands of bad-guys. They'll still get illegal guns on the black-market."

"I see what you're saying... but we're a long way from agreeing on this issue." She stared into his eyes. "Do you think for now we can agree to disagree?"

"I think we should try. I'd hate to have different opinions on certain issues ruin our day. You're too much fun to hang out with."

She beamed up at him. "I'd hate that too. Now, let's go again."

AFTER TWO HOURS OF SHOOTING, THEY'D BUILT UP AN appetite. Burke took her to a Brazilian steakhouse for dinner.

"Isn't this the kind of place where they bring huge chunks of meat around to your table and carve you off a slab?"

"Yeah, have you ever been here?"

"No. It's a lot of meat." Susan wrinkled her nose.

Burke smiled and opened the door for her. "There's a salad bar too, I think."

Half way through the meal, Burke had devoured close to a pound of various savory, roasted meats, and Susan was on her second round of soup and salad.

"How can you eat that much meat? Doesn't it make you feel sick?"

"I need the protein." Burke laughed.

"What was today about?" Susan tore a chunk from a whole-wheat roll. "I feel like there's a message in your choice of activities. Are you trying to prove something to me?"

"No, I don't want to prove anything. I just want you to

know who I am. If you don't like these things about me, then it's better to realize that up front."

She nodded. "I get it. I've dated my fair share of guys I thought were wonderful until six-months later when I found out they were into dog-fighting, or drugs, or worse."

"Well, I love dogs and I don't do drugs, so it sounds like I'm ahead so far." Burke took a drink of his beer. "Did you have fun today? Or," nerves danced on his vocal chords. Her answer mattered more to him than he expected. "Do you want to pull the brakes?"

Susan cocked her head to the side and gave him an impish grin. Her eyes sparkled. "I had a really good time today, and you haven't shown me anything I can't handle. But..."

"But... what?" Burke reached for her hand and threaded his fingers through hers.

"But now it's my turn to plan a date. We'll see how well you do with the things *I* love."

Burke laughed. "That sounds like a threat." He didn't want to think about what kind of crazy plot she was hatching. He didn't care. She wanted to go out with him again. That was all that mattered.

Chapter Four

❦

Susan parked her light blue Prius in the driveway of the address Burke had texted her. He lived in a house off of Hampden and I-25, only about twenty minutes from her apartment. The home was probably built in the 70s, but he maintained it well. Burke kept his lawn cut and cared for, and an old Elm tree graced the front yard with abundant shade.

It surprised her to see a pot of flowers on the porch, cheerfully bobbing their faces in the breeze. Susan rang the doorbell and then reached into the mass of red and white petunias and pinched off three spent blooms. The front door swung open to Burke buttoning the last few buttons of a blue checked dress shirt. The color set off his eyes.

"Am I early?" Susan couldn't move her gaze from his thick fingers fumbling with the small plastic discs.

"No, come on in. I'll be ready in two shakes." He stood aside for her to enter. The subtle cologne he wore suggested she nuzzle in for a deeper breath, but she walked past him into the living room. "Can I get you a drink? A beer?" He shook his head slightly. "Or a glass of wine?"

"Do you have wine?"

"Yeah, I think so. Let me check."

Susan giggled. "A beer would be great."

Burke flashed her a bright smile. "Good. I know I have that." He went into the kitchen.

Susan glanced around the space. People's homes always interested her. They told so much about the people who lived there. Burke's living room was done in blues and browns, though probably unintentionally. There were two leather recliners pointed toward a huge flat screen TV, a small brown and tan flecked couch sat behind a coffee table that appeared to be the frequent recipient of half-time snacks and un-coastered drinks. Seemingly out-of-place, a beautiful oil landscape painting hung on the side wall.

Burke returned with two open beers. He handed her one, but drew the bottle back. "Do you want a glass? I should have poured yours in a pint glass. Sorry." He turned toward the kitchen.

"No, thanks. A bottle is fine."

His brows bobbed upward as he glanced at her. "Are you sure? It's no problem."

"I'm sure." Susan took a swig of beer to show him she truly didn't mind and wondered if his concern came from his mother's teaching him good manners or another woman who demanded such things.

"I'll be right back, I need to grab my tie."

"Thanks for being willing to dress up for an unknown experience." Susan enjoyed watching him walk down the hallway, his broad shoulders straining the fabric of his shirt before tapering nicely down to a trim waist. He wore well-tailored slacks, which surprised her a little. She assumed FBI agents were more "off the rack" types. There was a hidden side to Burke Cameron, and Susan looked forward to discovering it.

He returned, knotting a patterned tie that was blue, gray, and burgundy. It looked sharp with his shirt and complimented Susan's burgundy dress. "Nice tie."

"Gorgeous dress." He sent her a dazzling smile that made her light-headed. "You're stunning. I don't care where you're taking me, as long as I get to look at you all evening."

Heat rushed up her neck. "Thank you." She touched her throat with her cool fingers and took another, bigger gulp of her beer. "I hope you have fun, though."

"How can I not?" He tightened the knot at his neck and tilted his head toward the door. "Want to sit on the front porch while we finish our beers?"

Susan stepped outside, and he followed her. She heard him chuckle under his breath. "What are you laughing at?"

"You drive a Prius?"

Her eyebrow shot up. "Yes. Why is that funny?"

He grinned and shrugged. "Worried about your carbon foot-print?"

"As a matter of fact..." A vague defensiveness swelled in her chest.

He held up a hand. "Don't get me wrong. I think that's great. It's just that it's Colorado. How does that thing do in the snow and ice?"

"Well..."

He laughed.

"There are three-hundred days of sunshine in Colorado every year. So, I do just fine."

"You can always call me if you need to be pulled out of

a snowdrift." He winked at her, and his kind eyes had her relaxing. He was only teasing, not judging. She hoped. In many ways they were as different as day and night, but she was undeniably drawn to him at the same time. It had shocked Susan when the first date he took her on was to the gun club, but maybe he would feel the same way about her plans. Burke was right. It's important to communicate who they really are.

"I'll keep that in mind." She sat next to Burke on a glider. "Any guesses about where we're going tonight?"

"I can only imagine, but you were a good sport about learning to shoot, so I promise to be open to whatever you have up your sleeve."

Susan laughed and tapped his bottle with hers.

AN HOUR LATER, SUSAN DROVE PAST THE HUGE BLUE bear leaning against the glass wall of the Denver Convention Center and pulled into a parking lot in the middle of downtown.

"First, we'll have a quick dinner. Have you ever been to Native Beet?"

Burke's brows bunched together. "What?"

"Native Beet. It's a vegan restaurant. It's a bit bohemian—fun—and the food is fantastic."

"Can't say that I have. Vegan, huh? I don't think I knew you were vegan."

"I'm not, but that doesn't mean that vegan meals aren't delicious."

"If you say so. Do I have to eat tofu?"

Susan smirked at him and grasped his elbow. "Come on. You promised to be open to new experiences."

They entered the restaurant, and Burkes' eyes

narrowed as he looked around. There was a definite odor of weed underpinning any aromas from the food, and Susan didn't figure that was going over very well with Burke.

They were seated side by side on a bench seat. Burke lifted the menu, and read it—twice—before looking askance at her. "What do you recommend?"

"Didn't you see anything that looked interesting?" Nerves nibbled along the edge of her stomach lining. When she planned the date, she'd been trying to make a point, but now she worried he wouldn't have a good time. She didn't want him to think they were *too* different. Her heart squeezed with regret. She should have taken him somewhere more moderate, somewhere he would have enjoyed.

"I don't really know what I'm looking at. I've never even heard of some of these foods. So, you choose. I trust you." He reached for her hand and held it.

Warmth radiated up her arm, and she wanted to lean into him, to kiss that brilliant smile. "If you like Mediterranean food, I suggest the chickpea stir-fry. Or, you might like the Portobello burger."

One blond eyebrow rose. "Why do they call it a burger, if it's really just a big mushroom?"

Susan bit her lip. "We can go somewhere else, if you want. I admit I was trying to push you a little."

His deep laugh vibrated inside her and woke something primal. "No way. I deserve every artsy-fartsy thing you plan on doing tonight. I totally pushed you with the gun-range thing. I've never taken a date there before."

"You haven't? Why did you take me?"

Burke lifted her hand to his lips. "I like you, Susan. A lot. Which seems kind of weird, doesn't it? I mean we come from opposite paradigms. We see the world so differently. I guess, I just want you to know what you're getting into if you decide to keep seeing me." He rubbed her knuckles across his mouth as he stared into her eyes.

"I feel the same way. I think about you all the time. I love being with you, and at the same time, I don't understand how you can view the world the way you do."

He nodded and kissed her hand before lowering it back to the table. "Do you think it's worth trying for us?"

"I do, but I want to get to know you better."

"Okay. Then sometimes one of us will have to choke down garbanzo beans and learn to like it." He smiled, and warmth bathed her skin.

Susan touched his cheek, and he pressed it into her palm. They gazed into each other's eyes for a wondrous moment before he brought his mouth to hers. Her body ignited, and she wished she hadn't spent so much on the tickets for the evening's main event. She'd rather she spent nothing and could take him home instead.

AFTER THE SUN WENT DOWN, THE TEMPERATURE dropped. Spring in Colorado was unpredictable, and it was always cold in the canyons between Denver's skyscrapers. Susan huddled into Burke's arm as they walked together toward the Denver Center for Performing Arts.

"Are you taking me to see Hair or something?" Burke chuckled.

"No, but if it were playing, I definitely would have. It'd be worth the ticket price just to watch your face."

Burke rolled his eyes playfully. When they got to the Boettcher Concert Hall, it surprised Susan when she noticed how comfortable Burke was in the symphony environment. She handed the tickets to the clerk, went through security, and Burke took Susan's coat to the coat-check.

"Would you like a cocktail?" He murmured in her ear, sending champagne tingles up her spine.

"Yes—would you? Remember, this is my treat."

"Let me at least get the drinks. What is the performance tonight?"

Susan tilted her head to consider him. "Beethoven's Piano Concerto, Number Four."

"Nice. Wine?" A laugh flirted with his mouth, and Susan raised up on her toes to kiss him.

"Yes, Chardonnay, please. Why do I feel like you know exactly what this concerto is?"

His laugh buoyed her. "Because I do." He returned her kiss and lingered before turning to the bar for their drinks.

They found their seats and Susan flipped through her program, too aware of Burke's body, his leg and shoulder touching hers, to focus on any of the words. He shifted and slid his arm around her shoulders drawing her closer.

Leaning into her hair he spoke over the cacophony of instruments warming up. "Thanks for bringing me here tonight. You couldn't have known I love the symphony." He chuckled. "Maybe we have more in common than we think."

Susan snuggled into him. "Maybe we do. I had never been target shooting, but I had a blast."

He grinned. "Pun intended?"

"No, but it's fitting," she giggled. "You surprise me though."

"Why's that?"

"Tell me about the painting in your living room." Susan canted her head to peer at him.

He laughed. "That was a gift from my mother when I bought the house. She's always trying to force culture on me. It's her fault I like the symphony, too."

Susan loved the warmth that glowed in his eyes when he spoke of his mom.

Burke bent down, bringing his lips a hair's breadth away from hers, and gazed at her. Her heart danced in prestissimo as she searched the depth of his eyes, her breath suspended. The audience erupted in applause around them as the conductor took the stage, but neither Susan nor Burke joined in.

Against her mouth, Burke whispered. "What do you have planned after the symphony?"

Susan breathed in the bourbon on his breath and pressed her mouth against his. She wished once more that they didn't have to sit through the concert after all. Burke raised his hand to her cheek and kissed her with promises she didn't want to wait for.

The conductor said a few words and then tapped his baton on his music stand. The pianist began the concerto, and still Burke kissed her. Susan's body hummed with the sweet heat of his whiskey mingling with her amped up desire. When he pulled away, his eyes searched hers before he sat back in his seat, and held her hand.

Susan knew music played for the next two hours, but she couldn't remember any of it. When the concert was over she stood with the crowd, clapping, happier it was over than with how wonderful the performance had been. She and Burke walked arm in arm to her car. Susan hated that they had to pull apart so she could drive, and she rushed through lights to get home.

"Do you want me to drive?" Burke slid his fingers over

her thigh, and she sped up. "Whoa." He took his hand back with a sly grin.

"Sorry. No, I'm fine. Your place?"

"Unless you have anything else planned."

Susan swallowed. If he only knew the things she was thinking.

She parked in his driveway and turned off her car. Burke pulled her toward him across the console. He kissed her, tasting, teasing and nibbling. He plunged his fingers into her hair. She spread her hands across his hard chest, feeling his heart race. She fumbled with the knot of his tie. His mouth left hers and tracked hot kisses along her jaw and down her throat. Susan could hardly contain the need screaming for release inside her body. She circled his neck with her arms and pushed into him. A groan escaped from deep inside him, and she responded with a mewling of her own.

Burke returned to her mouth. His kisses were so hot she thought she might dissolve. He gripped her shoulders and drew away, breathing hard. He blinked several times and swallowed. "Thanks for tonight. I had a great time. Can I see you again tomorrow?"

Confused, Susan tried to steady her own breath. "Tomorrow?"

He nodded. "I've already got a plan."

She shook her head to clear the haze of desire clouding her mind. "You do?"

"Yeah. Are you free?"

She nodded, dumbly.

"Great." He kissed her quick. "I'll pick you up early, at six. Wear jeans and a sweatshirt." He kissed her again and offered her a soft smile. "Really. Thanks for tonight, Susan. I had a great time. I'll see you in the morning." The parting kiss he gave her was so tender and sweet, her heart ached. "Good night. Text me when you get home."

She could only nod. He got out of the car and stood by the drive, lifting one hand in farewell.

Susan put her car in reverse and raised her hand back. *This boy scout thing is killing me. It has to stop.*

Chapter Five

S usan's alarm rudely blared against her eardrums at 5:15 am. What kind of crazy person gets up this early for a date? *The kind who's obsessed with a sizzling hot FBI agent, that's who.* She stumbled into the bathroom and cranked on the warm water for her shower.

The doorbell rang promptly at 6:00 am, as promised, and Susan hurried to answer. She opened her door to Burke holding two steaming paper cups and a bag of fast-food breakfast sandwiches. The rich scent of roasted coffee floated inside her apartment.

"Good morning." His gaze traveled over her, and he kissed her cheek. "Coffee?"

She didn't have the heart to tell him she preferred tea in the morning. Besides, she'd drink any type of potion this Norse god wanted to give her. "Good morning. Thank you." She reached for the cup he offered.

"Are you ready?"

"I think so. Do I need anything?"

"Nope, I've got all the gear."

"Gear?" Oh no. It was too early in the day to do something strenuous that involved gear.

A quick smile brightened Burke's face. "What's the matter? Are you worried?"

"Should I be?" In the end, she knew along with drinking whatever he gave her, she'd also follow him wherever he wanted her to go. She behaved like Pavlov's dogs. Burke smiled, and she salivated, panting after any crumbs. Eying the greasy bag he held, Susan grabbed an apple from the bowl on her counter. "Let's go."

As they drove, the sun rose and bathed the front range in gold and peach. Burke took a state highway leading into the mountains. After about an hour, they left the pavement for a winding dirt road which eventually panned out to an open grassy area that overlooked a breathtaking mountain lake. The early sun skipped across gentle ripples in the water as it made its ascent. Dawn cast the pine trees and newly budding aspen in purple-gray silhouettes. Birds sang their morning arias into the soft breeze that stirred the leaves.

Burke watched her as she took in the scenery, and she turned to him. Her soul overflowed with the beauty of their surroundings. "This is magnificent, Burke. What is this lake?"

"It doesn't have a name yet." He stared out at the view with the eyes of a lover.

She might have felt envious of the adoration in his gaze if she didn't share his awe. "No name?"

"It's a private lake." He opened his door and pushed a button to unlock the back door. He glanced at her with a mischievous smile. "Ever been fly-fishing?"

Susan's mouth fell open. *Fly-fishing?* "No, I never have."
She smirked. "What are we doing, Burke? It's like we're
trying to find reasons to prove we shouldn't be together."

"What do you mean? You hate fishing?"

She laughed. "No. I don't know if I hate it or not. It's
just, first you take me shooting and now fishing. I took you
to a vegan restaurant when I know you're a dyed-in-the-
wool beef eater and then to the symphony. To be honest, I
was pushing you outside what I thought was your comfort
zone. I think you're doing the same. It's weird. Why are
we doing this instead of trying to convince each other
we're perfect for each other?"

"It's a good question." He pulled gear from the bed of
his truck and organized it before he continued. "I really
like being with you. I'm already convinced of that, so
maybe I want to be sure you know the real me and want
that before we go much farther. We're not in high school
anymore."

He sounded serious. Susan wasn't sure about anything
beyond the next couple of months. She had professional
goals and a dream of running her own company, but she
hadn't considered much beyond that. Well, besides
knowing that she wanted her relationship with Burke to
progress to a more physical level. Didn't this stuff work
itself out, *without* a strategy?

She shaded her view with her hand to see him better in
the brightening morning. "So, you're looking for forever?"

"Aren't you?" His eyes sparked blue light. "I know I
want a family. If you don't want to move in that direction,
it's better if we both realize that now. Don't you think?"
His gaze fixed on her, and he waited for her to answer.

"Do you have your whole future planned out? Is there
any room for natural progression?" Susan's throat tight-

ened. "I don't even know where we stand with each other. I mean, an agent friend of Kendra's asked me out the other day and I don't know how to answer him."

Burke's eyes hardened to blue glass, and his knuckles whitened in his grip. "Who?"

"A guy named Clay Jennings." She twisted her toes into the dirt. "Do you know him?"

"Yeah, I know him. Well—I know who he is." He swallowed and his Adam's apple bolted up and down in his throat. "Do you *want* to go out with Jennings?"

Susan released an exasperated groan. "Not if you and I are seeing each other exclusively. Are we?"

"I'd like to be. You're the only one I want to be with." A muscle bunched in his jaw.

"I just don't have everything figured out already. Sometimes it's good to take chances. For example, I just quit my job to start a new career—my own business." Burke was light years ahead of her in his planning. For now, she simply wanted to spend time with him, get to know him. "You're moving way too fast for me."

"Wait a minute—did you just say you quit your job? Before you can support yourself with your new one?" His eyes widened under drawn brows. "How will you pay your bills? What about rent?"

"I have some savings." Susan suddenly felt less sure of her decision. Burke clearly didn't approve.

He shook his head and stared at her. "How long is that going to last? Do you have a budget planned out so you know how many months you can go without an income?"

"I have one in my head..." Susan squirmed. "Anyway, I'm going to the conference to celebrate."

His jaw flexed again, and he lowered his gaze down to the gear he held in his hands. "Let me ask you a question.

Last night, when we kissed goodnight, if I would have asked you to come in, to stay over, would you have?"

Her body shuddered at the memory of her frustrated desire. The truth was, she would have jumped at the chance. She wanted him like a starving person wants a meal. Her voice was soft when she answered. "Yes."

He nodded and re-gripped his fishing rod. He peered up at her from under concerned brows. "So, you quit your job on a whim, you're considering dating Clay, and you're ready to sleep with me. And you think *I'm* moving too fast because I want something serious? Something permanent? Seems kinda backwards to me."

Heat flooded Susan's cheeks, and she crossed her arms, turning away from him. *Not only a boy scout, but one from fifty years ago.* Obviously he thought she was foolish, loose, and easy. She wasn't, but she'd be lying if she didn't admit her attraction to him—how drawn she was to him.

"Look, I'm sorry if I've made you angry." His tone lightened. "I only meant that I'd like to see if we can mean more to each other than that. It's better, easier to cope with, if we find out we're not suited for each other before we cloud things up with sex."

This was not getting any better, and she was stuck out here with him until he decided to take her home. Susan spun back to face him. "I'm not angry. A little embarrassed, maybe. I only told you about Clay for the sake of honesty, but I think you're looking for someone very different from me. I mean, you're crazy conservative. You love guns and," she gestured at the world around them, "all this fishing and hunting stuff. You eat fast food and drink coffee..." Susan's voice became shrill and under the pressure of her shame she veered off the course of the rational. She swallowed and refocused. "It seems to me you're looking for a friend. You think I'm easy, and you don't want me." Unexpected tears blurred her vision.

Burke's head tilted to the side, and he dropped his gear on the ground. In two long strides he came to her and pulled her tight into his body, his mouth crushing hers. Strong, solid arms wrapped around her shoulders and one of his hands held the back of her head, pressing her deeper into his dominating kiss. He drew in a ragged breath as his lips burned her skin with his exploration of her ear and the length of her neck. One rough hand pulled at the neckline of her top, almost tearing the fabric to get it out of his way. His teeth grazed her collarbone, and Susan's knees nearly buckled. Sparks shot throughout her body igniting a ravenous hunger for him.

"Don't want you? Are you insane?" His hand roamed her curves and yanked at the hem of her shirt. She heard the material tear and was glad of it. Burke's grip around her waist tightened, and he lifted her, turning until he had her pressed up against the side of his truck. He crushed her between his rock-hard body and the equally solid metal. "You couldn't be more wrong." He pulled back slightly so he could look in her eyes. "I want you so bad, it hurts. But I don't want to let all these feelings loose, if we are too different. If we both aren't wanting something real. Can you understand that?" He kissed her again, searching out the curves and angles of her mouth. "The truth is," he spoke against her lips. "You already mean too much to me to take you for granted." He stared into her eyes. "I want to cherish you, Susan... to savor you."

His rough thumb brushed a tear away from Susan's cheek she was unaware had fallen. No one had ever spoken to her like this. No one had ever made her crazy with a searing desire that mixed with a yearning she didn't understand. A strange sort of home-sickness washed over her as Burke pushed himself back, though it was only by a mere inch or two.

When she spoke her voice hid, and she had to clear her throat. Still weak, her words tripped out. "We're so different. Do you really think we could make it?"

The vulnerability that lay bare in his eyes cracked her heart wide open. She touched his cheek with her fingertips. His tone was low, gruff. "I don't know, but I want to try."

THIS WOMAN IS GOING TO KILL ME WITHOUT EVEN BREAKING a sweat. Burke grasped onto his self-control by a thin strand of one-pound fishing line. His hormones demanded he ignore his ethics and morals and take what she offered. Susan wanted him, she said so with her words and her body. He sucked in a cool breath and held it while his frame shuddered in his denial of its fierce desire. Her fingers tracked flames down his cheek to his chin, and she tipped his face so she could look into his eyes.

"I want to try too." She blinked at the drops threatening to spill over her lower lids. "I... you make me feel... I've never really felt like I do right now." Her gaze searched his, asking hundreds of questions he wanted to answer. "So, we slow down to move ahead? Is that your plan?" A soft smile curved her lips.

Burke braced himself against the truck door, his hands on either side of her. His muscles trembled one last time, shaking off the testosterone overload, and he let loose a great sigh. "I honestly don't think I can go slow for much longer. Not after that kiss." He grinned, hoping to ease the weight of the moment. "We should take some time to talk through the things we completely disagree on. Like, I don't care if you want to eat beans and seeds, but I personally will starve to death without a good steak."

Her giggle eased the tension in his gut. His shoulders relaxed, and he stood tall. Susan reached forward and placed her hand on his chest. Her touch branded his heart.

"I can live with that, but you've got to cut down on the fast food. If I'm going to fall in love with you, then you have to take better care of yourself."

What? Did she say she's thinking about falling in love with me? Burke gave her a double take, and she laughed.

"Come on. You're supposed to be teaching me how to fish, aren't you?" She picked up one of the poles and walked away toward the water. Stunned by the whipping turns of emotions, Burke scrambled to collect the rest of the gear and follow the sway of Susan's enticing hips as she hiked down to the lake.

She called to him over her shoulder. "What do you do with all the meat you get from hunting and fishing? Ever think about donating it to a shelter to feed the poor?"

Burke chuckled to himself at the challenge. The fact was, he had an arrangement with a rural food bank where he donated his processed game, but he wanted to spar with her some more, so he didn't let on. "Is this when I have to tell you the parable about how I could give a man a fish and he'd eat for one night, or I could teach a man to fish and he'd eat forever?"

Susan stopped, turned, and glared at him with a teasing glint in her eye. "Is that why you're teaching me to fish? So you don't have to take me out for dinner anymore?" She laughed, and his whole day brightened. "Here's the thing about your parable. You can teach a man to fish, sure, but he still needs fishing gear, and a place and means to cook his meal. If he doesn't have any of those things, then the knowledge he gained from you is of no benefit to his empty belly except to cause a longing he can't fill."

Burke's eyebrows rose as he considered her. How was it possible that he was falling in love with an irresponsible, impulsive liberal?

Chapter Six

Monday evening, Susan put her kettle on the stove and stared at the voicemail reminders on her phone. She chewed her lip while she waited for the water to boil. When the steam whistled, she jumped out of her reverie and poured the water over the teabag in her mug.

Susan paced around her dining-room table working herself up to make the phone call she wished she could dodge. She hated these types of conversations, but knew it had to be done. Pulling out a chair, she sat sipping her tea while she re-listened to Clay's messages. He'd called her two times wanting to take her out. The first call she had genuinely missed. The second call she purposefully sent to messages to avoid talking to him. Now, she could no longer put him off. Her relationship with Burke was moving forward, and it was time to make a commitment.

She tapped the call button on his voicemail. Clay's phone rang three times before he answered. "Jennings here."

Her stomach tightened. "Oh, hi. Clay? It's Susan Bell."

Warmth entered his tone. "Susan, hey. Glad you called."

"I'm returning your messages. Sorry it took me so long."

"No problem. I was just hoping to find a time we could get together. Are you free this weekend? I'd like to take you out for dinner."

Susan took a deep breath and swallowed. "That's really nice, but the thing is, I'm seeing someone." There was a pause on the line. Susan bit her lip and closed her eyes, waiting for his response.

"Oh. You should have said something."

"It's kind of new."

"Okay, I get it. Well, you've got my number. Let me know if anything changes."

"Thanks for understanding."

"He's a lucky man, whoever he is. Make sure he treats you well."

"Okay, bye Clay.

"Take care, Susan. See you around." He ended the call.

That was easier than I thought it was going to be. Susan realized she'd never told Clay that Burke was the man she was seeing, but it wasn't like they were good friends, or anything. Burke only said he knew who Clay was, that was all. She rolled her eyes at herself, hoping this wouldn't become "a thing." Either way, she'd made the situation clear and knew Burke would feel good about that.

Susan's shoulders relaxed and she let go of a deep tension she didn't know she'd been holding. She drew in a full breath and was free. She wondered at the excitement swirling through her body at the direction she and Burke were headed. Before, she'd always thought freedom meant seeing whoever, whenever, and not being committed to any one person. Now, though, a deep sense of peace and anticipation settled in her heart.

THE FOLLOWING WEEKEND SUSAN PICKED BURKE UP FOR a sunrise picnic. The morning was fresh and crisp and overflowing with promise. Susan marveled at the sense of contentment humming through her body whenever she spent time with Burke. In contrast, when they were apart she seemed strangely adrift. He filled her mind and something more—a space inside she hadn't noticed before, but that he now occupied. When he was away, that space yearned for him.

Together, they set up their picnic and reclined on a green plaid blanket to watch the sun embrace the day with peachy-pink arms stretching across the sky. Susan tasted a spoonful of tart Greek yogurt mixed with juicy strawberries and sweetened with a touch of honey. A drip of the sticky nectar slid down her lip onto her chin. When Susan moved to wipe it away, Burke clasped her wrist.

"Let me." His husky voice sent a tremor straight to her core. He pulled her toward him and licked the honey from her skin, nibbling his way to her lips. He kissed her, savoring her as though she were dessert. Susan didn't fully understand why Burke wanted to wait to make love to her, but one thing was becoming uncomfortably clear. The longer they waited, the stronger her desire for him grew. Her whole body trembled with wanting him. When he finished torturing her, he sat up and gazed at her with longing. *Maybe he feels it too.*

"In about twenty minutes, we will meet up with a group that practices Tai Chi in the park."

He drew his chin back and cocked his head. "What?"

Susan giggled at the incredulous expression that took over his features. "We're going to do Tai Chi. Have you ever tried it?"

Burke rolled his eyes and chuckled. "No, I can't say that I have." He sat up and packed the dirty dishes and trash into Susan's backpack. He gave her a sideways glance. "We have to do it out here in the park, in front of everyone?"

"In front of whom? There's hardly anyone here this time of day."

"Hmm," he grumbled.

"It's a wonderful way to get in touch with your body and nature. It's peaceful."

Burke shook his head, but his grin let her know he was open to her lead. It was one of the traits she liked the most about him. He had set ideas on a lot of things, but he could hear someone else's opinions and he was willing to try new experiences.

Together, they found a spot at the back of the small group of mostly older people. Before attempting the different exercises, Burke watched the guide go through her sequence first. On the next rotation, he tried it. His athletic frame performed with strength and balance, if not grace. His movements were punctuated with stiff jerks, but he laughed at his own awkwardness. Yet another thing to love about Burke.

What is it about this woman that makes me willing do crazy shit like this for her? Burke watched Susan's lithe body go through the elegant motions of Tai Chi. He pictured his hands running up her sides as she stretched her arms to the sky. That's when he lost his balance and had to refocus on the routine. Susan's soft laugh made him want to become a Tai Chi master. He'd do anything for her. Christ, he was in way over his head.

An hour later, they shared a water bottle and took their things back to Susan's car. Burke closed the hatch. "Kendra invited us to come for dinner tonight, if you'd like. She and Rick are grilling steaks." Burke liked that his friends included Susan. It was as though they thought of them as an official couple.

"That sounds fun. She lives in the mountains, doesn't she?"

"At the base of the foothills. It's nice."

"What time?"

"She said come any time after four."

"Perfect. Then we'll have the afternoon to go to the Contemporary Art Museum. That's the next activity I have planned for us today."

Burke sighed. "Regular art museums are one thing. I have to tell you ahead of time, I don't like modern art. It's just a bunch of weird shit a three-year-old could make, that someone decided to call art. How about we compromise and go to the real Art Museum? They have a particularly nice Renoir collection."

Susan's mouth opened, but she didn't say anything. Her brows furrowed, and Burke figured he'd said the wrong thing.

"You never stop surprising me. First, the symphony, and now you know about the Renoir collection?" A mischievous smirk played on her lips. "I guess there's a lot more to you than a pretty face and incredible pecs."

"Incredible, huh?" The way she looked at him made him feel like Captain America.

She spun away, but not before he saw her bite her lower lip. Burke moved up behind her and wrapped his arms around her, nuzzling her neck. "I'll go with you wherever you want, but don't expect me to have an enlightened discussion of how toilet paper rolls glued to a canvas and gobbed with bright paint colors means anything more than that people are ridiculously gullible."

Susan twisted around in his embrace until she faced him and circled her arms behind his neck. He thought of many things he'd rather do than wander through a room full of junk. When she stretched up to kiss him, his body as much as told her what he had on his mind. He pulled her tight, and they pressed against each other. Burke released her and snatched up the water bottle, guzzling the rest of the cold drink. He needed some space because what he wanted to do right then and there—was illegal.

Susan eyed him with humor skipping in her eyes. "Ready to go?"

He could only manage a nod.

Even Susan had to admit that the museum was a disappointment. Or, maybe the game of trying to find things that would push Burke out of his conservative, good-old-boy mind-set was getting tiresome. Something had shifted. Suddenly, all she wanted was to do what pleased him. Susan was happy to spend the evening with Rick and Kendra, but she hoped the hours would pass quickly. Perhaps tonight Burke would finally ask her to stay.

A chocolate Lab bounded out of the front door toward Burke's truck when they pulled up in front of Kendra's house. Kendra and Rick followed the young dog outside, and Rick paused and held the door for a three-legged bloodhound.

Susan glanced at Burke, and the corners of his mouth pinched. "That's Baxter, the dog who Abbot Lee shot."

Susan shook her head with sorrow. "I'm so relieved that creep will spend the rest of his life in prison." A dull pain darted through Susan's heart. "Poor dog, and poor Kendra. That must have broken her heart."

"It did. Not only did Bax have to retire, but she lost her partner." When Burke opened Susan's door, Annie hopped and leaped around his legs. He bent down to rub her head and ears when he could grasp ahold of her. "This is Annie, Kendra's new partner."

Susan held her hand out for a sniff and lick. "We've met. I met Annie on my tour of Kendra's work."

Burke's jaw bunched. "Same day you met Jennings?"

She shrugged but before she could reassure him, Kendra commanded, "Annie, *knoze*." The dog sprinted to Kendra's side and sat down. "Good girl Annie." Kendra looked back up at Susan. "Hi, Susan. Welcome. We're so glad you guys could make it. You've met Annie, and this is Baxter."

The bloodhound ambled up to Burke first and then sat politely at Susan's feet to receive her greeting strokes. "Nice to meet you, Baxter." Susan glanced at Kendra. "What does *No-Say* mean?"

"*Knoze* basically means heel. It's Czech." Kendra scratched her Labrador's ears.

"How's the training going with Annie?" Burke walked toward them, and he and Rick shook hands.

Kendra turned her head from side to side and laughed. "Well, the good news is that Annie is smart and willing. The bad news is she'll behave like a puppy for about another seven to ten years and then she'll retire. To be honest, it's hard to get used to all of her extra energy. I take her swimming at the reservoir almost daily just to wear the edge off."

Susan knelt down before Annie and stroked her soft ears. "She's beautiful." Annie responded with a sloppy lick across Susan's cheek. She laughed and wiped her face on her sleeve.

Kendra patted the dog's head. "She has an incredible nose. I'd put her up against Baxter anytime, and I never thought any dogs had as good of noses as Bloodhounds."

Annie lapped at Susan's hands and bumped them to encourage more petting when Susan stood.

Rick chuckled. "She sure seems to like you, Susan."

"The feeling is mutual."

Kendra led the group around the side yard to the back deck where the patio table was set for dinner and the grill was heating up. "You guys want a beer or a glass of wine?"

"Wine for me," Susan said. "Burke? Beer?"

"Thanks." He grabbed a bottle from a cooler on the deck, kissed Susan's cheek, and went out into the yard with Rick.

The men stood together on the lawn playing with the puppy and tossing humorous insults back and forth. They threw a tennis ball for Annie who raced after it like a greyhound chases a rabbit. Kendra and Susan went in through the back door to the kitchen to get their wine and bring out the food.

"Something smells amazing in here." Susan sniffed at the air.

Kendra pointed to the counter with her chin. "Apple pie. Burke's favorite." Kendra handed Susan the salad bowl and tongs. "Things seem to be going well between you two."

Susan smiled. "I think they are. I wondered at first because we're so different in many ways, but we're figuring it out."

"Is it an 'opposites attract' sort of thing?"

"I don't know." Susan laughed and leaned into Kendra's ear. "It's definitely a 'hot, gorgeous guy attracting me' sort of a thing, that much I know."

Kendra laughed. "Burke's a great guy. He's a bit straight-laced, but I've seen him loosen up, so I know it can happen."

"I can't wait." Susan giggled.

Over dinner, Kendra asked, "How are things going with building your online business?"

"Awesome. In fact, I'm gradually growing a following. I've been working on creating an online survey to see what people's needs are. Then my goal is to build some courses that will help clients accomplish their own health goals. It's a huge process to get everything set up, but once it's in motion, it should be much simpler to manage it. I'll handle a lot of it with automations."

Rick sat forward and leaned his forearms against the table. "What kind of health goals? Do you mean diets?"

"No, more like learning how to eat healthier. First of all, there are always the people who think they need to lose weight. The thing is, that might not be what they really need or even want. Sometimes, what people mean when they say they'd like to lose weight, is that they actually want to be stronger and leaner. Which can often mean eating *more* of the right foods." Susan laughed at her own enthusiasm. "I'm not telling you three anything you don't already know. You guys are all in great physical condition."

"We have to be, for our jobs." Rick reached for Kendra and pulled her over to sit in his lap. "Except Kendra. She's just naturally perfect."

Kendra swatted at him. "Whatever." But the glow in her eyes told Susan she loved his attention. Susan wanted this kind of relationship in her life, and she snuck a glance at Burke. He answered her look with a slow, suggestive smile that sparked a flame deep inside.

Kendra stacked Rick's plate on hers and stood to gather the others. "So what's your next step?"

Susan helped with the dishes. "Well, I'm going to the Women Entrepreneurs Strength Building Conference this week. I hope to learn a ton from ladies who've already found a way to be successful in their businesses. I'm super excited."

"I didn't realize that was so soon." Burke sat up, a line furrowing between his brows.

"I thought I told you." Susan's heart missed a beat. She hadn't considered how Burke would feel about being apart for over a week. They wouldn't even be able to talk on the phone. That was part of the conference format. They had to surrender their phones and watches at the door.

"You did, only I thought it was later, like next month. When do you leave?" Burke stood and took the dishes out of her hands.

"Tomorrow. It's for ten days, and I'll be totally incommunicado." Susan grimaced, the full impact of her words causing her to realize the bad timing of the trip. She didn't want to be away from Burke that long.

Burke's jaw flexed, and his brows scrunched together. He followed Kendra into the kitchen with the plates but was back in seconds. Burke reached for her, and Susan moved into his arms.

"Ten days is a long time."

"I know, I'm sorry. Maybe I should cancel—go another time?" Confused by the swirl of powerful emotions flooding through her, Susan wanted Burke to tell her what to do. Which was weird. She had never wanted *anyone* telling her what to do, but some small part of her hoped he'd ask her to stay home.

"No way." His strong voice rolled over her. "This is your dream. I'll hate not seeing or talking to you for that long, but you need to do this. You'll regret it if you don't."

Kendra nudged him. "Good answer, Cameron. I thought I might have to punch you, but lucky for you, you said the right thing." She carried the last of the dinnerware into the kitchen while Rick cleaned up the grill.

"Let's have a celebration dinner when you get back." Rick leaned against the deck railing. "That'll give our poor lonely boy here something to look forward to while you're off having the time of your life."

Burke chuckled. "I'd tell you where you could get off, but for once you've had a good idea." He pressed his lips into Susan's hair. "I'll plan something while you're gone and we can celebrate when you get home."

BURKE'S CHEST ACHED AT THE THOUGHT OF SUSAN BEING gone. He'd never viewed ten days as a long time before but now it seemed like an eternity. Susan slid her arm around him and leaned into him. She tilted her face to his and kissed his jaw. Blood surged through his body like a Tsunami. It was time to go.

"Pie, anyone?" Kendra's voice sang out from the kitchen.

Burke barked a short. "No."

Susan's gaze snapped to his, and they stared at each other. She cleared her throat to answer, her eyes never leaving his. "None for me either, thanks though."

"It's getting late. We should probably be going." Burke wanted to have Susan to himself. Alone. Now. Vaguely he heard Rick chuckle as he went to join Kendra, leaving them on the deck.

Susan's eyes were dreamy as they plunged into his. She pressed herself against his chest, gazing up. "Are you ready?"

A growl rose from his throat. He was beyond ready. Burke hoped he could make it back to her place without getting pulled over for speeding. He tightened his hold on Susan, and she burrowed her head in his neck.

"Take me home."

They went inside to thank Kendra for dinner, and Burke kissed her on the cheek. "Sorry to be leaving so soon, but Susan has an early morning drive up to Buena Vista."

Kendra's eyes held laughter and warmth. "I understand, and I'm happy for you." She reached for Susan's hand. "Have fun at your conference. I hope you come home all hyped-up and inspired with new ideas."

"I'm sure I will." The women embraced.

Rick shook Burke's hand. "Drive safe—no speeding. You have plenty of time, it's still early." His almost black eyes sparked humor. Burke didn't care if he and Susan were being obvious about why they wanted to leave. His urgency was louder than his sense of decorum at the moment.

Susan dropped to her knees to bid the dogs a good-night. Annie flopped onto her side in Susan's lap wanting her belly scratched, but Kendra cut the rambunctious behavior short. "*Knoze*." Annie hopped to her feet, sat down next to Kendra, and looked at Susan with a wide Labrador grin.

"Good night, and thanks for everything. We'll have you guys over after I get back from the mountains." Susan waved, and she and Burke left through the front door.

Hand in hand they made their way down the walk. A phone rang in the house behind them as Burke opened Susan's door for her. He longed to get her somewhere private. Burke wanted to make her his before she left on her trip. As Susan climbed up into the cab, he ran his fingers over her cheek and drew her into a kiss he hoped would communicate his desire for her and a promise of more. She responded with a heated passion that caused his heart to race.

"Burke."

He thought he heard his name, but he ignored it—intent on the swirling whirlpool of ravenous need whipping around inside him.

"Hey, Cameron."

He delved deeper in the kiss, his brain separating input and discarding anything that wasn't Susan and the sensations she induced. His hand roamed from her back to grasp her narrow waist, edging up to the curve of her breast.

"Agent Cameron!" Rick's commanding voice finally broke through, and Burke's head snapped up. His breath ragged, he turned with undisguised irritation toward his boss.

"What?"

Rick had come halfway down the front walk. He glanced at Susan. "I'm sorry, Susan." His eyes leveled on Burke. "I know this sucks, man, but we just got called in. We have to go—right away. There's been a murder connected with drugs and human trafficking down in Pueblo. It'll take us a good hour and a half to get there, if we leave right now."

Burke's energy deflated like a popped balloon, and he swallowed hard.

"What's going on?" Susan's voice was small beside him.

Rick answered. "Burke and I are working a case and something's come up. Kendra can drive you home."

Susan's eyes were large in the moonlight. "I understand." She reached her hands up and held both sides of Burke's face. A gentle laugh sighed through her words. "I guess I'll see you in ten days. We certainly have something to look forward to." She slid out of the truck and raised up on her toes to kiss him.

The extra testosterone in Burke's system pinged through him like a summer hailstorm. Cut short from burning it off in the way nature intended, Burke was edgy, and frustrated. "You have no idea how sorry I am." He glanced at Rick.

"I'll uh, wait inside." Rick took the hint and left.

"I think I do." She tugged on his lower lip with her teeth.

"Now you're just torturing me." Burke tried to laugh, but a wave of unspent desire choked his words. "I'll make this up to you. I promise."

Susan blinked up at him. "I'll hold you to that."

The engine of Rick's Explorer roared to life. "I've got to go."

"I'm going back inside to eat my emotions with a huge

piece of Kendra's apple pie." Susan gave Burke a final peck. "Be safe." She glanced down before raising her eyes to meet his gaze once again. "If you get back before midnight..."

Burke took her mouth with a promise of hope that he would.

Chapter Seven

B urke flung himself into Rick's Explorer and slammed the door. His body was slow to re-absorb the hormones flooding his system.

"Hey, man, don't take it out on my car."

"This sucks."

"I agree." Rick turned out onto the road and headed for the highway.

"What's happened?"

"All I know at this point, is the local Pueblo police pulled over a truck as it was leaving a rest stop on I-25 headed north. They suspected the driver was hauling drugs and possibly working a human trafficking line. They packed the truck with drugs, but no people. However, they found two dead bodies at the rest stop the guy just left. Now they're trying to make a connection between the two."

Burke's analytical mind snapped back into work mode. He considered the case they were assigned to. Drugs from marijuana to heroin had been running up and down the I-25 corridor from Mexico to Montana and spreading east and west on I-70. "It's ironic that Coloradans voted to make pot legal, and all that happened was that the illegal side of the drug trade got worse. Did people think drug lords would simply smile and be glad they could now grow their weed legally—happy to pay the US government taxes for the privilege? It's more dangerous now than ever."

"You're right, and this case is taking another dark turn."

"What do you mean?"

"Apparently, the man who was murdered, shot in the back of the head by the way, was found without any clothes on, laying prostrate on top of a young girl, also naked. She's estimated to be around twelve years old. The execution style killing has drug cartel written all over it."

"That's sick." Burke's gut curled in on itself.

"It gets sicker. I'm afraid this is only a gust of the tornado headed our way."

Rick made a quick stop at a drive-through coffee shop for caffeine, then they made their way south to the bloody scene of the drug world. The coffee was stale and left a flat, bitter taste on Burke's tongue that matched his mood.

BY THE TIME THEY FINISHED THE LONG DRIVE TO Pueblo, the arrest was made and the drugs had been confiscated. Burke and Rick met the Officer in Charge and the Crime Scene Investigators at the rest-stop murder scene. They parked behind two cop cars with their red and blue lights still flashing and walked toward a brightly lit area roped off with yellow crime scene tape.

"About time the Feds show up," the Sergeant, a short, stocky man, chuckled and stretched out his thick hand toward Rick.

Rick shook it. "Yeah, sorry we didn't get here sooner. We had to drive down from Denver. I'm Agent Sanchez, and this is Agent Cameron."

"Sergeant Muñoz." He nodded a greeting before turning around to face the crime scene. His radio squawked, and he paused to listen before explaining the situation. "We were sure these guys were smuggling people, but all we found inside the vehicle were drugs."

Burke watched as two bodies were zipped into body bags and loaded on gurneys. "Did the truck come up from El Paso?"

"Yep. Twenty kilos of what we think is China White were stacked and wrapped in plastic on a pallet in the trailer on the back. We suspect it's laced with fentanyl. Of course, we won't know that for sure until we get the lab results."

Rick rubbed his chin. "Do you think the cartel is trying to open new markets? Fentanyl is more prevalent in California and the east coast."

"Could be." The Sergeant rocked back on his heels. "What do you fellas think?" He held up his phone to show them photos of the truck being loaded and towed to the impound lot.

"I think that's an awfully big trailer for hauling only twenty kilos of heroin." Burke peered at the small screen.

Rick took the phone and enlarged the photo. "Could they have already delivered a load? Maybe downloaded some girls somewhere too?"

"It's possible, but the New Mexican State Police started tracking them just north of Las Cruces. We received word from them that they suspected the truck was carrying women and children. The Colorado State Troopers took over once the vehicle drove across our border, and our city police joined up with them when they got near Pueblo." The Sergeant took his phone back from Rick and slid it into its holster on his belt. "No one saw anyone getting out of the truck except to pump gas. The driver pulled over at several rest stops along the way, but apparently he remained in the cab." Muñoz lifted his chin and rolled his eyes skyward. "Of course, no one saw the murders happen either." The lawman shook his head. "We're hoping to connect the deaths with the driver of the truck, which I don't think will be too hard. But even still, that's only one girl—hardly a harem. It's possible we had bum intel."

Ragged frustration packed Burke's chest and throat. They'd driven down to Pueblo to further their investigation on the increasing problem of human trafficking in Colorado, especially along the I-25 corridor, only to find a relatively small amount of drugs and two dead bodies. "So, why did you guys call us all the way down here for this? We could have done all this over the phone and email."

Rick gripped his shoulder and pulled him backward. Subtly edging himself in front of Burke, he asked, "Are these the only photos you have? Do you have any of the murder scene? Or more of the truck?"

"That's it. The truck is in impound though, if you want to have a look at it. The crime investigators have the murder scene evidence."

"Thanks. We'll look into it in the morning. Where's a good place to rack out for the night?"

"There's a motel about three miles south, if you're not too picky."

Burke's gut bunched. "We're staying down here?"

"Yeah, it's too late to drive back to Denver tonight, and

I want to see the evidence and interview the suspect in the morning."

A sigh pushed its way out of Burke's chest, and he perched his hands on his hips. "Okay."

"Hey, man. I'm sorry about you and Susan, but—"

"It's the job, I get it. I was just hoping to stop by her place tonight to say goodbye. She leaves tomorrow morning for ten days."

Rick chuckled. "I guess you can look forward to the reunion when she gets back. Don't they say, absence makes the heart grow fonder?"

Burke swallowed back his physical frustration. He'd already waited a long time to be intimate with Susan and now that he was ready to take that step, ten days seemed like forever.

SUSAN SKOOTCHED ONTO THE BLACK LEATHER SEAT OF Kendra's Jeep and waited for her to load her dogs. "Thanks for driving me home."

"It's no problem." Kendra closed her door. "Sorry about Burke having to leave."

"Is it like this a lot? You guys getting called into work at the drop of a hat?" Susan buckled her seatbelt.

Kendra turned the key and started her engine. "It can be. Mostly Burke works eight to five unless something happens."

"Is he in danger?" A painful lump expanded inside Susan's throat. She'd come to care about him more than she realized over the past month.

Kendra smiled at her and squeezed her hand. "I don't

think so. He and Rick are just investigating a situation the local police have already handled. They'll be fine."

"Want to have a glass of wine with me at my place while we wait to hear?"

Kendra's smile broadened. "Sure, why not? If you don't mind the dogs in your apartment."

"I'm happy to have them." In fact, she'd be more than happy for the distraction while she waited for Burke to call.

SUSAN OPENED HER APARTMENT DOOR, AND THE WOMEN sidestepped her luggage that sat packed and waiting for her trip in the morning. Baxter and Annie scampered in behind them. "Come on in. Red or white?"

"Red would be great." Kendra followed Susan into the galley kitchen.

"I have some chocolates we can share too, even though we did just have some of your pie." Susan twisted the bottle opener into the cork and pulled. "Too bad the guys missed out."

Kendra laughed. "Yeah, Burke was sure in a hurry to leave with you tonight. I've never known him to walk away from apple pie before."

Susan's face warmed. "I hope you weren't offended. It's just that I'm leaving tomorrow, and..."

"No, I get it. You guys must be getting serious, then?"

Waiting to answer until the glasses were full, Susan handed one to Kendra. She held her glass to her nose and breathed in. "Mmm, black currants." Susan gestured toward the living room and followed her new friend with the box of chocolate. "I don't know exactly how serious we are. I have a hard time getting a read on Burke's feelings."

She and Kendra sat opposite each other in the living room. The dogs curled up at their feet.

"That's funny. Burke's a pretty straightforward guy."

"Yes, I agree, but every time I think we're going to... to extend our evening, he curls my toes with an incredible kiss and then says goodnight and leaves."

One of Kendra's dark brows spiked. "You mean..."

Susan shook her head. "So, tonight would have been the first time. At least that's what I hoped was happening, but now I'll never know."

"Hm." Kendra reached for a piece of candy.

"What do you mean by *that?*"

"You guys have been dating for weeks now."

Susan's heart sank. Kendra and Burke were close friends, and if his lack of progress on the intimate level surprised her, then something had to be wrong. "Yes. So it seems strange to you too? His not moving forward, intimately?"

Kendra pursed her lips into a thinking frown. "Have you given him any indication that *you* wanted to wait? 'Cuz one thing I know about Burke is he'd never push himself on a woman."

"No. In fact, if anything, I've been the assertive one. Maybe he just doesn't feel the same way I do?" Susan's chest ached at the thought. *Maybe he doesn't want to be with me.*

Kendra shook her head. "No. No, I think it might be the exact opposite. I know he cares for you. He talks about you all the time. The thing about Burke is, as good-looking as he is, he's not in any way, a lady's man. He wants to get married and have a family—the whole nine yards. So, he's probably taking it slow to be sure you guys want the same things."

"He has talked about that."

"See? I bet that's it." Kendra tucked one of her legs underneath her and stretched to pet Baxter's flank. "So, do you? Want the same things?"

Susan's pulse skipped a beat, and she felt the pressurized weight of Kendra's question. "I do—eventually, but right now I'm focused on trying to start my business. I guess I just want to have fun for a while. I'm not ready to settle down yet."

Kendra shrugged. "There's nothing wrong with that, Susan, but I'm betting that's why Burke is slow to make his move."

"But, how will we know if we want a life together if we don't try it out?"

Kendra shrugged. "Burke takes his relationships seriously. I can't see him just fooling around for the fun of it. He's a stand-up guy."

"That's so old-fashioned." Susan plucked at a loose loop in the upholstery's weave, then smoothed her hand across the nubby fabric. Her body warmed with her thoughts of Burke. "I told him I thought he was a boy scout."

Kendra snickered. "Yes. That's Burke, to a T. I tease him all the time that he could be cast in that old FBI TV show, Dragnet." She screwed up her face and lowered her voice. "Just the facts, ma'am." Laughing at her own joke, Kendra reached out, and touched Susan's knee. "If you understand that about Burke, then you know precisely who you're dealing with. He's the kind of man a woman wants to settle down with when she's ready. The kind of man a woman can depend on, one she wants to grow old with."

"I know—but I'm just not in that place right now. Maybe our timing is off?"

"Could be. It'll be good for you both to have a few days away from each other—to think. You'll figure it out. Either way though, don't believe for a second that because he hasn't made the move, he's not hot for you. Oh, my god—did you see the fire in his eyes when Rick called him back to go to work?"

Susan giggled. "I'd hoped that wasn't just my imagination."

Kendra grinned but then chewed her lower lip. "Promise me one thing though. I know Burke doesn't need me to be his big sister, but he's a good friend. He doesn't let too many people in, so whatever happens between you two, just be honest with him. Don't play games."

A flash of pure indignation washed through Susan. "I realize you don't know me very well, but I am not someone who plays games. I care about Burke. I would never hurt him on purpose." Annie responded to Susan's agitation by sitting up and resting her chin on Susan's knee. Susan stroked the spot between the Lab's eyes.

"Did Clay ever call you?"

"Yes, but I told him I was seeing someone."

"Good." Kendra's grin re-emerged, "Just don't get too caught up in Burke's baby-blues and bulging biceps to remember that he's a man whose feelings run deep."

"I hear you." Susan reached for the box of candy and held it toward Kendra to change the focus. "Another chocolate?"

Susan and Kendra talked until early in the morning, sharing tales of their childhoods and the struggles they each had growing up. Finally, Kendra called to her sleeping dogs. "It's time to get these two sleepy-heads home. Not to mention, sleepy-me."

Susan walked her to the door and gave her a hug. "Thanks for the ride home, and the friendship. I'm really having fun getting to know you."

"Me too. I don't have many women friends. It's nice."

Chapter Eight

Susan slapped at her phone when the alarm sounded. It had been the early morning hours before Kendra went home, and the wine they shared now resulted in reluctant eyelids. She pushed herself up and sat on the edge of her bed wiping the weariness away. Stretching, Susan turned the hot water on in the shower and waited for it to heat. She was already packed, so all she had left to do was get dressed and have breakfast.

Her thoughts returned to Burke. They were never off of him for long. Susan glanced at her phone again, checking to see if he had texted or called. He hadn't. She chewed the inside of her cheek. If he didn't call her in the next forty-five minutes, she'd phone him. Then that would be it for ten whole days. This long-awaited conference now sat plumb in the middle of bad timing. She and Burke were just about to take a serious turn in their relationship, and she was leaving.

"Ugghhh!" Susan growled aloud into the silence of her apartment. She checked her phone one more time before she plunged herself under the warm stream of water.

Dressed and fed, Susan packed her last bag into the trunk of her Prius. She pulled her phone from her back pocket and tapped the screen. Still no Burke. *He's the old-fashioned one. Why hasn't he called me?* She eased herself into the driver's seat, clicked on his contact information, and listened while his device rang miles to the south.

"H'lo?" Burke's muffled voice came over the line.

"Burke? It's eight o'clock. Did I wake you?" Susan would have sworn Burke Cameron had never slept past six in the morning his whole life.

"Susan?" Undiscernible sounds and muted swearing aired through her speaker. "Damn. My alarm didn't go off. I'm sorry. Rick and I interviewed the suspect till four this morning." He coughed, and his voice cleared. "I'm so glad you called. I'd have been totally bummed if I missed you."

"Sorry I woke you, but I'm getting ready to leave. I wanted to hear your voice once more before I drive up in the mountains."

"Me too. You're all set? Your gas tank's full and everything?"

Susan giggled. "Yes, Dad." Actually, she'd have to check that. She forgot to think about gas.

"You have directions to get where you're going?"

"Jeeze. I have Google maps, you know." She felt his chuckle roll over her and wanted to feel his strong arms around her.

"Sorry, I can't help myself. I want you to be safe."

Susan smiled and closed her eyes. "Thanks. You're sweet. I'll be fine though, I promise."

"I hate that I couldn't make it back up there last night." His tone dropped and drew her in.

"Me too, but it's only ten days. Let's plan a whole day together when I get back."

"Deal." He went silent. The moment lengthened. "Susan?"

"Yes?"

"I..." he cleared his throat. "I'm really starting to care about you. A lot."

"I feel the same, Burke. It will be a long ten days, but then we have the entire summer ahead of us."

"I'm going to miss you."

"It's strange isn't it? I mean we've only been together a little over a month, but I'll miss you too—like crazy."

"Yeah. Well, drive safe. I can't wait till you get home."

"Me too."

***

BURKE ENDED THE CALL AND RAN A HAND ACROSS HIS face. He needed a jolt in the form of a hot shower and an even hotter cup of coffee. He and Rick were going to take a final crack at the driver. For two hours last night, the guy pretended not to know English, which didn't do him much good since Rick was fluent in Spanish. Yet he still played dumb. With any luck, the schmuck didn't get any sleep in his cell and would have to face their next interview exhausted.

Rick was already in the lobby eating from a container of yogurt provided from the complimentary continental breakfast set out on the counter. It was a paltry offering, but it was available, and Burke needed food. He filled a

Styrofoam cup with coffee, grabbed a dry non-descript pastry, and slid into a chair across from Rick.

"Get any sleep?"

"Sure, like a baby." Rick gave him a wry expression.

"I slept hard and almost didn't wake up. Luckily Susan called before she left."

Rick nodded and jammed his napkin into the empty container. "I don't think we'll get much from this guy today. He's just a drug mule, hired to drive the truck."

"And murder?"

"Probably. I think the killing was meant to send a message. The staging was obviously deliberate. I mean, I doubt the guy was actually screwing that girl right on the sidewalk of the rest stop."

Burke's stomach rolled. It was too early to think about the horrific scene from the night before, especially before breakfast. "You never know. Some people are beyond disgusting."

"True, but still. It looked contrived to me. I'll keep an open mind, but I'm going into the interview with that theory this morning."

RAGGED WITH LACK OF SLEEP, THE SUSPECT SAT FACING the camera in the small interview room at the Pueblo Police Department sub-station. Someone from the Colorado State Police had kept him up for the past couple of hours with their own investigation. The local PD had at him in the times between. Sometimes it was awkward to be involved in a case with federal, state, and local police interest, but in this situation it worked to keep the driver tired and off balance. Burke and Rick were only interested in information that would lead them to the next step up the food chain. They'd get what they could and leave the dirt-bag to the state and local cops to deal with.

Rick slapped a notebook down on the tabletop, causing the suspect to jolt awake. Both he and Burke carried cups of coffee into the small room with them knowing the enticing aroma might become a bargaining chip. The man sniffed at the air. Rick sat across from the suspect and Burke took a standing position behind him, leaning against the wall.

"I'm thirsty, man." The driver peered into Rick's cup then stared up at him with dark eyes.

Rick raised his chin to Burke. "Have them bring in a cup of water."

"Oh, come on, man. I've been awake all night. *Dame un café. Por favor.*"

Smirking, Rick shook his head.

Burke stepped out and asked one of the local officers to bring a paper cup of water. "And make it lukewarm."

The cop smirked and left on the errand. Burke returned to the room.

"So," Rick opened the file, but stared at the suspect over the top. "Where did you get the drugs?"

"I told you, man. They hired me to drive the truck up to Colorado Springs. That's all I know. I didn't know there were drugs in there."

"Then why did you kill that man and the young girl?"

"I didn't."

"Why don't you tell me what happened between Thursday morning, when you woke up and now. Every detail."

The man was heavy on mundane details and sketchy on the ones that mattered, but that was fine. Burke knew that Rick would eventually ask him to tell his story backwards starting from the interrogation, and the lies would stand out.

"The keys were in my post office box with directions to the truck. I found the truck, got in, and started driving. That's it. Until I got pulled over."

Rick scribbled words on a pad of paper. "Where did you pick the truck up?"

"In a Walmart parking lot."

"In El Paso?"

"No. Las Cruces."

"You didn't once stop for gas or food?" Burke asked from behind the man's head.

The man jumped and shifted to look at Burke. "Well, yeah, I mean, I guess I stopped for gas."

"How many times?"

"Uh... once."

Rick leaned back in his chair. "Just once?"

"Yeah."

"But your tank was full when the cops hauled the truck to the impound lot."

"Cuz I just filled up."

Burke had him swinging around again. "So you can go 500 miles on a tank of gas in that crap truck?"

The suspects eyes narrowed. "I guess, sure. I never measured. It's not my truck."

Rick took a long drink of his coffee and sighed with contentment.

"Come on, man." The suspect leaned forward. "Can't I get some coffee in this hellhole?"

"You want me to give you something, but you refuse to offer me anything." Rick took another swallow.

"I'm telling you what happened. What do you want from me?"

Burke pulled a chair out from the table, turned it around and straddled it. "We want the truth."

The man elevated his tone. "I'm telling the truth."

Rick bent forward, braced his arms on the table, and stared into the man's eyes. "Okay, so, tell me the sequence of events backwards. Start with you sitting here, begging for coffee."

"*Jesu*—fine. I'm here asking to be treated fairly. The cops brought me here last night and have been grilling me all night long. I'm fucking tired."

Burke interrupted, "Yeah, yeah, we don't want your sob story."

"I got pulled over, and the cops yanked me out of my truck. They told me to open the back, so I did, and it was full of drugs, but I didn't know anything about them." He eyed both Burke and Rick. When neither responded, he continued.

"I stopped for gas, like I said, and—"

Rick jumped in. "Was that before or after you were at the rest stop?"

"Before—" the suspect's eyes ping-ponged back-and-forth between Burke and Rick. "I mean..."

"What happened at the rest stop?"

The man's face paled. "Look, the girl was already dead, man. I didn't kill her."

"She was in the back with the drugs?"

He broke and held his hand over his eyes. "Yes—I mean no. She was back there, but she was alive."

Burke stood and rested his hands on his hips. "I thought you said you didn't look in the back."

"I lied, all right? But now I'm telling the truth. I didn't kill that girl."

"Then, who did?"

"That fat bastard who was on top of her." The man yelled, his exhausted desperation etched on his face. "We took a break, and he wanted to... test the merchandise. But he started choking her, and she was screaming, trying to fight him off."

"So you shot him?"

"It wasn't me. I didn't shoot him. I was in the truck—I swear."

"Who shot him then?"

"I don't know. I heard the shots, and I rammed the truck into gear and sped away. I didn't want to be next."

Rick brought the attention back to his line of questioning. "What happened right before you opened the back of the truck?"

The man jerked his head around. His eyes pivoted back and forth looking as though his brain struggled to stay on his invented time-line. "We were driving. We'd just stopped for dinner at a truck stop."

"What did you have for dinner?"

The man's face went blank. He stared at Rick.

"A... burger."

"Where did you keep the gun?"

"Under the seat." The words were out, and he couldn't take them back. He shook his head and closed his eyes. "Shit."

Rick kept hammering. "How many other girls were in the truck?"

The man's shoulders slumped, and he leaned his head forward on his arm. His voice sounded with defeat. "None. She was it. Supposed to be like a gift or something."

"Where were you taking her? Who were you taking her to?"

"I swear to God, we were just supposed to drive into

Colorado Springs and drop the car off at the airport.
That's it."

"How are you getting paid?"

"I got half up front, and I was gonna get the other half
when I got back home."

"Give me a name."

"I don't got a name."

"Bull shit."

"I don't, I swear. Just notes and cash. That's all."

Rick pushed his chair back and stood. Burke opened
the door to the interrogation room and gestured for the
local cop waiting in the hallway to come in.

"He's all yours."

"Mr. Muñoz, you are under arrest for the murder of..."

Burke and Rick didn't need to stay to hear the guy
being read his Miranda rights. They stopped in the
captain's office on their way out.

Rick knocked on the open-door frame. "You have the
tape and his confession. Will you email me copies?"

The captain stood to shake hands. "You got it. Did you
get everything you were looking for?"

Rick clasped the back of his neck. "Nope. This guy was
a drug mule, but I believe he doesn't know who hired him.
We might have to go down to Las Cruces and see what we
can dig up down there."

"Well, good luck."

Burke stuck out his hand. "Thanks, Captain. We'll
keep you posted." Burke followed Rick out to his car. "So
why did that dirt bag murder the fat guy? Surely not to
protect the girl."

"No. That guy was dying no matter what. It just
happened to be when he had his pants down - literally."

"Why?"

"I think the murder is probably a message. Now we need to figure out who the message is from and who it's to."

"And the girl?" Burke closed his eyes against the image of the naked pre-teen crushed by the obese monster.

"Just an inconsequential life to these pigs." Rick got in behind the steering wheel and slammed his door so hard the vehicle shook. "Hopefully we'll have an ID soon and someone can let her family know."

"This whole thing is twisted."

Rick stared at Burke. "This is nothing. Put on your seatbelt."

Chapter Nine

Back in the city, Rick took a cross-town route to the office. Driving through the gentrified, old neighborhoods east of downtown Denver, Burke appreciated the mature trees shading the narrow streets. They made their way past a park where a group of older people gathered together, practicing Tai Chi. Burke chuckled under his breath.

"What's funny?" Rick glanced out Burke's window.

"See those people doing Tai Chi in the park?"

Rick nodded and returned his focus to driving.

"Susan made me go with her to try that yesterday morning." Burke shook his head and rubbed his chin. "Man, can that have just been yesterday? Seems like a week ago."

Black brows shot up and laughing, Rick gave Burke a sideways glance. "Are you kidding me?"

"It's totally a Susan kinda thing."

"Yeah, I can see her doing it, but you? Priceless."

"It was ridiculous, for sure." A lopsided smirk twisted his lips as Burke remembered his times with Susan. He was still skeptical about their chances as a couple. They were like night and day, but... then again, there couldn't be a night without day, so—maybe.

Rick broke into his thoughts. "Wipe that silly grin off your face, you look like Goofy."

The teasing only caused Burke's smile to broaden. "Can't help it, man."

"Good. In fact, it's great to see you two so happy." Rick turned in front of the United Airlines Training Center and drove several more blocks to the parking garage of the FBI building. His phone rang as the entry bar lifted.

As soon as Rick parked, Burke got out of the car to give Rick privacy for his conversation and to enjoy some fresh air before having to go inside. June was one of Colorado's best months as far as he was concerned. Warm, gorgeous days that weren't yet too hot. A slight breeze filled with the scent of faded lilac blooms brushed across his face. He leaned against a cement column and breathed the fragrance in.

Rick slid out of his car and slammed the door, the sound echoing in the empty garage. "You won't believe this."

Burke turned to listen.

"That was the Pueblo PD. They just got word from the New Mexico State Police that two other girls were found at different rest stops along I-25. Both looked to be about the same age as the girl in Pueblo. When they discovered them, both bodies were naked and appeared to have been strangled. No definitive reports from the medical examiner yet." Rick pounded his hand against the frame of the Explorer's door. "Damn it. We have to find the head of this snake."

"Did they question the driver again?"

"They're interrogating him right now. Too bad we already left."

"If those girls started out in the same truck, and it seems likely they did, whoever sent them will view them as his property. Penalty for stealing from a cartel is death—execution style."

"Exactly." Rick dragged a hand over his face. "This entire thing makes me sick. Those girls were just children."

Burke swallowed against a surge of bile burning his throat. "What's our next step?"

The men walked together toward the building's entrance. Rick glanced at his watch. "We have kidnapping and murders that cross state lines, so we certainly have jurisdiction. The execution of the dead guy will serve as a powerful message to other mules. With any luck we can find the trafficking routes and rescue some children before any more harm comes to them. We have to do something to shut this crap down."

"What about setting up highway check points? Pull over trucks that might be carrying human cargo?"

"It could be a place to start, but I'd like to work alongside the special task force that focuses on these crimes exclusively. I'm going to see if I can get assigned over there."

"I'm in too. Now that I've seen just a minor piece of human trafficking in person, I'll never be able to look the other way."

"Good, let's do it. I'll call Jennings over at K9. It'll help to have some dogs on the job too."

Burke nodded. He ground his teeth against a rush of territorialism that pricked the inside of his chest. *Jennings —the guy who wants to take Susan out.*

. . .

SINCE IT WAS SUNDAY, THE BUILDING WAS EMPTY. BURKE organized his desk and studied a roadmap of the United States while Rick made phone calls from his office. Burke narrowed his eyes as he considered the border towns of El Paso and the Mexican town of Juarez. He tapped his pen on the edge of his desk and was deep in thought when Rick leaned against the wall of his cubicle.

"What're you thinking?"

Burke sat up. "Why are the guards at the border not finding the drugs and kidnapped kids when they go through the checkpoint?"

"Well, they do find some. But there will always be those that get through."

"Maybe. Or maybe they're bringing the people in through different entry points? I'm just brain-storming, but the driver said he drove up from Las Cruces - not El Paso. I mean he could be lying, but what if he's telling the truth about that? If he picked up the truck in Las Cruces, we don't know for sure where the girls came from. We're assuming they're from Mexico, but what if they're not?"

"Go on." Rick braced his hands on the back of Burke's chair and stared at the map on the monitor.

"I was just thinking it would be really hard to sneak people past the dogs at the border. Wouldn't it? In fact, I think I read somewhere that most of the human traf-ficking in America actually involves American citizens and not people smuggled into the country."

A feminine tone answered his question. "They could get past the border patrol dogs fairly easily—if they weren't smuggling drugs."

Burke's pulse spiked at the unexpected voice. Both he

and Rick spun around. "Kendra—what are you doing here?"

Rick kissed her in greeting. "Hey, there. We didn't hear you come in."

She smiled up at Rick but answered Burke. "Sorry to startle you. I drove your truck up so you wouldn't have to drive with Rick all the way out to my place to pick it up. Rick can give me a ride home."

"Thanks." Burke's heart thudded hard as it slowed back down. "Why do you think the smugglers could sneak past the dogs?"

"Those dogs are trained to sniff out drugs, firearms, and explosives. That's their job. They smell people all the time—all the people. So they wouldn't necessarily alert at their scent."

"Could you teach them to?"

"Yes, but it's different—a different skill. Still, if the human trafficking happens in conjunction with drug smuggling, the drug sniffing dogs might inadvertently find both. We should be able to use K9s not only at the border, but anywhere there's a check-point set up."

"What if it's just people?"

Kendra bit her lower lip in concentration. "That's a good question. I'll talk with Clay about it and see what his thoughts are, but I don't see why we couldn't."

Acid nipped at the lining in Burke's stomach. "Clay *Jennings*?"

"Yeah..." Kendra's voice sounded wary which rubbed Burke wrong.

He held up his hand. "Don't worry, Susan told me he asked her out."

Rick's head snapped toward him. "What? Clay's interested in Susan? How does he even know her?"

Kendra placed a hand on his arm. "She came by for a tour of the K9 facility a couple of weeks ago. They met then."

Rick's dark eyes slid to Burke. "So? What are you going to do about it?"

Burke figured Rick was the type of guy who would stake his claim and defend it, but despite the persistent gritty-edged jealousy he had to tamp down, Burke wanted the woman he dated to make that choice on her own. "Susan told me she wasn't going to go out with him, so why would I do anything?"

Rick huffed. "Will you be able to work with him on the task force?"

"It won't be a problem for me."

Rick cocked his head. "Have you ever met Jennings?"

"I know who he is." Burke's gut tightened with unease.

"Kendra?" Rick pushed a loose strand of hair behind her ear. "Is there going to be a problem?"

She shrugged. "I'll talk to Clay."

Chapter Ten

Susan thought about Burke on her long winding drive through the Rockies, spending time considering his values versus hers. She pictured his eyes, his perpetually fresh haircut, his square jaw and solid chest. Those images led to an hour of fantasizing about her homecoming. She would have to marshal her thoughts if she was going to survive this separation.

With a firm hand, she forced herself to think about her new business. She ran through her marketing plan and her process for acquiring more clients. The remainder of the drive flew by and before long, Susan turned down a curving dirt road that led to a huge log cabin retreat center. There was a main lodge in the middle of the campus surrounded by ten or so smaller cabins. Gravel paths connected the buildings. Susan parked her car and got out to stretch and breathe in the refreshing pine-scented mountain air.

When she entered the lodge, women of all ages filled the lobby. Someone directed her to the sign-in table where she received her name-tag lanyard and a packet of information. She picked up her room key and went to her cabin to unpack.

Cocktails and networking started at four in the court-yard. Susan had signed up for a team-building, white-water rafting excursion scheduled for the first two days of the conference, and she hoped to find some of the other women who were going too. She slipped a soft sweater over her t-shirt, brushed through her hair, and returned to the main event.

With a generously poured Cabernet in her possession, Susan drew a deep breath. Time to meet new people.

A dark-haired woman who stood several inches taller than Susan approached her. "Hi. Are you signed up for the river trip tomorrow?" The elegant lady held out her hand. "I'm Prue Wilkens."

"Susan Bell." They shook. "How did you know I was going on the rafting trip?"

Prue pointed long tapered fingers toward Susan's name tag. "Color of lanyard. We adventurers are yellow."

"Got it." Susan ran her fingers down the ribbon. "What kind of business are you in?"

Prue touched Susan's elbow and indicated they move to an open bench. "I own a woman's boutique, where I sell clothing, accessories and a few decorative items."

"Wow. How long have you owned your own business?"

Prue grinned. "I think I've always had some type of business or another. This particular one, I've operated for about ten years."

"That's impressive. I'm just starting out, myself. I want to have an online health and nutrition counseling business."

"Interesting idea. What's your background?"

"I recently left a job as the nutritionist for an elderly

care facility. I didn't like working there, but it gave me a front-row view of the long-term effect of nutrition choices. Some of the older folks are in good shape because of their history of a healthy diet and regular exercise. Others are really struggling." She sipped her wine. "Of course, there are lots of extenuating circumstances, but the work helped me to realize I want to be on the front-end helping people to make better health decisions now so they can have a higher quality of life in their later years."

Prue nodded, her smooth dark hair bobbing. "That's far more inspiring than selling clothes."

"I think owning and running your own business is inspiring—no matter what it is. How did you get started?"

"Well, like I said, I've always had something in the works, but I finally got serious with the boutique. I took some design courses, but I never actually finished college. I began with renting some space in a consignment market and built up a clientele before jumping into leasing my own shop. That was terrifying, but it was also the turning point for me."

"Wow. Where is your boutique located?"

"I'm down in old-town Littleton."

"I know right where that is. I'll have to stop in." A server came by with appetizers, and the women each chose caprese skewers. Susan bit into the juicy cherry tomato, savoring its tang blended with the earthy flavor of basil and the cool rubbery texture of the fresh mozzarella. Her stomach growled for more, and she smirked. "What has been the biggest challenge for you in owning your own business?"

"Honestly? The bookkeeping. Especially the taxes. I'm trying to make enough to justify hiring someone, but for now, it's just me. My hair may be all gray within a year though." Prue winked. "I wish I had taken some business classes in school before I dropped out, but I didn't know."

"You can still take a course, I bet."

"Yeah, except right now time is a commodity." Prue cocked her head. "But... maybe one online. I'm going to think about that."

Their conversation lasted until the staff served dinner. During the meal, the leaders of the event presented the basic convention guidelines and expectations. After dessert, a short stocky woman wearing denim from shoulder-to-toe, climbed up on the platform and stood behind the microphone.

"My name is Nora James. I'm the lead guide for the rafting trip tomorrow. Those of you who are attending that event, please meet me in the lobby after dinner."

Susan and Prue shrugged at each other and gathered their things. They moved to the foyer and met with several other women who signed up for the excursion.

Nora approached them. She was shorter than the others, but her confidence and gruff exterior let everyone know she was in charge. "Thanks for meeting me. We've had a mishap and now have a decision to make. My assistant guide broke her arm rappelling down a mountain earlier today. So, we need to decide whether to cancel our rafting excursion or take a calmer river route and have only one guide. If we do that, our trip will be approximately six hours shorter, but we'll still camp in the woods overnight." Her frank eyes assessed each face in the group.

A petite woman with fiery red hair spoke up. "Hi, I'm Audrey Collins. I'm a realtor with my own agency."

Several voices greeted her.

"I say we go, anyway. I'd hate to miss the experience."

"Me too," said Prue, and others nodded.

Nora met each woman's gaze. "Everyone feel the same way? If not, we can make alternate plans for anyone who doesn't want to come along."

All the women agreed to attend the excursion, and they made plans to meet in the lobby before breakfast the following morning. Nora passed out a list of items to bring. "Don't pack anything that's not on this list. We have very limited space on the raft. The camp is already setup for us, so all we need to do is float down the rapids and then find our tents." She clapped her hands together. "Okay. I'll see you ladies in the morning."

"Well, that's bad karma." A young woman in purple tie-dye leggings stretched her arms into the sky. "But, this group has a positive energy. If anyone wants to, you can meet me in the lobby tomorrow morning an hour early for morning yoga."

"That sounds great." Susan raised her hand. "I'll be there."

"Wonderful." The yogi swung her straight, multi-colored, streaked, blonde hair over her shoulder. "I'm Keira." She reached for Susan's hand with both of hers and a kind smile lit her eyes.

Susan introduced herself and then Prue.

"My name is Nancy." A meek woman approached the group. "I'd like to try yoga. I've never done it before."

Keira clasped her hands together in front of her chest and inclined her head slightly. "Beautiful. I'm happy to have you."

"Do I need anything special?" Nancy's brow furrowed, and her eyes darted to each face.

"No. Just wear something loose and comfortable tomorrow. If you like it, then you may want to get some stretchy yoga clothing."

"I have some cute things at my boutique. I can show you online." Surprised faces turned to Prue. "What? We're supposed to be networking aren't we?" She laughed.

Audrey twisted her red hair into a knot at the top of her head. "I'll be here in the morning too, but I'm turning in for now. Good night everyone."

The small team dispersed.

Chapter Eleven

The morning sun steamed in through stained-glass windows decorating their makeshift yoga studio in a rainbow of light. Susan moved into downward dog and noticed Nora standing behind them watching their yoga practice. The stout woman stood with her arms crossed, leaning against a wall in the lobby. Keira instructed the women to step through and stand tall in mountain pose and Susan glanced at the clock. It was seven o'clock.

"We don't have time to end with savasana this morning, I apologize. But at least our bodies have had a chance to wake up nicely." Keira placed her hands in a prayer position and bowed her head. "Namaste."

The group murmured "Namaste," in return, and Susan noticed Nancy nervously glancing around the room before she took part in the blessing.

Nora shoved herself from the wall and approached the women. "Looks like everyone's packed and ready to go. Get changed into your rafting clothes, then we'll have breakfast in the bus on the way."

The women loaded their bags in the back of a fifteen-passenger van and then climbed in. Susan sat next to Prue and Audrey. The morning meal was better than she expected. Nora offered them a selection of yogurt, fruit and granola. Forty-five minutes later, they pulled onto a gravel road that led up to the bank of the Arkansas River. Two men and a large yellow raft awaited them.

Nora got out of the van first and spoke with the young men preparing the float. She lifted a sturdy zippered bag and carried it toward their group.

"Everyone put your things in this pouch. We will secure it to the raft, so we won't lose anything—as long as we don't capsize the float." She chuckled at what she must have thought was a joke, but the others didn't join in her humor. Susan swallowed hard and shoved her small pack of items into the larger bag, suddenly nervous about the excursion.

Each woman received a helmet, a life jacket, and an oar. One of the men gave them instructions. "If for any reason you fall out of the boat, the first thing to remember is Do Not Panic. Usually, you'll still be right next to the raft. Grab ahold of it so you don't float away." He paused to look at each face. "If you end up having to swim in the river to get to a safe spot, roll to your back and point your feet downstream. This way you can push away from rocks with your feet."

None of his directions gave Susan any comfort, and her stomach tightened with nerves. *Why did I sign up for this again?*

Prue gripped her arm. "It'll be okay. I've done this before. It's fun. Plus, with only one guide, they will only take us on an easy, beginner route. There's nothing to worry about. I promise."

Susan smiled at her new friend. "If you say so."

"Come on." Prue led the way to the raft.

Wearing quick-drying nylon shorts and a tank, Susan stood with the others knee-deep in the cold water of the river. Each woman hung on to the edge of the boat until it was time to load up. Nora took the rear position with her larger oar.

When everyone was secure, Nora gave the nod and the men holding the raft steady, released it. They were off. It was a slow, gentle float from the launch point, but Susan saw ripples of white water at the bend up ahead. She glanced at Prue who responded with an encouraging grin.

"See, no big deal."

"Not yet, anyway." Susan laughed. She relaxed with the flowing rhythm of the river.

For the first hour, the ride was smooth and gave the opportunity to enjoy the breath-taking scenery of the surrounding Colorado Rockies. This part of the wilderness was seemingly untouched by man. Susan peered up the steep edges of mountains on both sides of the river to the sun sparkling through the trees.

Instead of relaxing, however, the back of Susan's neck prickled. She wondered for a minute if she was having a premonition, but then she chastised herself for her nerves and tried simply to enjoy the experience.

Nora called out from behind. "Up around the next bend, we'll be running into slightly rougher water. Move with the raft and enjoy the ride."

Susan saw the rapids up ahead, but they didn't appear too daunting. Nothing like the niggling that kept nipping at her spine and plucking at her gut. She had the oddest sensation she was being watched. Of course, that was silly as they were moving at a decent clip down the river.

Prue leaned toward her. "Are you feeling all right? Motion sickness?"

"I'm fine." Susan smiled but glanced around the tops of the ridges they passed by, anyway. She couldn't tell Prue her feelings without sounding crazy and she tried once again to shake off the sensation.

At noon, Nora steered the raft to a still pool at the edge of the river. "We'll stop here for lunch. Feel free to swim here where it's calm, if it isn't too cold. We'll be here for about an hour and then head down toward our camping spot."

Susan slid over the edge of the craft to help pull it to the edge and held it while Nora tied it to a tree. The river was freezing and she couldn't wait to get out and dry off in the sun on a warm rock. The women ate turkey sandwiches, chips, fruit, and Oreos for lunch. Water and juice boxes were the offered drinks.

"What I wouldn't give for a nice cold beer about now." Audrey sat down next to Susan.

"Or hot tea." Susan laughed as she shivered in the cool mountain breeze. Glad of the instructions not to wear cotton, Susan's nylon outfit was dry within minutes.

The simple lunch was surprisingly satisfying and had filled Susan's empty stomach. Her only complaint was no milk to dip the Oreo cookies into. Sated, Susan lay back on the rough surface of the large, warm rock and soaked in the sunshine. She was almost asleep when a cold foreboding breezed over her. Her skin prickled up in gooseflesh and she sat up, staring into the shadowy trees across the river.

"What's the matter? Bad dream?" Prue pushed herself up next to her and stared into her face.

"No, I just..." Susan didn't know how to explain her

experience. She leaned close to Prue's ear and whispered. "I've just got a weird feeling, that all. What's that saying? 'It feels like someone just stepped over my grave?'"

Prue squinted her eyes and scanned the ridge across from them. "I don't see anything. Are you sure you didn't doze off for a second and have a weird dream?"

Susan wasn't certain, so she shrugged. "Maybe that's it. It's probably my self-doubt haunting me." She laughed away her apprehension.

Nora shook her thick legs out. "Time to pack up and get back on the river. We have another couple of hours on the water before we pull out and hike up to our camp."

"I love camping in the mountains." Prue stood and gathered her trash. "But it's been a long time since I've slept on the ground in a tent."

"I've never done it." Susan got to her feet and stretched. "The only camping I've done was in a pop-up camper."

"Glamping?" Prue grinned at her. "Don't worry. We'll survive. It's only one night."

Susan laughed, "Right. We can do anything for just one night." She couldn't help staring back into the thick forest of pines across the river. There was something... but she couldn't see it.

Back in the river and into the raft, Susan's sun-warmed skin tightened against the frigid water. She couldn't climb into the boat fast enough. It wasn't long before they faced their first set of real rapids, even though they were only Class I. The ride thrilled her and soon Susan was ready to ride some Class II rapids.

Nora yelled over the tumbling water. "Once you get your feet wet and realize you survived, it's common to want a greater challenge. Think about that in context of your business goals. Where are you in that process? Have you jumped in? Ready for more difficult rapids? What will you need to navigate your next steps?"

Susan loved the metaphor. It was exactly what she was experiencing on the river and in her life. She'd jumped in all right—head first. By quitting her job she'd forced herself to sink or swim.

Rougher water demanded greater attention and their afternoon tumbled down the river. Susan was relieved when Nora pointed out their next landing spot. Her muscles were tired, and she was ready for solid ground. They secured the float to two trees, front and back, then retrieving their personal packs from the raft bag, the women hiked up a steep trail toward their campsite.

The hike was tough and longer than Susan had expected. As they hiked through the aspen and pines, the ominous sense of an unknown presence returned. Susan stilled her breathing and tried to gauge where the inkling came from, but she couldn't pin-point it. She stared up the sides of the valley. *What if we're being followed by a mountain lion?* Ever since she'd moved to Colorado, Susan had heard terrifying stories of how the great cats stalked their prey for miles on hiking trails.

She shuddered. "Hey, Nora. Are there mountain lions around here?"

"Sure—and black bears too. But don't worry. If we stay together as a group, we'll be fine. Wildlife does its best to avoid humans."

Somehow that didn't help Susan feel any better. She glanced at Prue who made a googly eyed face at her. "Don't worry. We'll be fine," she mimicked. Especially once we get a campfire started."

Susan rubbed the back of her neck. "If you say so."

Chapter Twelve

ancy's piercing scream echoed through the forest and vibrated through Susan's bones. Her body chilled, and for a moment she couldn't move. Deliberately, Susan pulled in a deep breath. Prue and Kiera stared at her until Nancy screamed again. The second shriek mobilized them and they rushed to the tent opening to see what had Nancy so upset.

Susan drew the flap open wider and peered inside. Audrey's small form was lying on top of a sleeping bag. Her red hair was mussed across her pillow, and her head tilted at an odd angle. Flat blue eyes stared straight out at nothing.

Nancy withered into a pile of trembling sobs. "She's dead. Audrey... and Nora... they're dead. Oh, my God..."

With tears smeared across her young face, Kiera knelt down and wrapped her arms around Nancy. She didn't talk, only hummed and tried to comfort the hysterical woman.

Susan shuddered. "What is happening?"

Prue shook her head and swallowed hard. "I don't

know, but no one goes anywhere by themselves anymore. Got it?"

"But what happened to her?" Susan gripped Prue's hand and spoke quietly so Nancy couldn't hear. "It looks like Audrey's neck is broken, but how?"

"I thought Nora's death was an accident, but now I'm not so sure." Prue zipped the tent closed. "We need to get out of here. Immediately."

Susan agreed. "Grab only essentials. We can get on the raft and make it down to the rendezvous point."

Nancy was in shock, and Susan took ahold of one of her arms, helping Kiera stabilize her on the trail. The distraught woman stumbled on the path between them. They all followed Prue down to the river. Susan's skin crawled with the sensation of stiff, rickety beetle's legs scratching along the surface. The hair on her neck and shoulders prickled with the sense that someone was about to grab her from behind at any second. She had an over-powering desire to bolt ahead, leaving the others in her dust, but she shook it off, tightened her grip on Nancy, and pressed on.

Together they tripped and lurched down the steep grade to the water. They rushed to the spot where they tied the boat earlier, but it was gone.

Prue stood still in the middle of the path. The blood left her cheeks, and she sent Susan a sickened look. "It's gone. The raft, with Nora... it was right here. Wasn't it?" Her eyes widened with fear.

"Maybe it was further down the trail?" Keira's soft voice shook.

"No, this is where we tied it." Susan touched the severed rope still knotted on the tree. "Someone cut the rope."

They looked out across the water. Prue pointed. "There. The boat is across the river caught in those rocks."

There was something odd about the way the yellow rubber bobbed and seemed to drape around the stones. Susan squinted to see better. "The raft is deflated. Look—someone slit the sides."

"Oh, my God! We're all going to die out here," Nancy wailed.

Keira moved to comfort her, but Susan nudged her away.

"Stop it, Nancy." Susan grasped the frantic woman by her shoulders. "Stand up and get a hold of yourself. We all need to stay calm and come up with a plan."

Both Nancy and Keira stared at her, stunned, but the firm and steady tone in her own voice bolstered Susan with an unexpected inner confidence. "We have to keep our heads about us." Prue joined the small circle and Susan continued. "The only choice we have is to hike down river. The river will lead back to people."

"But what about whoever is trying to kill us?" Nancy whimpered.

Prue lifted her chin high. "We don't know that anyone is trying to kill us. Let's just get out of here. That's what we must focus on."

"And we have to stay together." Susan ordered.

Prue struck out in the lead, down the path. Susan followed with Keira and Nancy close behind. Over-whelmed with her sense of being watched, Susan continued to keep her feelings to herself. No need to add to the terror. A quarter of a mile father along the trail, Susan found a sturdy walking stick. She tried it out, knowing she could use it as a weapon, if it came to that.

. . .

As the morning wore on, the physical reality of muscle exhaustion was undeniable. The women agreed to stop for a break and to eat a snack for energy.

Keira stared back the way they'd come. About an hour ago, they'd run out of trail and were now just following the river through raw forest. "Any idea how many miles we've gone?"

"My guess is four or five." Prue untied her boot and rubbed her toes. "I think I'm getting a blister."

Sitting on a boulder at the side of the water, Nancy fidgeted. She crossed and uncrossed her legs.

Susan sat next to her. "Are you okay?"

"I have to go to the bathroom."

"Oh, well, now's a good chance, since we're stopped." Susan glanced around for a suitable spot.

"I'm scared."

"I'll go with you and keep an eye out."

Nancy's cheeks flared a bright red. "No. I can't. Not with you standing there."

Susan stifled a sigh of irritation. Now was not the time for modesty. "Okay, why don't you just step behind that bush." She pointed at a large wild shrub on the mountainside. "And we'll keep watch from down here."

"Okay." Nancy crept up the hill to the back side of the large shrub.

Susan couldn't see her, but they could hear her if she cried out.

Prue sat down next to her and offered her a protein bar. "I wish we had more water. We're low and I think we should start rationing since we don't have any idea how much farther we have to go."

"Good plan." The rapids tumbled by, taunting Susan's

thirst. "Do you think the river water is safe to drink way up here?"

"Maybe, but probably not worth the risk. I should have bought one of those water purifying drink bottles."

"Hind-sight's twenty-twenty." Susan stood and walked toward the bush. "Nancy? Are you about done?"

There was no answer. Sharp nerves scraped across Susan's psyche. "Nancy?"

Just then the women heard a scream, shrill in the distance.

"Nancy!" Susan bolted in the direction of the shriek.

Prue was after her in a shot. "Wait, Susan. We all go together or we don't go at all."

"Why did she wander off? I told her to stay right by the bush." Panic and dread swamped Susan's brain. She couldn't think, and her heart threatened to gallop away.

"I don't know, but let's go find her. Together." Prue took one of Susan's hands and held the other out toward Keira. Hand in hand they hiked until the mountain forced them to release their grip to keep their balance on the rough terrain. After about fifteen minutes of uphill climbing, they came to the edge of a steep cliff. They called out to Nancy and looked at the wilderness around them for hints she'd passed by.

"Here, look!" Keira pointed at the pine-needle covered ground. "A footprint."

"Nancy!" Susan shouted another time, her throat dry and sore.

Prue studied the print and then cast her gaze in the direction it led. The cliff.

The warm pine mulch infused the air with a keen earthy dust. Susan closed her eyes and shook her head—already knowing.

"No. No, no, no." Keira fell to her knees.

Prue grasped Susan's hand and together they peered over the edge of the precipice. There, far below, was Nancy's body, broken against the rocks she landed on. Susan's tears came then. No amount of self-control could stop them.

"How?" She sniffled. "Why did she hike all the way up here? If someone was after her, why didn't she scream out or just come back to our side of the bush?"

Prue's breath rushed in and out. "How did we not hear anyone that close?"

Kiera took their hands. "What do we do? Do we try to climb down there?"

Susan touched the young woman's soft cheek. "No. There's no way she could have survived that fall. We need to get out of these mountains right now."

"But we can't just leave her," Keira wept.

Prue gripped Keira's hand tight, squeezing her fingers. "When we get to safety, we'll send the sheriff back. But right now, we have to go."

Susan gritted her teeth. She'd never felt so helplessly terrified in all her life. Someone or something was after them. Killing them off one by one. They were lost, and all she had to defend herself with was a big stick.

The women hiked together for hours in a general down-hill direction, searching for the river or any sign of civilization. They stopped for breaks when they couldn't walk anymore, and their water supply had dwindled to dangerously low levels.

Prue limped to a fallen tree trunk and sat down heavily. She untied her boot and peeled her sock away from her skin. Her toes were pink and bloody. "Damn, this hurts."

Susan knelt before her. "I'd pour water over your blisters, but we barely have four ounces left."

"How could we lose a huge river? I don't know how we got so turned around." Prue blew on her blistered foot.

Susan kicked a dry branch off the tree trunk with a satisfying snap. "I guess we were in such a hurry to get to Nancy we didn't pay much attention to our route or how long it was."

Kiera stretched each of her limbs before she sat cross-legged on the ground. "Are we just going to keep walking? We might wander farther into the wilderness making it impossible for anyone to find us."

"But if we stop moving, we become sitting ducks for whoever is hunting us." Prue removed her second boot.

Susan sat next to Prue and leaned forward with her arms on her knees. "We can keep hiking until dark, but it's dangerous to travel at night. Plus, we will eventually have to sleep, at some point."

Kiera's voice weakened. "I hope we find the retreat center before then."

"We all do, but I think we ought to look for a place to rest. Prue's feet need a break." Susan stood and paced the clearing. "We have to locate a spot to camp that we can defend. One of us will have to stay awake at all times. We'll take turns."

The other two nodded in weary agreement. Prue lifted her head. "Do we have any food left?"

"A few bars, but we need to ration them. Who knows how long we'll be out here before help finds us." Susan prayed someone would find them before the killer did. They were being hunted and knocked off one-at-a-time.

As though reading Susan's thoughts, tears flooded Kiera eyes, and she cried, "I'm so scared."

Susan squatted and hugged the young woman. "We're all scared, but we need to hold it together. It's how we'll keep each other safe."

Keira nodded into Susan's chest, and she threw her arms around her waist.

Prue forced her feet back into her boots. "Okay, let's find a place to make camp for the night."

The women hiked another hour before they found a flat spot that backed up against a rock wall. If they slept there, they could at least be sure that no one could approach them from behind. They sat leaning against the cool stone and shared a protein bar, each taking only one sip of the remaining water. They had no means to make a fire, and nothing to cover themselves with, so they huddled together for warmth wishing they would have brought a tent with them.

Prue pulled away and stood. "I'll take the first watch. I'll wake you in a couple of hours, Susan. Kiera, you can hold the third shift."

"Sounds good. Be careful." Susan drew Kiera closer.

At first, sleep eluded Susan. It was too terrifying to relax. It would have been better for her to take the initial shift. At this rate, she'd be awake for both Prue's and her watch. Eventually, her muscles ignored the danger and slackened, begging for rest. Before long, Susan's eyelids joined the campaign and drooped over her gritty eyes.

THE CAW OF A BLUE JAY CALLING ACROSS THE DAWN brought the first awareness of daylight to Susan's sleep drenched brain. Golden tendrils of sunshine stretched out and warmed her cheek. Slowly, consciousness returned to her. She bolted upright, jolting Kiera who slept curled next to her. It was morning.

"Prue!" Susan yelled.

Keira startled and sat up, rubbing her eyes.

"Prue, where are you?" Susan's heart tumbled like a rockslide. She couldn't breathe. *Where is Prue?* Susan grabbed Kiera's shoulders and shook her. "Did Prue wake you for a shift in the night?"

Kiera's eyes were huge, and she shook her head no.

"Prue!" Susan screamed. "Oh, my God."

"Maybe she just went to pee?" Kiera's fear-pinched features belied the hope of her words.

"She never woke me. And if she never woke you either, she's gone."

"Gone?" Tears filled Kiera's eyes. "You mean…"

"Come on." Susan stood and pulled Kiera up with her. "Let's see if we can find her."

The women hooked arms and crept out of their semi-sheltered spot. Susan searched, hoping with all her heart she wouldn't find Prue dead at the hands of whatever was stalking them. *Why didn't I tell Nora I thought someone was watching us? Following us?* They hunted for over an hour but found no trace of Prue. Susan pitched to the side and retched with dry heaves. There was nothing more than bitter bile in her stomach to expel.

Kiera wiped her forehead with her bare hand. "Are you okay, Susan? Can you keep going?"

"Yes." She wiped her mouth with the back of her wrist. "We have to keep going. It's our only chance." Susan took several deep breaths, wishing she had water. Her whole body screamed for moisture. "Let's try to head downhill. If we're anywhere near the river, it will be at the bottom of a valley."

"Okay, but what about Prue?"

"I don't know." An overwhelming desire to burst into tears washed through Susan's body. She bit down on her lip and blotted her eyes on her sleeve. "We've got to keep it together and get out of here."

Susan and Kiera walked next to each other down the slope, holding hands, and praying they would find help. Susan's skin maintained a thin coat of sweat, and she shivered uncontrollably. She'd never known such fear. The constant adrenaline spikes left her depleted and exhausted, and she wondered if the odor she breathed in was the scent of terror.

The women finally stopped to rest at the bottom of a narrow valley that, unfortunately, did not host a river. But there were some puddles at the base of a stand of aspen trees. Susan dropped to her knees and scooped water into her hand. She held the cool liquid to her lips and drank.

"Susan." Keira sounded worried.

"I don't even care if this makes me sick. I'm desperate." Susan scooped another mouthful. "It tastes so good, almost sweet."

Kiera fell to her knees by Susan's side and joined her in drinking. They filled their bottles with the now cloudy water and stuffed them into Susan's pack before both bending down for one last long drink.

On the other side of the puddle a stick snapped. Susan's body tensed and went completely still after an initial chill. She sucked in a breath and looked up.

Chapter Thirteen

B urke wore jeans to the office since they were going to the K9 facility to talk about a new K9 division for the Human and Drug Trafficking Task Force. He and Rick were partnering with Kendra and Clay Jennings to discuss how K9 teams might help combat the growing issue of the trafficking of women and children. Colorado's junction of I-70 and I-25 in Denver was a main thoroughfare for the whole country.

Opioids were on the rise, and both synthetic drugs and the real thing, when laced with fentanyl, were deadly. Young men, women, and children of both genders were stolen and sold along the same routes, to all kinds of customers. Evidence showed that the sex trade not only pandered to everyday dirt-bags, but also businessmen, professors, professional athletes, politicians, and even corrupt judges. Burke ground his teeth together at the thought of children being exploited by these disgusting predators.

Burke pushed the button for the elevator, but when the doors opened, Rick stepped out. "Good timing. You can drive over to the K9 facility with me. Our meeting's in thirty minutes."

Burke turned on his heel and fell in step with his boss. "What's the plan for including the federal K9 units? I figured the local PD K9 teams would handle the search and seizure aspects."

"They'll be involved too. My hope is that this will end up being a massive cooperative effort. Dogs could really be an effective way to cripple this insidious evil in Colorado. The FBI-K9 teams will work both in the areas where they've already been assigned and be available to assist where smaller departments don't have K9 teams on staff."

The agents pulled into the parking lot. Burke had never visited this facility before. They entered the building, showed their identification, and signed in. Kendra met them at the door to the back area where the offices were. Annie was at her side. She glanced around, and seeing no one besides the three of them, Kendra stretched up on her toes, held Rick's face and kissed him.

"Good morning." She smiled up at him.

He chuckled, "Good morning." He pressed his mouth to her ear and whispered, "Again."

Burke snickered. "I can still hear you."

Rick laughed and gave him a joking shove. "Quit eavesdropping."

"Can't help it. I'm trained in surveillance." Burke winked at Kendra.

She smirked and led the way to her boss's office and rapped on the door frame. "Agents Sanchez and Cameron are here. Are you ready for us?"

Burke sucked in a deep breath. He was about to meet the man who was interested in his girl. Well, maybe Susan wouldn't consider herself *his girl*, but that was how he liked to think of her.

A hulking agent wearing FBI fatigues walked out of the office. He was an easy two or three inches taller than Burke's own six-foot two-inch frame. He wore his fair hair cut short in what the Marines referred to as a high-and-tight. The man shook Rick's hand and greeted him as a friend before he turned his ice-blue Nordic eyes toward Burke. The force of his Viking-like gaze dug into Burke making him want to step back. Instead, Burke stepped forward and gripped the man's hand with all the strength he had.

Kendra rolled her eyes at Rick who shrugged. "Let's go out and meet the dogs and their handlers." She led the way with Annie in lock step.

Rick followed her, and Clay held out his hand gesturing for Burke to proceed. The last thing Burke wanted was to have Clay Jennings on his flank. Though he'd be hard pressed to explain why.

They went through the door to the training yard, walking past the line of empty kennels. All the dogs were at work by this time in the morning. The small group lined up along a chain-link fence and watched the exercises going on before them.

"Looks a lot like the obstacle course at basic training." Burke leaned on the rail with his forearms.

Clay slid aviator sunglasses over his eyes. "It's very similar. In fact, we train these dogs to do all the things their handlers can do."

"Except scuba-dive." Kendra added.

Clay nodded. "True. Balance and agility work is part of their daily routine." He pointed at a dark, short-haired shepherd-looking dog who leapt to the top of a seven-foot-high wooden wall, caught himself on the edge, and pulled himself over. "That's the unit's newest K9, Ranger. He's a biter like my dog, Gunner, but he's also trained for sniffing. I hope that dogs with this dual training will become the back-bone of the K9 side of this task force."

Burke watched the amazing dog as he flew through the course seemingly without effort. "So, you use sniffer dogs to find drugs, explosives, and ammunition, along with searching for people, but Agent Dean explained that they most often search for people by using their particular scent."

Clay turned his head toward Burke, but the mirrored glasses hid his eyes. "That's right, those are trailing dogs, like Baxter."

Burke didn't appreciate not being able to see behind the reflective lenses so he looked back out to the course. "So, how will the dogs know to alert us to people who are being smuggled around?"

"It's a good question. Most often, when people are being trafficked, they accompany illegal drugs of some sort. Either in an actual shipment or merely drugs used for personal use by the drivers."

"And if not? Will the K9s alert their handlers to smuggled people that don't have drugs traveling with them?"

Kendra spoke in a low tone. "*Lehne.*" Annie laid down by her foot, and Kendra turned to Burke. "That's what we're working on. It's challenging because there will definitely be people in the transports—at a minimum, the drivers. Sometimes, the victims are drugged and appear asleep, or are doped and hidden in trunks or trailers— whatever. So, we'll separate the drivers and any other passengers from the vehicle and ask the dog to search again."

Clay interrupted. "That's where Ranger's training comes in. He's an apprehension dog. He'll alert us to any person still in the vehicle who is hiding or being smuggled. He's trained to search for the human scent."

Burke turned to watch Ranger maneuver over a balancing obstacle. "Don't all people smell a little different though? How do you train a dog to search for someone you don't have a scent for?"

A proud smile spread across Clay's face. "Honestly, only the dogs know what it is they're smelling. We think it might be pheromones, or skin rafts."

"Skin rafts?" Burke tilted his head.

"Yeah. Humans have thousands of tiny flecks of themselves leaving their bodies all the time."

"Like skin cells?"

Clay nodded. "And other stuff—hygiene products, bacteria, parasites, sweat, and hormones. Around forty-thousand microscopic particles fall from us every minute, which gives dogs a good nose full. But it could be any type of secretion that humans emit. All I know is that Ranger can find someone who's hiding or is being hidden, and I trust him to do it."

Kendra bobbed her head in agreement. "Ranger's an incredible K9."

Rick ran a hand across his jaw. "So, once you perfect the training system, you'll train other dogs to do the same thing?"

"That's the idea." Clay stood tall, towering over everyone. He whistled an ear-piercing squeal, and the handlers all instructed their K9 partners to stop and sit by their sides. Clay's command voice echoed across the field. "Come on over and meet the new members of the team."

"Will Annie be ready to join the task force with Agent Dean?" Rick asked.

Kendra reached down to ruffle the fur on the top of Annie's head.

Clay answered. "Her nose is certainly up to the job, but we're going to ply the team with dogs that are also biters. This particular criminal element is often violent. Labradors don't make great attack animals." He chuckled.

"You could do it if you wanted to, couldn't you, Annie." Kendra spoke to her dog like one would a child.

Clay shook his head. "Not likely. However, Agent Dean, I would like you to train with the team using one of the cross-trained K9s."

"Yes, sir."

"It will mean double duty. We don't want Annie's training to go by the wayside."

"No, sir. I'll keep her up to task."

Rick rested his hands on his hips. "Will Agent Dean have to take both dogs home with her at night? She already has Baxter there."

Kendra's color heightened, and Clay's mouth twitched. "You worried about being crowded out at Dean's place, Sanchez? Don't worry, we'll expand the custom kennel in her yard."

"Man, these dogs live better than we do—heating and air-conditioning, not to mention beef at every meal." Rick teased.

Kendra glared at Rick, and he held his arms out and mouthed. "What?"

Burke chuckled at his friends.

The rest of the team approached, and Clay introduced everyone around. After shaking hands, the training resumed. "I think we should station teams at checkpoints along I-25 and I-70. We can post them randomly and change positions daily so their locations aren't predictable."

Rick nodded. "I agree. We'll work in conjunction with local and state police. I'd like to start with two right away —one south of Pueblo and the second south of Colorado Springs, before the junction with Highway 34. That's another hot route, out through Limon."

Burke crossed his arms. "Only two?"

Rick checked his watch. "To start. We can gauge how they go and make any necessary adjustments before we add more teams."

The group made their way back to the building. Clay opened the door and held it for Kendra. "How's your friend, Susan?"

Kendra's eyes darted toward Burke. He did his best to keep his expression neutral though he thought he might break a molar clenching them together.

"She's fine."

"I talked to her a couple of days ago. She left for some mountain get away, but I think we'll hang out after she gets back."

Kendra ducked into the hallway without responding. Burke's gut rolled into a tight fist, and his fingers reflected the emotion. He thought Susan said she'd tell Clay she *didn't* want to go out with him. Did she change her mind? Burke was the last one through the door, and he closed it with much more force than necessary. The other three turned to look at him in question.

"Sorry." Burke murmured.

They said their goodbyes, and Rick squeezed Kendra's shoulder. "I'll see you later."

She smiled up at him as though they were alone.

Rick and Burke made their way back to the black Explorer. "Man, you need to cool your jets."

Burke tossed his arms out to his sides. "What?"

"Don't give me that. You practically yanked that door off the hinges."

"I did not."

One dark brow rose over skeptical eyes. "Look, you can't talk to Susan about them going out until she gets home from the mountains. But, on the bright side— neither can he. So chill out until then."

"She told me he'd asked her out, but she said she was going to say no."

"Do you trust her?"

"I want to."

"Then stop looking at Agent Jennings like you're going to rip his throat out." Rick laughed. "'Cuz I don't like your odds in a brawl with that guy."

Burke forced a laugh that held no mirth. Rick was right though, Burke had to get past his jealousy if he and Jennings were going to work on the same team.

The men drove through the fast-food line at Chic-fil-A, a close-by favorite for lunch on their way back to the office.

"What do you say we take our food to the park? I don't know about you, but I'm in no rush to lock myself inside for the rest of the afternoon." Rick clicked his signal and turned toward the open space.

"You're singing my tune." Burke pressed his tie against his chest out of habit. "It's hard to want to go back to work on such a beautiful day."

"Right? We get an hour, so let's take it. I think Kendra left a frisbee in the back of the car that she uses to play with Annie. It may have a few teeth marks, but it might be fun."

"You're on. I haven't tossed a frisbee in years. Not since college—on the quad."

Rick grinned, turned off the air conditioning and rolled down his window instead. Fresh air breezed through the car. "What did you think of the K9 Unit? Those dogs could really make a difference in putting a stop to the trafficking."

"For sure. I'd feel a lot better about stopping those dirt bags with a dog like Ranger on the team."

"Do you remember how Gunner, Jennings's other K9, yanked Abbot out of his van the night Kendra was attacked? Right through the window?" Rick pulled into the mostly empty parking lot at the park. "Those dogs are fricken' amazing."

"Yeah, even though you blasted the back tire, that psycho still might have gotten away if Gunner hadn't grabbed him."

"By the way." Rick glanced at Burke. "Clay Jennings is a good guy. I doubt he knows about you and Susan, or he wouldn't have said anything to Kendra. She'll set him straight."

Burke gave a casual shrug, trying to disguise his inner agitation. "I'd rather Susan set him straight. I'm not sure how to feel about the fact that she didn't."

"She probably just hasn't talked to him—which is a good thing."

"Sure." Burke didn't want to talk about Clay Jennings at all, and certainly not in the same conversation involving Susan. He'd gulped down his chicken sandwich, but it sat in his belly like a lump of mud. No longer hungry, he wadded up the rest of his fries inside the bag.

Rick eyed him, but said nothing and finished his lunch. He tossed his key fob to Burke. "See if you can find that frisbee in the back while I throw this garbage away."

Burke found the disc and threw it straight at Rick's back. At the last second, Rick turned and snatched the frisbee out of the air. "Good try, but I have ninja-like reflexes." Rick snapped his wrist and sent the saucer flying toward Burke who had to leap to the side to catch it.

The men played and ribbed each other for a half-hour, and feeling better about returning to work, wound up their game.

"I guess we better get back to the office. I have to coordinate our investigation efforts across the states." Rick glanced down at his sweat-stained clothes. "Good thing I live close by. I'm going to swing by my place for a fresh shirt." He gave Burke a baleful look. "You can borrow one too."

Burke laughed. "Yeah, maybe next time we should play in our work-out gear?"

By the time they returned to work, it was already one-thirty. Burke and Rick batted friendly insults back and forth on their way to their respective offices.

"Agent Cameron. There you are." Lucinda glided toward them from the reception area. It was next to impossible not to notice her long legs and swinging hips.

Rick lifted a hand at Burke. "I'm out. Next time, let's make it a competition. Loser pays for happy hour."

Burke raised his chin toward Rick. "You're on."

"Agent Cameron, I have several messages for you."

Burke gave Lucinda his full attention. No one called him at work unless there was an emergency, and the people on that list were few. His parents, his brother and sister, and maybe Susan. "Who are they from?"

"Some southern lady." Lucinda peered at the yellow message notes she held. "A Mrs. Bell." She looked up and met Burke's gaze. "She said it was urgent and wants you to call her back immediately."

"Did she say what it was about?" Burke's stomach turned to stone.

"No, but she's called every fifteen minutes for the last two hours."

An icy-cold wash of panic sluiced through him followed by a surge of boiling adrenaline. Burke sprinted toward his desk. He punched the number from the messages into his phone.

"Mrs. Bell? This is Burke Cameron. How can I help you? Is something wrong?"

"Oh, thank God, you called me back. I'm worried sick."

"What's happened, Mrs. Bell. Is it Susan?"

"Yes! I'm sorry to call you at work, but I don't have your cell phone number and well, I know you and Susan are... friends."

"It's fine. You can call me anytime. In fact, I'm calling you from my cell now, capture the number and you can use it to call me direct."

"Yes, well, I need your help."

"Of course. What's the problem?"

"Susan is missing!"

The world around Burke stopped for several long seconds. He took a calming breath. The sound of his heart bashing against his ribs made it difficult for him to hear. He blinked his eyes and swallowed hard. "What do you mean she's missing?"

"From the conference. She went on a rafting trip, and the group never came back. They're all missing."

His heart catapulted into his throat and beat so hard it hurt. "Was there an accident? Or... tell me everything you know." He mentally cursed himself for fooling around for an hour with Rick at the park.

Mrs. Bell started crying, and it was difficult for Burke to understand her. "The group was supposed to meet their transport back to the convention center at noon yesterday." Sobs and a gulp sounded over the line. "They never showed up." Mrs. Bell blew her nose. "They waited for four hours before they launched another raft to see if they could find them."

"And did they?"

"No..." Mrs. Bell's sobs were muffled and while Burke waited for her to return to the call, he googled the retreat center that Susan went to. "They... they found the raft—shredded and caught on the side of the river in some sticks."

"They located the boat but none of the women?" Burke squeezed his temples between his thumb and middle finger.

"No... they discovered the guide caught up in the raft and scrub... she—she was dead. The last I heard, they were going to search out the women's campsite." Mrs. Bell dissolved into incoherent whimpers. Someone on her end of the call tried to reassure her.

The unknown voice picked up the phone. "Hello? I'm sorry, but Mrs. Bell will have to call you back."

"But—" the call disconnected. Burke dropped his phone on the desk and clicked on the Women Entrepreneurs' website until he found a contact number. He dialed it from his work phone.

"Hello, Peak to Peak Retreats. How may I direct your call?"

"This is Agent Burke Cameron of the FBI. Put me in touch with whoever is in charge of your missing persons' investigation."

"Oh, yes, sir. One minute, please." The line went still.

"Come on... come on..." Burke stood and tapped agitated fingers on the top of the cubicle wall.

"Hello? Agent..."

"Yes, this is Agent Cameron with the FBI, badge number 2547. With whom am I speaking?"

"This is Marion Wells, director of the retreat center."

"Ms. Wells, what can you tell me about the missing persons' situation you have?"

"Well, not much. The sheriff is handling it. I think he's called in the Search and Rescue team."

"Okay, that's good. What information do you have so far?"

"Not much, I'm afraid. Our own search team found their ruined raft. Unfortunately, the guide was also found, she was..." the woman's voice dropped to a whisper. "Dead."

A freezing shudder coursed through Burke's entire body. "Did you call the sheriff?"

"Yes, the search team called him to join them at the overnight campsite. I haven't heard back from anyone yet."

"Can you give me the contact information for the Sheriff in charge of the investigation?"

"Of course, one minute, please."

Burke thought he would burst through his own skin. *Come on, lady!*

"Here it is..." She gave Burke the number, and he copied it down, reading the digits back to her to be sure he had it right. He hung up and ran to Rick's office.

"Susan's missing. She's lost—maybe injured—up in the mountains."

"What?" Rick rose to his feet. "Slow down."

Burke reiterated the information he had. "I'm going up there."

"You're pretty upset, I don't think you should drive."

"I'm fine." Burke spun and raced to the elevator. He sprinted to his car, punched the retreat address into his GPS, and peeled out of the parking lot. As soon as he merged onto I-70 headed west, he called the Sheriff's office in Chaffee County.

The deputy who answered gave Burke basically the same information as Marion Wells did, only calmer and with a few more details. "Sheriff Rathburn is on his way up to the ladies' campsite right now. If they don't find the other women there, they'll call Rocky Mountain Search and Rescue before they start to hunt for anyone in earnest. Our best guess is the rafters made it to the bank of the river and were trying to hike out, but got lost."

"So far you haven't seen any sign of anyone else injured or..." Burke forced the words across his lips. "Or killed?"

"No, sir. No sign of the other five ladies as of yet. They were on a calm part of the river, but the mountains in that area are awfully rugged. Fairly easy to get turned around in the woods. Don't worry, we'll find them. I'll call you back as soon as I know anything."

"That'll be good, but I'm on my way up."

"It's not really a case for the FBI." The deputy sounded wary.

"This is personal. I know one of the women who was on that raft."

. . .

TWO HOURS INTO HIS DRIVE, BURKE'S PHONE BUZZED. He answered through his car. "Burke here."

"Agent Burke, this is Sheriff Rathburn up in Chaffee County. My deputy told me you called."

"Yes, Sheriff. I'm almost to the Peak to Peak Retreat Center."

"Good. I'll have one of my deputies meet you there and drive you up this way. We're at the campsite where the rafters camped on their first night."

"What did you find?"

"Seems we have another dead body on our hands."

A cold sweat covered Burke's skin. He swerved and slowed down. "Who... do you know who it is?""

"Yes, the director has given a preliminary ID. The woman is likely Audrey Collins—a realtor from the Denver area. We'll have to get a family member to officially ID her of course, but that's what we're going with for now."

"Thank God!"

"Pardon me?"

"I'm sorry. That isn't what I meant." Burke rubbed his damp face on the sleeve of his borrowed shirt. "No sign of any other women?"

"No. Not yet."

"What caused Ms. Collins's death? Do you know?"

"My best guess is a broken neck. There is bruising, looks like we might have a hand print, but I'm not sure the marks are consistent with a strangulation. Hard to tell, and it certainly isn't my expertise."

"What's happening up there, Sheriff?"

"Don't know yet, but I must admit, I'm concerned."

Chapter Fourteen

✦❧✦

Keira screamed high and shrill, piercing Susan's eardrums. Susan instinctively reached her arm out in front of Kiera and pushed the woman back behind her. Across the puddle, at the base of the opposite side of the narrow valley, stood the largest, hulking man Susan had ever seen. Her body remained still as she stared at him. The giant's long tangled dark brown hair matched an unkempt beard. He wore leather from head to toe.

Holding up a hand, he said, "Don't scream."

"Where did you come from?" Susan's palm dripped with the water she'd been drinking. "Who are you?"

The man took a step toward them, and Susan sprang to her feet, pulling Kiera with her. She edged backward. He stopped and raised both hands, palms out. "Don't run. I don't want to hurt you."

Keira whimpered behind Susan and clutched at her t-shirt. Susan reached an arm back and wrapped it around Keira to offer courage. "I asked who you are?"

The man stared at her for a moment before he answered. "My name is Jerrod."

"Okay, Jerrod. Where did you come from?"

He took another step toward the women. "I live in the mountains, about a two- or three-day's hike from here."

"Do you have a car?"

He stepped forward again but didn't answer. His dark brown eyes watched her from under waves of wild hair. His beard held beads of water as though he too had been drinking recently. The man edged his way toward one of the puddles and knelt down. Never taking his gaze from Susan's, he dipped his massive hand in and pulled out a drink for himself.

"We're lost. Can you help us?" Susan's entire interior alert system screamed for her to run, but there was a glimmer of hope that this was just a man out on a hike. A stranger who could help them get home.

The man's lips twitched, but a smile never emerged. "I want to help you." He stood, and Susan guessed he was six foot six or seven. His form reminded her of the Hulk dressed in leather clothing. His entire outfit was made from roughhewn animal skins, and he looked like a mountain man from the eighteenth century.

Without warning, he sprang over the puddle toward them.

Susan screamed, "Run!" She turned away and pushed Kiera to get her moving. Susan bolted like a deer with a mountain lion on her tail, blindly running to get away.

"Susan!" Keira's voice cried out. "Susan, please don't leave me."

Susan glanced over her shoulder as her legs continued to pump, sprinting up the mountainside. Her feet came to a complete stop. She turned around. The man had hold of Kiera. He held her off the ground in one arm not affected in the least by her kicking and clawing to get free. Jerrod gestured to Susan with his other hand to come back.

"Let go of her! What do you want with us?" Adrenaline made her limbs jumpy, her body insisting that she run.

"Come here, and I'll tell you."

"You can explain with me up here. And let her go!" Susan's terror echoed between the mountain sides.

Jerrod turned and walked back the way he had come. He stomped through the puddle, kicking aside the walking stick Susan had been carrying. He sat on a rock out-cropping, and swung Keira's legs around, resting her on his lap like a child, and waited.

"Just let us go." Susan yelled again.

"Come down and talk to me."

Her heart careened inside her chest wall. Nerves cleated across her scalp. Susan didn't know what to do. Her survival instinct demanded she run. Maybe she could get a way and find help. Only, she was lost, and she knew she wouldn't be able to get help in time. The giant had a hold of Keira, and he flopped her around like a great doll. If there was a chance, any chance at all, that Susan could save her, she had to try.

Susan chewed her lip until she drew blood. *He's big and strong, but he might not be able to handle us both at the same time.* She stepped downward onto a wobbly leg. The urge to cry was as overwhelming as her fear.

Jerrod watched and waited.

"If I come down there, will you let her go?"

His dark eyes assessed her and then looked down at Keira. She was faint with fear. Jerrod, with a gentle and careful movement, brushed Kiera's hair from her face. He rubbed some strands between his fingers. "Why is your hair all these different colors? I don't like it."

Keira stared at him, seemingly frozen in space, and offered no answer.

He said something to her that Susan couldn't hear. Kiera gave a slight nod, and then Jerrod lifted her to a spot next to him on the rock. He held his hands up so Susan could see he wasn't holding her friend.

Run! Susan's mind screamed at Kiera. Why was she just sitting there? Now was her chance.

Jerrod cupped his hand toward Susan again, gesturing for her to come.

"Keira, climb up here to me."

The young woman's shoulders shook silently before she broke into uncontrollable sobs. She was paralyzed with fear. Susan realized that Keira's only opportunity to get away would be if Susan offered herself in exchange. She marveled at the thought. Never having considered herself a person who would sacrifice her life for someone else's. Yet, when she found herself in this situation, Susan knew in her soul she couldn't make any other choice.

"Listen, Jerrod. I'll come down there, but you have to let Kiera go."

He cocked his head to the side and stared at her, then he took his time looking at Kiera. Then he nodded. He scooted away from Kiera until there was a foot of space between them.

"Keira, get up and walk away from him."

Keira tried to stand, but her legs didn't hold her. She balled herself up and hugged her knees to her chest, rocking herself and sobbing.

Susan ran plan after plan through her mind on how they might escape this man. Keira was useless at this point, but if Susan went with Jerrod, she would eventually calm down and could try to find help. Or the smarter option might be to leave her and run. Susan would have a better chance of survival in the wilderness and finding help. With her mind so occupied, Susan took another step but slipped on loose pine thatch and fell on her butt.

In the same second, Jerrod sprang toward her. Before she could recover from her fall and get back to her feet, he was on her. He covered her body with his bulk. She screamed.

"Hold still. I told you, I don't want to hurt you."

Susan's blood boiled, and it filled her with an animalistic rage. She pressed against Jerrod's weight, she scratched, tried to kick and knee him. He was too heavy to budge, and as he allowed his full weight to press into her, she could hardly breathe.

He grasped one of her wrists and then the other and slid a thin lace of leather around them, binding her hands together.

"Let me go!"

"That's not going to happen. It will be easier on you if you stop fighting." He eased some of his girth off of her. Susan sucked in a desperate breath and used the renewed energy to fight against him once again. He responded by resting his considerable weight on her until her struggle stilled.

Frustration and anger distracted her from her fear, and Susan groaned. "Get off me!"

"Are you done fighting me?"

She didn't answer and instead tried to see around his huge shoulders to get a glimpse of Kiera. Maybe she had come to her senses and run.

Jerrod pushed himself into a sitting position next to

Susan. She filled her lungs with the air they craved and took several deep breaths. Kiera remained huddled in a ball at the bottom of the slope.

"Come." Jerrod stood and helped Susan to stand. He tied her hands with another longer leather strap and held the end like a leash. He tugged on it so she would follow him. She pulled back, refusing. He spun in a fluid motion and grabbed her bound wrists and jerked her forward. She flew off her feet and landed on her knees, skinning them on the dirt.

Susan cried out in pain. She'd been unable to catch herself with her hands tied. Jerrod stepped off again, and she hurried to stand before he dragged her by her arms. He stopped at the pooled water and lifted her, setting her on a rock at the edge nearby. Then he scooped up handfuls of water, and gently and with unusual care, rinsed the scrapes on her knees. She could only stare at this strange man and remind herself that he was a murderer.

He blotted her cleaned wounds with his sleeve and then turned to Keira and said, "Come."

To Susan's utter shock, Kiera stood and walked to him. *What the hell?* "Keira, run! Get away!"

Before she could respond, Jerrod caught the girl's wrist and bound her hands in a similar fashion to Susan's. Then he took the long end of the strap and tied it around Susan's waist. With the leather lashed to Susan's wrists in his hand, Jerrod struck off up the side of the mountain, pulling the captive women behind him.

He kept a demanding pace considering that Susan and Keira took two strides to his one. He seemed to have boundless energy and stamina. After walking mostly uphill for what had to be two or three hours, Susan pulled back on her tether.

"Can we stop a minute?"

He stilled and glanced toward his prisoners. "Yes. Hungry?"

Susan was limp with hunger, but she wanted nothing from him. "No." She turned away from him, defiant.

Keira hadn't said a word since their capture. Susan worried for her mental state. Jerrod rummaged through Susan's pack he had brought along and pulled out her water bottle. He helped her curl her fingers around it and hold it to her lips. She gulped desperately. When she'd had her fill, Jerrod held the container to Keira's mouth. He supported her head like an infant and helped her drink.

They emptied the bottle, and Jerrod leaned against a thick pine tree. "Sit."

Susan was beyond exhausted. The long hike was hard enough, but she'd already spent her energy trying to fight against Jerrod in the beginning. Still she didn't want to cooperate with him in anything. So she stood.

A slight smile crossed his mouth as he watched her, which only inflamed her rage. She would bide her time, but she was going to escape, and she and Keira would survive.

Keira sat down and stuck her knees up through her arms and rested her head on them.

"Where are you taking us?" Susan glared at Jerrod.

"Home."

"Home, where?"

He pointed his head in the direction they were travelling.

"Why?"

"It's time I had a wife."

"What?" Susan sucked in air. "You can't just steal someone and make her your wife." Her mind spun at the permanency of what he said. But with her shock came an awareness of opportunity. If Jerrod didn't plan to kill them right away, they had a better chance of survival and escape.

"Your name is Susan?"

She turned her back to him.

"And she's Keira?"

Susan looked down at the young woman. Her eyes were distant, and she hummed quietly to herself as though she had gone somewhere else in her mind to avoid what was happening to her. Susan crouched down and tried to catch her eye.

"Keira? Are you all right, honey?"

The younger woman didn't respond.

"We're going to be okay. Don't be afraid. We'll be fine." Susan had no right to make such a promise, but what could it hurt? She wanted to offer the girl some hope to hang onto.

"Ready?" Jerrod stood.

"How much farther? I don't think she can hike much more."

"We'll rest at dusk. Come." The hulking man stepped off and left it to Susan and Keira to scramble on their feet before he dragged them.

He was good to his word. Jerrod didn't stop again until twilight sparkled in the sky. He found a flat spot and tied the women to a tree before going about setting up a simple camp. After building a small fire, near enough to them they could feel its heat, Jerrod left.

"Keira. Keira!" Susan tried to get the woman to focus. "Now's our chance. We've got to get our hands free so we can run."

Keira cast her gaze toward the flames, but her eyes remained blank. Susan shook her head and attacked the leather binding with her teeth. She'd made no progress on the tight knots by the time Jerrod returned carrying some kind of creature by its tail. Susan watched in horrified fascination as he pulled a blade from his belt and skinned and gutted the animal before her.

His movements were swift and skilled, and before long the remaining meat was turning on a handmade spit. Susan had no idea what type of meat it was, and at this point she didn't care. She'd been working on a third of a protein bar and after their exhausting day, she would have eaten anything.

When Jerrod deemed the meal cooked, he removed it from the spit and let it cool a minute or two. He grasped the lower back leg, pulled it off, and handed it to Susan. "Eat."

She held the greasy leg bone between her hands and tore into the flesh with her teeth. The roasted meat smelled surprisingly good and tasted even better. Susan figured that was only because she was so hungry. Jerrod tenderly held a chunk of meat he pulled from the carcass up to Kiera's mouth. She turned away.

"You must eat. You need strength." He tried again, but she buried her face in her knees. Jerrod's gaze moved to Susan. "Make her eat."

Susan didn't know what to think of a murderer who was also gentle and caring. A butcher who wanted to force one of them to be his bride, after killing all the others. Her mind turned in on itself, threatening to shut down. On some level, Susan wished she could escape into herself the way Keira had, but she was far too pragmatic. She had to keep her wits about her because she was the only one she could depend on to find a way out.

Night fell, and the thick pines hid the stars behind

their black canopy. Susan shivered. She and Kiera huddled together at the base of the tree he tied them to. Jerrod approached, and Susan's body jumped to a five-bell alarm. He knelt next to her and brushed loose strands of hair from her face. She jerked her chin away from him.

"Why do you cut your hair short?" He spoke in a quiet tone, his deep voice blending with the night.

Susan didn't answer him.

"It's pretty. You'll grow it out." He leaned toward her, and Susan's chest squeezed tight. Every muscle in her body tensed, prepared to fight.

Chapter Fifteen

❦

Burke squealed to a stop and jumped out of his truck next to a deputy's sedan. The smell of burnt rubber from his abrupt skid singed the inside of his nose. "Deputy," Burke flashed his badge and ID. "I'm special agent Cameron—FBI."

"Yes, sir. I have orders to get you up to the campsite as soon as possible."

"Let's go." Burke hopped into the front seat of the squad car and sat, tapping his thumb on his thigh. The two lawmen sailed up the winding mountain road. They pulled off near the river and changed from the police vehicle to an ATV. Burke was vaguely grateful he'd worn jeans to work today with his hiking boots since he never went home.

The deputy drove, and Burke sat behind him, hanging onto the rack. They crossed the water at a low, wide spot and zipped along a trail that followed the river for several miles.

The deputy finally stopped the vehicle and turned off the engine. He pointed to the opposite bank, downstream.

"See that yellow plastic bobbing up and down in the water?"

Burke squinted his eyes. About a half-mile away he saw what was left of the float. "Yeah."

"That's where we found the ruined raft and the body of Nora James, the rafting guide."

Unable to force any words past the rock lodged in his throat, Burke nodded.

"We have to hike from here. The terrain is too steep and rugged to drive. The campsite is about a mile up this trail."

Burke studied the area. "Is this where they would have come off the river for the night?"

"Most likely."

"It looks like someone cut the raft's tie rope from the tree."

The deputy leaned in close. "It sure does." He shared a solemn look with Burke and jotted a note in a book. "Let's go."

Burke followed the man up the steep climb. He slipped and landed with his knee against a jagged rock and grunted.

"You doing okay, back there?"

The deputy had to be part mountain goat, and Burke wasn't about to let on that his joint screamed in pain. "I'm good. How much farther?"

"Almost there."

Spotlights flooded the camp area though it was only dusk. It could be full on dark in a matter of minutes up in the hills. The sheriff approached. "Agent Cameron?" The men shook hands. "Did my deputy catch you up on the latest findings?"

"Yes, he did. Where's the second body?"

"Over there, in the tent. I'm limiting the people who enter until a team of investigators can get up here. But that won't likely be until tomorrow."

"No sign of the other women?"

"No, sir." The sheriff pointed out the fire ring, and the abandoned breakfast. "Hard to say what happened. I'll leave some men up here to guard the site, but there's not much we can do now until morning. It's a treacherous mountain range to be wandering around on, even in the daytime, let alone in the pitch-black of night."

"We can't stop looking, just because it's dark. Those women are out there somewhere and could be in danger."

"Oh, they're definitely in danger, even if it's just from the mountain herself. But we're not doing them any good if we get ourselves killed looking for them." The older man clapped Burke's shoulder. "We'll be back out here before dawn. Now let's go."

"I'm not leaving." Helpless resistance tensed his ridged muscles.

The Sheriff cocked his head at Burke and considered him for a moment. "You know son, you may out rank me in town, but up here in the hills, I'm the boss. I understand you have someone you care about up here, but you won't be any good to her if you get yourself killed. Now— we're going back down to Peak to Peak, and we'll return in the morning. Rocky Mountain Rescue is meeting us first thing."

Burke reluctantly acquiesced to the older lawman and returned with him to the facility. It was well past dark by the time the retreat staff showed him to a room for the night. As soon as he shut the door, he called Kendra.

"Burke, what's the matter? Where are you?"

"I'm up at the Peak to Peak Retreat Center. Susan's missing, somewhere on the mountain."

"Oh, my God. Okay, try not to worry. She's a smart girl and they'll find her, I'm sure of it."

"There's more, Ken." His voice caught, and he hesitated until he gained control.

"What is it?"

"The sheriff found the rafting guide dead. At first, they thought she had drowned, but then they discovered another woman, also deceased, inside a tent at the campsite where the group slept the first night. The other women are all missing."

"What?"

"It looks to me like foul play."

"What do you need?"

"Can you come up here with Annie?"

"Don't they already have search dogs?"

"I don't know. Rocky Mountain Rescue is meeting us up there in the morning. Apparently it's too rugged and dangerous to search at night."

"Right. Good thinking. I'll call Jennings and let him know I won't be at work tomorrow, and I'll drive up tonight."

"Ken?"

"Yeah?"

"Thank you."

"No question. I'll be there in less than three hours."

IT WAS MORE LIKE FOUR HOURS BEFORE KENDRA ARRIVED with Annie, and she came with reinforcements. It was late when Burke opened the door to his room to let Kendra and her dog in, and it dismayed him to see Clay Jennings and Ranger following close behind them.

"Cameron." Clay clasped Burke's hand. "We'll find her. Don't you worry."

Burke glanced at Kendra, and she turned away to look out the window. "We've talked with our contact on RMSR, and they know we're pitching in." She angled back to face Burke. "One of the staff here at the retreat center is going to Susan's and the other women's rooms right now to gather articles of clothing to give the dogs their scents to track."

A knock sounded on the door, and Clay opened it. A woman, holding burgundy fabric draped over her arm, peered in and seeing Ranger, backed up two steps. "I have a dress from Ms. Bell's room. The other ladies on the list were staying in a different lodge. Their clothes will be here shortly."

Kendra reached for the clothing and thanked the woman. She knelt down to her dog. "Let's let Annie focus on Susan's scent. They've met in person too, so Annie will remember her smell." She encouraged Annie to sniff the fabric. The dog wagged her tail and looked at Kendra before sniffing it more. "Good girl, Annie. You remember, Susan, don't you?" Annie's tail waved faster as though she understood the question.

Burke's head floated like it was filled with helium. The dress that Annie had her nose in was the same silky one he'd run his hands all over the night Susan dropped him off after the symphony. He gripped the back of the desk chair for balance.

Without a word, Clay reached into his bag and tossed Burke a Power Bar. "When was the last time you ate something? Rule number one. You can't help others if you don't take care of yourself."

Burke wanted to hate the guy. He was a total stud, always prepared, always in control. Who was he anyway, Captain America? "Thanks."

Kendra stood and narrowed her eyes at him as he bit into the chewy chocolate flavored protein. "You need to get some rest too. I know you understand how imperative that is, if you're going to be firing on all pistons in the morning. I have a room down the hall. You two are bunking together."

You've got to be kidding me. Burke nodded like it was an obvious decision. "Sounds good."

Burke couldn't sleep. His imagination turned over every possible scenario and several impossible ones. His darkest thoughts frosted his bones. Still, his body had a chance to rest even if his mind didn't. In the morning, an hour before sunup, the search team met outside in the parking lot. Someone from the kitchen passed spicy breakfast burritos around for the crew. Kendra shook hands with the man in charge of RMSR. There were two other volunteer dog and handler teams on hand, and it encouraged Burke when he realized that Kendra had worked together with both of them in the past.

After a briefing about protocol and not destroying any evidence in what might be a crime scene, the team loaded up in several vehicles and drove to the shallow part of the river. They crossed on foot and made their way to the campsite where they set up their base camp. Kendra and Clay both fitted devices to their dog's collars.

"What're those?" Burke pointed to the gadgets.

Kendra held up a fist-sized monitor. "These are Garmin electronic trackers which allow us to know the exact location of our dogs when they're tracking off lead. We can see where they are and if they've given more attention to one area more than others. They also record all of this information back here at the base camp."

The sheriff's voice rang out to the group. "My men removed the decedent's body last night, but they left everything else where it was." He showed the search and rescue team the various evidence he thought might be important.

"This is the women's last known location." The SAR Commander pointed out. "We'll set up the base camp here. Everyone check your radios before you head out. Be sure you have plenty of gloves and evidence bags in case you find anything. This nice weather is supposed to hold, and the breeze is blowing out of the northeast. Be safe and stay in touch."

After a long and impatient hour of preparation and combing the site, the SAR team started off to search the surrounding area. Kendra opened her pack and pulled out Susan's dress. Burke's throat went dry. He wanted to bury his face in the fabric right next to Annie's.

"Okay, girl. Today's your day to show us your skills." Kendra stuffed the clothing back in the bag. "Find her, Annie. Seek." Annie sniffed all around the site where, of course, she indicated several locations. Clay went through a similar procedure with his dog, only they started nearer the trail. First, he held what looked to Burke like a baby-powder container up at shoulder height and squeezed a puff of white talc into the air.

Burke leaned close to Kendra. "What's that for?"

"He's determining the direction of the breeze. Then

he'll point Ranger in that angle so he can catch a scent. Ranger's skill and experience is in locating human-based scent from the air."

Clay then held a sweatshirt belonging to one of the missing women out for Ranger to smell before turning him toward the morning breeze. He sniffed and was off, back down the path. The two other SAR-K9 teams headed off in the opposite direction to see if they could catch any human scents from the far side of the camp.

Kendra spiraled out from the center of the clearing until Annie, who was a tracking dog, no longer reacted except at the trail. She tracked scent from the ground. When she indicated the path as well, Kendra and Annie followed Clay. "Come on, Cameron. Let's go. We can be reasonably certain Susan left the campsite in this direction. Annie's on it."

Annie was fast on her feet with her nose to the ground. She sniffed both sides of the route and sat down and barked at the water's edge. Kendra pointed. "There are lots of boot prints near the bank over here."

One of the SAR members pulled a broken oar from behind a tangle of scrub.

"Hey, careful. Don't pick stuff like that up without gloves," Kendra directed. "There could be fingerprints."

"Do you think they got into the water here and floated a mile before the raft sank?" Burke kneeled next to Kendra.

"Maybe..." She walked Annie further down the path, and in seconds Annie was off on the trail again.

Burke ran after them, leaving the rest of the team to determine if there was any evidence left behind. What felt like miles later, Annie circled a rock and sat down. She whined and barked. "Good girl, Annie." Kendra rubbed her head. She looked back at Burke. "I need to force Annie to take a break. I'll have her get some water from the river."

"Okay." Burke unzipped his pack and pulled out some Gatorade and handed a bottle to Kendra.

"Thanks."

After a short rest, Kendra let Annie smell the dress again and headed down the path, but Annie turned back. "What is it girl?" Kendra began again from the spot where Annie first indicated and slowly circled out. After three circles, Annie took off straight up the mountain.

"Are you kidding me?" Burke puffed.

"This is a tough slope. I'd have never guessed she'd leave the path and head uphill." Before long, they met up with Clay and Ranger. They had come to the same conclusion.

"Whose clothing do you have Ranger tracking?" Burke asked.

Clay held the sweatshirt for Ranger to smell. "A lady named Prue Wilkens".

"So at least up to this point, we can assume the women stayed together."

"Looks that way." Ranger pulled against the lead in Clay's hand. "What is it, boy?" The Belgian Malinois led Clay up the slope another twenty feet to a cliff with a sheer drop off. Ranger lay down and whined. Clay followed and knelt by his dog. Ranger low crawled several inches closer to the edge. Clay took the hint and peered over the edge.

"Oh, shit." He glanced back at Kendra, and some unspoken communication passed between them.

Hundreds of needles shot through the top of Burke's scalp, and he lurched toward the precipice. Kendra jumped in front of him. "Agent Cameron, stop." She shouted at him.

He blinked at her.

"Burke. Hold Annie's leash and stand right here." She forced the lead into his hand. He stood, stunned into stillness. Kendra held her palms up as if telling him to stay, then made her way to the cliff and lowered herself to her hands and knees. She looked over the edge. "There's a woman's body down below, but Burke, she has brown hair. It is *not* Susan." She turned and ran back to Burke. "Did you hear me? It isn't Susan."

One of Burke's knees buckled, and he collapsed onto the forest floor.

Clay called someone on his radio and gave coordinates asking for the RMR helicopter. After he signed off, he approached. "Look, Dean." He spoke as though Burke were not kneeling right next to them. "I know Cameron is a friend of yours, but I don't think he should be out here with us."

"I'm staying with you." Burke glared up at Jennings. No way in hell was he bailing on Susan now. He closed his eyes and said a quick prayer asking that they could find Susan before... He shook his head and stood. Burke stroked the top of Annie's head. "Let's go. Come on, Annie. Help us find Susan."

Chapter Sixteen

✥

To Susan's incredible relief, Jerrod simply spread his coat over Keira and her before he stretched himself out by the fire. He was asleep in minutes as his soft snore attested. Still, Susan couldn't sleep. Her mind rehearsed plan after plan of escape until she settled on one. Morning came too early, and Jerrod rose with the first bird song.

Susan pretended to sleep so she could surreptitiously spy on their captor. He stood over them for several minutes before he strode out of the camp leaving them alone.

"Keira? Are you awake?" Susan nudged her co-prisoner. "Keira?" Her whisper was harsh in the soft morning mist.

Keira shifted and rolled her head to face Susan. She nodded, and then her eyes filled with tears.

"Oh, Keira, don't cry." Susan tried to rub her arm with her numb, bound hands that had lost circulation long ago. "Listen. I have a plan. For whatever reason, this Jerrod person isn't planning on killing us." She swallowed. "At least, not right away. I have friends who are FBI agents."

Susan's chest ached at the thought of Burke's warm, sexy smile. God how she hoped she'd see him again. "One of my friends, her name is Kendra, is a pro at finding people. She has a K9 partner, a chocolate Lab named Annie. Their whole job is finding lost people."

Keira whispered. "What's your plan?"

Tears sprang to Susan's eyes in gratitude that Keira had come back to her mentally. "We need to leave a trail for them to follow. Annie can pick up our scent, but it will be even better if we break sticks or loosen rocks along our way. We want to make our path as obvious as we can for them."

"But how do you know they'll come looking for us?"

Susan smiled as her thoughts returned to Burke. "Because, the man I'm seeing—"

"Your boyfriend?"

Susan knit her brow and then grinned. "Yes, my boyfriend. He'll make them come, and he won't quit until he finds us."

"Really?"

"Absolutely." The idea comforted her as well as Kiera. When Susan thought about it, she knew it was true. It was Burke they were talking about, after all. The same guy who asked if she had enough gas to drive to the mountains. He was fiercely protective and though that might have bothered her a little before, she was supremely thankful for it now.

"You've found your voice." Jerrod stood at the fire ring.

Susan jumped, not having heard him approach. She hoped he hadn't listened to her plan. Kiera turned her face to the ground, hiding from him.

He sighed. "Breakfast." He held two squirrels up to show them.

Susan's stomach curdled, and she swallowed as her mouth flooded in preparation of retching. That must have been what they ate last night, and honestly, it wasn't bad. She worked to force her mind over matter because she would need all the energy she could get today.

"Will you untie us? We need to..."

Jerrod's dark eyes rested on Susan for a long time before he answered. "You can go behind those rocks, but I will hold the strap."

"What about our hands? I've lost circulation, and I can't feel my fingers."

"If I untie your hands, you'll have to do your business in front of me so I can keep an eye on you. Your choice."

Susan shuddered at the thought of him watching her pee. "Never mind, come on Kiera." She helped the young woman to her feet, and they made their way, still tethered, behind the rocks.

When they finished, the women stood close to the fire for warmth. The smoke from the meat was savory, and Susan's belly begged for food. "Please, untie our hands, just for a little while." She asked when Jerrod offered her a hunk of squirrel.

Those eyes, as if he could see inside and read her intentions, stared at her. "Okay, but don't try anything or I'll tie them tighter and not undo them again."

She nodded, and he pulled out his razor-sharp blade. She held as still as possible when he slid the knife between her wrists and loosened the knots with the tip of the blade. Instantly, blood rushed into her starved veins. Her hands heated and then tingled with painfully sharp prickles. Susan shook her arms out and then accepted the meal, licking every drip of rich grease from her fingers.

Keira didn't lift her hands toward Jerrod to be untied.

She refused to look at him, and she turned away when he tried to help her eat.

His jaw rippled, and apprehension flowed through Susan's blood. "Keira, please. You must eat." She leaned closer and whispered. "Don't make him angry."

"Leave her be," Jerrod spoke. "We have about twenty miles to go today. If she doesn't want to eat, she'll regret it. That's how she'll learn."

"Please, Keira. For me?" Susan shook Keira's shoulder, but she still refused to accept the food.

After their simple meal, Jerrod passed Susan a leather-bound flask filled with water.

"Thank you." She wanted him to see her as cooperative. Maybe she could lull him into complacency.

He nodded, staring at her in that disconcerting manner. "I'm gonna leave your hands apart today. One tied to her." He pointed at Kiera with his chin. "And one tied to me. Should be more comfortable."

Such a simple reward brought tears to her eyes, and Susan felt a tremendous amount of gratitude toward her captor. She shook her head against the emotion. *No! He's not being kind. Jerrod's a killer, and he's kidnapped you!* Her mind screamed.

Jerrod dumped scoops of dirt over the fire spot and tossed the rocks from the ring back out into the forest. He sprinkled pine thatch over the top, and by the time he finished, no one could tell there had ever been a fire laid there. When Jerrod turned his back, Susan pulled a small chunk of hair from her head and tucked the strands into the bark of the tree she leaned against.

"Let's go." Jerrod tugged on the strap attached to Susan's right hand and she stood. She reached to help

Keira up but the young woman refused. Jerrod marched on, stretching Susan between them.

"Keira, come on." Susan's arms were pulled from both directions until she gripped the tether in her left hand and yanked hard. "Keira, all you're doing is hurting me."

Keira got to her knees but was hauled off balance by the bear of a man who kept moving whether or not they willingly followed him. Keira cried out, but he did not even turn to look and she scrambled to catch up or be dragged.

Susan experienced a strange shift that she was quick to shut down. She found herself angrier at Kiera than at Jerrod. As they hiked, Susan gave herself a mental shake and kept her eye out for ways to leave subtle signs for anyone who was trying to track them. She'd thought of breaking small branches, but with her arms stretched out, one forward and one to the back, that was impossible. Along the way, she managed to turn several rocks over, exposing the dark, moist dirt underneath.

Around mid-day, they stopped for a break near a small spring. Jerrod filled all the water containers he carried and lapped the cold liquid from his cupped hand. Susan followed suit, though she considered dipping her whole mouth in and just sucking in the water, as thirsty as she was. Even Keira sipped a little, but if she didn't start giving her body more nutrients to go on, she would pass out. Maybe that was her plan, but Susan hoped not. She suspected that if Keira became too much of a liability, Jerrod would cut her loose. Literally.

Before they left, Susan was careful to press her boots down firmly into the damp ground and the dirt near the water, hoping to leave footprints. She shifted her weight to one leg to deepen an imprint, but when she looked up, she saw Jerrod watching her. He considered her for so long a cold sweat broke out across the surface of her skin.

Without a word, he approached her and pulled her hands together. He pulled another strap from a bag on his belt and tied her wrists together. Then he stared into her eyes. She couldn't hold his gaze and looked away.

Jerrod snapped a branch from a bush and swept over the boot prints she'd made in the wet dirt, erasing them. When he was satisfied, he grunted and started off. This time his pace was faster—a punishment for her attempt.

He moved down the side of the mountain with quick, sure steps that the women couldn't keep up with. They stumbled and tripped behind him.

"Jerrod, please." Susan cried out to him. "What's going on?"

"You want to walk in the water. So we'll walk in the water."

At the bottom of the hill, they came upon a creek. It was about six feet wide and moved lazily over stones smoothed by the current over centuries. He pulled the women into the river behind him and without slowing, he walked upstream about ten paces before he yanked them out again. He took Susan by the shoulders and pushed her back and forth, scuffing the dirt on the bank.

When he reached into a pocket and pulled out the chunk of hair she'd left behind where they'd slept, Susan's stomach filled with bile and her head swam. He'd known her plan all along. She watched him tangle the strands in a branch at shoulder height. His eyes held anger when his gaze met hers, and she looked away.

"Look at me."

She refused.

"I said, look at me." He reached for her face, but the

fingers that tilted her chin were gentle. "Don't try something like that again."

Susan gulped in a breath of air, blinked against sudden tears, and nodded.

Jerrod pulled them about fifty feet along the bank of the creek before he led them back down into the water. He traipsed in and out of the stream several more times before he entered for the final time and turned back, walking with the current. They passed the place where they first entered the creek and continued on, in the water, for miles.

Susan lost hope of ever being tracked. Jerrod made it look as though they had gone in the opposite direction. If only she wouldn't have been so obvious, the dogs might have found them anyway, but not now.

When Jerrod was finally ready to walk back on dry land, the sun was high in the sky. He dug in and climbed straight up the side of the mountain. They arrived on the top ridge exhausted, Keira barely holding on to consciousness.

"Jerrod, Keira needs a break and food."

"She refuses to eat."

"May I try? There's a bar in my bag."

He rifled through the pack and handed Susan the wrapped protein bar. She tried to open it, but couldn't manage with her hands tied together. She held the edge of the wrapper to her teeth and attempted to pull it open. Jerrod's vigilant gaze took in every attempt. He moved up behind her and put his arms around her, covering her small hands with his large, rough ones. Spiders skittered across her skin, and she shuddered.

"Let me help." He tore open the bar. Susan handed it to Keira, and she accepted it this time. Relief washed over

Susan's shoulders. One of Jerrod's hands left hers, and he reached for his knife. Swiftly, he released her bound hands. Completely.

Susan stared up at him as she rubbed her worn and tender skin. He bent to pick up the piece of leather and stashed it away. From one of his many pockets, he removed a cloth-wrapped package. He unfolded it and held some beef jerky out to her. *Well, probably not beef jerky, but jerky nonetheless.* Susan reached for a strip. "Thank you."

He nodded and stuffed a piece in his mouth. They rested while they ate. "Jerrod, why are you doing this?"

"I told you. I need a wife."

Susan's eyes closed briefly. "You can't just steal a woman and force her to marry you."

He tilted his head sideways, and his dark bushy brows came together in the middle. "That's how it's done. A man goes out, gets a wife, and brings her home."

"No, Jerrod. It's not. What about falling in love? What about a woman *wanting* to be your wife, not being forced to?"

He pulled in a great breath and let it out through his mouth. "It's the way my pa got my first wife, and that worked out pretty good."

Susan's jaw dropped. "Your first wife?"

Jerrod shrugged. "I was about nineteen, I guess, when Pa left. He was gone a week and when he came home, he brought me a wife."

"Did she *want* to marry you?"

"I suppose. She didn't speak out against it." He spit into the dirt. "Course, she didn't speak much at all for the first year."

Susan pinched the bridge of her nose. *The first year?*

"What happened to her?" She tried to give strength to her voice, but she failed and it came out in a hoarse whisper.

"'Bout a year after my ma and pa died of chest sickness, Lorilee died in childbirth."

Keira drew her arms up to cover her ears and started moaning. Susan reached for her and rubbed her leg. This whole story was surreal.

"And the child?"

Jerrod kept his focus on his hands, but when he looked up, his eyes were glassy. "He died too." His eyes darted to a scab healing on his knuckle. "I didn't know how to help," he whispered.

Susan's initial reaction was to comfort him. Her heart broke at the pain that filled his eyes. Yet, he was her enemy. One she would kill to get away from if she had the chance.

"She'd lost two other babes before that, but earlier in her time."

"How—" Susan cleared her throat. "How old was, Lorilee?"

Jerrod rubbed his face on his shoulder and turned to meet her eye. "She told me she was thirteen when Pa brought her home to me."

"Oh, my god." She was someone's daughter, stolen from them. Her parents didn't know where she was the whole time or that she was now dead. Susan's stomach coiled up like a cobra. "She was just a child."

Jerrod's gaze held no shame. In fact, he showed no understanding of her reaction at all. "No, she was my wife. My pa married us."

Keira keened, "Oh God, oh God, oh God, oh God." Like a mantra in the background.

"I miss her something terrible, but it's time now for me to move on."

"How long ago did she die?"

"It's been about four years, I reckon."

"I can understand wanting to get married, Jerrod, but why did you kill all those women? That, I don't understand." Hysteria was hovering in her throat. Susan's voice strained, and her breath came fast.

Jerrod sat up like a jack-rabbit. "I didn't kill those women." He and Susan stared at each other until his shoulders drooped slightly. "Not on purpose, anyway." He dropped his gaze and for all the world looked like a little boy caught ditching school.

"What do you mean?"

"Nothing. I don't want to talk about that. We have to go." He jumped to his feet and offered a hand to help Susan up. "Can I trust you to have your hands free?" He narrowed his eyes at her. "You won't like it if I catch you at your games again."

"I won't try anything." Susan's heart sank as she sold out for the simple relief of having her hands free.

"Get your friend. Let's go."

Susan knelt next to Keira. "Ready?"

"Susan, he will keep us in some cabin in the woods and make us have his babies until we die." Keira whimpered.

"Keira, I need you to pull yourself together. We'll get away before that can happen, but not if you can't keep it together." Susan's patience with Keira was fraying, and her whispered words were harsh.

Jerrod didn't speak again for most of the afternoon, and Susan mulled over his story in the silence. The way Jerrod told his tale, it was as if stealing a bride was the most natural thing on earth. And, if that was what his parents had taught him, unless he had some other outside influence, why would he question it?

"Jerrod, do you have any brothers or sisters?"

His shoulders stiffened, but he answered. "I had a brother once, but the mountain took him. I was just a boy."

"What do you mean, the mountain took him?"

"Lightning storm."

"I'm sorry."

He shrugged but didn't turn to look at her. They hiked on. Susan's legs shook with muscle exhaustion. They'd been walking at a brisk pace for a day and a half. She stepped on a loose stone and didn't have the strength to catch herself. Falling, she twisted her ankle and skinned the side of her knee down the length of her calf.

Susan cried out, and in a flash, Jerrod was next to her. "Are you hurt?" His gaze roamed her body and landed on the blood oozing down her leg. "It's okay, I'll take care of you." He scooped her up like she weighed thirty pounds and carried her to a soft shady spot on the forest floor where he laid her down. One of the many pouches he strapped across his shoulders held a mountain man's version of medical supplies.

First, he poured cool water over her scrape, and then he lifted a small, brown glass bottle to his mouth and yanked the cork out with his teeth. He poured a clear, pungent liquid over her wound, and Susan screeched. The smile he gave her was full of compassion, and he held the bottle to her mouth. She thankfully took a hit of who knew what kind of hooch. Then, with tender presses, he blotted her injury until the bleeding stopped.

"How's your ankle? Can you walk?"

"I think so." His kindness confused her.

He gazed down at her and touched her cheek with the tips of his fingers. "We'll rest here for the night."

After eating a mystery meat dinner with some wild greens that Jerrod scavenged, he tied Keira by herself to a tree close enough to the fire to feel the warmth. He prodded Susan's ankle with his fingers and wrapped it snug with a cloth. She'd only twisted it, but she could work it to her advantage if he thought she had sprained it. She might be able to take him off guard.

He tied her hands together, but not as tightly as before and then secured a line between her wrists and his belt. She would have much preferred to be tied up with Kiera. Susan didn't want to think about why he'd made this particular change.

Chapter Seventeen

***

Kendra sent her boss a pleading look, and Jennings shook his head and stepped away to talk on the radio. Burke didn't care what the man thought. Three women out of six were dead and Burke wasn't leaving these mountains without Susan. One way, or the other.

"Okay, Burke." Kendra gripped his arm. "But you have to stay with me, behind Annie. You have to remember your training. This whole mountain could be a crime scene, so be careful not to mess up any possible evidence. Okay?"

"Got it. Let's go."

"In a minute. We're waiting for Jennings to finish coordinating the body retrieval of the woman at the bottom of the cliff."

"Why do we have to wait for him? He's got his own dog." Burke fought against just taking off and screaming out Susan's name. He knew that was foolish, but he couldn't stand the delay.

Kendra's eyes filled with compassion. "Burke, honestly,

I think you're too close to this. It might be better—you might be of more help—back at the base-camp tent. You could keep Susan's parents apprised."

"No way in hell, Ken. Come on."

"Then you need to get a grip. Seriously."

Clay and Ranger approached. Ranger kept tightly to his partner's side, watching his every move. He was ready for the next command. "Listen, Cameron. Because I respect Agent Dean, I'm giving you one more chance to be out here with us. But if you do anything impulsive or don't stay behind us, I'm sending you in. Is that clear?"

"Yes, sir." Burke understood—he knew better. He was too close, but he wouldn't admit it. Instead, he would force himself to behave like the agent the FBI trained him to be, rather than a man in love. God, he prayed for the chance to tell Susan how much she had come to mean to him.

Clay narrowed his eyes at Burke and drew one side of his mouth back in skepticism. He glanced at Kendra. "Okay, let's head out." He unclipped his dog's leash. "Ranger, find 'em."

Kendra gave Annie her command too, and the dogs wove back and forth around the immediate area with their noses on the ground. Annie caught the scent and followed her nose, angling down the mountainside. Ranger was quick to follow, and the K9s took turns in the lead, but both were on to something.

"This is all so strange... So, the women came up to the cliff and what? One of them fell off, or was pushed? But then the others just left her there?" Kendra spoke her thoughts out loud.

"Maybe they went to find help." Burke pulled off his

lightweight jacket. He was sweating with the strenuous pace.

After five miles, Kendra and Clay called their dogs back for water and a rest. Left to themselves they would follow their noses until they found their quarry, or collapsed of heat exhaustion and dehydration, whichever came first.

Even though he too was tired, Burke couldn't make himself sit still. He wandered through the trees nearby looking for any kind of sign. A silver glint reflected the sun and caught his eye. Burke bent low to see what caused the flash. Tucked under a few leaves was a piece of foil-lined paper.

Remembering not to touch anything, he stood. "Kendra! I think I found something."

Kendra and Clay joined him as he knelt down where he pointed. Clay pulled a plastic bag from one of the cargo pockets on his pants and reached for the shiny paper. "Looks like a candy wrapper."

"Whatever it is, it's a good sign. Two things—one, we're on their trail, and two, they at least have some food."

A deep growl sounded from Clay's throat. "Why don't people sit still and wait for rescuers to find them? If they followed that rule, we would have found them already."

Kendra turned her back to Burke and spoke softly to Clay. He was sure she didn't intend for him to hear her, but he did. "They might have been running from someone."

Clay's eyes darted to Burke's. There was a stiff kindness in his gaze before he stuffed the wrapper in another pocket. "Let's get going. We don't have much daylight left."

The agents released the dogs to search again, and the K9s led their handlers to a flat, somewhat sheltered spot up against a high rock wall. The grass at the base of the granite appeared to be matted down. Both Annie and Ranger sat and barked.

"Good girl, Annie." Kendra stroked her dog's head. "If I was a betting woman, I'd say they spent the night here."

"I agree, and it's as useful a place as any for us to do the same." Clay shrugged his pack from his shoulders and eased it to the ground. "Let's look for any evidence before we set up our own camp."

The three of them traversed the area using a grid pattern to be sure they didn't miss anything. They found nothing, so Clay and Kendra tended to their dogs with water and food. Burke pulled a light-weight sleeping bag from his pack and helped with the others.

"I'll get some firewood." Burke left the others in search of wood. As he walked, he thought of Susan's feisty manner and heard her laugh inside his heart. "Susan," he whispered into the gloaming. "Please be alive."

In the morning, Burke stretched out his stiff muscles. He kept himself in excellent condition, but they'd covered at least fifteen miles yesterday. Today, he'd start off well energized with a military MRE, meal-ready-to-eat. It was calorie dense and would provide the fuel he needed to hike to the end of the mountain range if need be.

Annie greeted him with a drooly kiss.

"Good morning to you too, girl." He ruffled her fur.

After a fast breakfast, their small team was prepared to head out again. Ranger caught a scent and was off. Annie also smelled a trail that matched the scent Kendra had given her, but it led in a different direction.

"Do you think they split up?" Burke looked after Ranger's racing form.

Kendra shrugged. "Maybe, or maybe one of these trails

is just them stepping away to go to the bathroom or something. Let's find out."

Burke followed Kendra and Annie. After about fifteen minutes, Kendra's radio squawked. "Ranger remains hot on a trail to the southeast."

"Roger. Annie's intently tracking south-southwest. Looks like they separated. Advise."

"Follow your partner and stay in touch. Remain alert."

"Will do. Out." Kendra stepped out after Annie. "You heard the man. Let's go," she called back to Burke.

Five miles into their track, Burke pulled his water bottle from his pack. "Why is Jennings up here, anyway? This isn't a formal FBI-SAR hunt. At least not yet."

"I had to ask him for time off to come up, and when I told him that Susan was missing, he wanted to help."

Burke was silent for a while, mulling over his envious thoughts. He preferred feelings of jealousy over those of abject fear, so he let his mind go. "You're friends with Susan, right?"

"Yeah."

"So you'd know if there was anything going on between Susan and Jennings?"

Kendra stopped and turned to face him. "Look, I know he wanted to ask her out. But that's all I know. Did Susan ever say anything to you about him?"

Burke clenched his jaw. "She told me he'd asked her out. She wanted to see if there was enough of an understanding between the two of us for her to tell him no."

"Okay, then. What did you say to her?"

"I said I wanted there to be, but it was up to her. She said she would talk to him, but maybe she didn't. Maybe she decided to go out with him after all." His gut turned to stone.

"Burke, you can't go there. Not during the search. Let's just find her first. Then you can figure it all out."

He offered Kendra a drink which she took. "I know you're right. But I can't help thinking about it with all this silence."

Kendra screwed the top on the bottle and handed it back to him. "Yes, you can. Take control of your thoughts and keep your eyes open. We *will* find her."

Burke gave her a grim smile and nodded before stepping off with Kendra to follow Annie.

Kendra's radio blared static into the quiet. "Dean? We've found something."

Burke's heart came to a full stop. He stared into Kendra's eyes as she spoke with Clay. "Did you find Susan?"

"Negative. But—"

Burke's tense muscles released, and he almost collapsed. Kendra whistled and called Annie back. "What did you discover?" she asked as she filled Annie's collapsible bowl with cool water.

"We have another body."

"Shit." Burke cursed under his breath. He sat down hard next to Annie. He listened to Kendra's side of the communication.

"Have you ID'd the individual?"

"No, but my best guess, if this is one of their group, it's Prue Wilkens. Tall, dark hair. Susan and the other woman are both blondes."

"Right. Any guesses as to the cause of death?"

Clay didn't answer right away. Burke looked up to gauge Kendra's expression. Finally, Clay's voice came back over the radio. "Inconclusive at this point. Looks like an animal attack, but I can't be certain if she was dead and then mauled or thrashed to death. That'll be the ME's call."

Burke closed his eyes against the too bright sun. A hot tear leaked out the corner of one eye, and he swiped it away. *Dear God, let me find her alive.*

Chapter Eighteen

❦

S usan woke to Jerrod walking into the camp from the forest. He held a large rabbit struggling in his hands. Before her eyes, he held the creature away from his body and with one hand on its head and the other around it's body, he twisted and wrung it's neck. Jerrod looked up then as Susan flinched.

"Morning." His gravelly voice scraped across the peaceful morning.

Her belly couldn't stomach such a brutal action, and she gagged. Jerrod didn't seem to notice as he pulled out his hunting knife and proceeded to prepare the rabbit to be cooked.

Susan pushed herself up and noticed that though her hands were still bound, Jerrod left her untied to anything when he went hunting. Stinging with regret that she hadn't woken earlier and realized she could escape, she turned her back to him to hide her emotions. Susan pulled her lower lip in between her teeth. *But he's starting to trust me, so maybe I'll get another chance.*

Keira stirred and rolled to face Susan. Dark circles

caused her eyes to look sunken in. She hardly spoke anymore at all, and Susan missed the chatty sparkly girl she met less than a week ago.

"Hey, how are you?" Susan knelt at Kiera's side.

"He's going to kill us, you know," she whispered. "It's only a matter of time."

"We'll find a way to escape. You have to hold on to hope," Susan murmured as she brushed hair out of the young woman's face.

"What are you two whispering about?" Jerrod's booming voice caused them both to jump. "You're talking about me, aren't you? What are you saying?" He stomped toward them, and Keira cowered behind Susan.

Susan pushed herself up to her feet. "No. I was just checking on her. She doesn't seem well. Maybe we could go a little slower today?"

Jerrod glowered at her, and she swallowed.

"How much farther do we have to go?"

He turned back to the fire and rammed a sharpened stick through the skinned rabbit carcass before propping it over the top of the flames. "We can be there by nightfall if we don't lose time." He grumbled.

Susan worried that she'd lost ground with him. Jerrod seemed suspicious now, and she'd have to be extra careful. She turned back to Keira and spoke loud enough to be heard by their captor. "Promise me you'll eat a good breakfast. You need to be strong for our hike."

Keira stared at her with round blank eyes.

Jerrod angled himself to face the women as he tended the meal. His eyes softened as he studied Susan. "How does your ankle feel this morning?"

Subtly, Susan shifted her weight off the ankle she'd turned. It was fine, but she might be able to buy Kiera a little ease in their pace if she said it hurt. "A bit sore, still." She took a step forward being sure to add a slight limp.

His eyes narrowed slightly, and Susan's gut twisted. But, he elected not to say any more.

After their meal, Jerrod gathered their things. He checked the laces securing Kiera's hands and strung a tether from her to his belt.

He held his arms out to Susan. "I'll carry you."

The skin on her neck and shoulders puckered with disgust at the idea of him touching her—of being so close to him. "I think I'll be okay. I just need to work it out a bit." She demonstrated her suddenly improved joint.

Jerrod, with Keira following, approached her and flashing his blade, cut through the leather binding on her wrists. Her body tremored every time he brought out his knife and she glanced up at his face. Bent down as he was, Jerrod looked like a huge bear. His dark eyes stared down at her from under burnt umber brows and tangles of unkempt hair.

He sheathed his knife and took her hand. Her arm reflexively pulled back, but he didn't release her. Instead, he stepped off with a giant stride, practically dragging Kiera behind him.

"YESTERDAY, YOU TOLD ME THAT YOU DIDN'T KILL THOSE other women. Or, that it was an accident." Susan squinted up at Jerrod. He made a terrifying silhouette in front of the brilliant sun. He tilted his head toward her, but said nothing.

She pressed on. "They were my friends, Jerrod. Will you tell me what happened?"

He kept his pace and didn't appear to want to talk.

Susan turned to check on Kiera who stumbled behind them. When she lost her footing, her wrists and knees were punished by Jerrod's unrelenting pace. The difference in his manner between the two women astonished Susan. He started off treating them the same, but the more Kiera rejected him, the more he treated her like an unwanted pet. Like a dog he didn't want but still had to feed.

"Can we stop a minute, please? I'd like a drink." Susan had to get Kiera a break.

Jerrod stopped. He released her hand and offered her his deerskin water flask. She drank deeply and handed the container to Kiera, but Jerrod grabbed her wrist. "If she's thirsty, she can ask me. Otherwise, she can go without."

"But—"

Jerrod snatched the water back and drank from it before sliding it back in his pouch. He held out his hand to Susan. She lifted her gaze to his and recognized the test she was being given in that moment. If she wanted to gain more of his trust, this was how. She placed her hand in his and it was instantly engulfed as he wrapped his fingers around hers.

They'd gone another mile when Jerrod said, "The woman by the boat struck me with the oar. I blocked her blows, but the third time she hit my head. I grabbed the paddle from her and struck back. I didn't mean to..."

Susan shuddered, picturing the scene.

"She fell in the water and didn't move."

Susan closed her eyes and tripped on a tree root. She felt herself fall and reached forward, but was lifted off her feet.

"I've got you." Jerrod pulled her into his chest.

"Put me down. I'm fine." She knew her voice was sharp and would probably cost her points with him, but her body recoiled at his proximity. He smelled like a filthy wild beast, and bile rose in her throat, burning the tender tissue.

He set her carefully on her feet, and she forced a smile she hoped didn't look like the grimace she felt inside her bones.

"We can rest for a minute."

He moved to a shady spot and unwrapped some of the greasy rabbit left over from breakfast. He held it out to Susan, but she lifted her palm at his offering and turned away. He glanced at Kiera, but she was lost in her mind, refusing to acknowledge the present. He rummaged in his pouch and came up with two strips of jerky.

"Thank you." Susan took those, and chewed on them ignoring that the jerky could have come from a skunk for all she knew. "What happened to the woman we found inside the tent at our camp?"

Jerrod took a large bite of meat, and grease dripped into his beard. He chewed while he thought. "I followed the smell of bacon cooking, and found her in the camp. I didn't touch her, but she screamed like a screech owl when I took the bacon. I told her to be quiet, but she screamed again, so I picked her up and covered her mouth."

He took another bite and swallowed it with a gulp of water. "She fought against me like a wild cat, and then all of a sudden she went still. I don't know what happened to her, but I laid her inside the tent to rest."

Susan thought of the rabbit whose neck was wrung this morning and Jerrod's lack of empathy when he killed it. *Was that how it was for poor Audrey? If so, he surely knew he'd broken her neck.*

Susan choked on a sob and dropped her chin. Without

looking up, she asked, "And the woman who fell over the cliff?"

Jerrod sat straight up. "I didn't even touch her. I was tracking you all from up high on the ridge when she came out of the trees. She saw me, screamed and ran. She ran right off the cliff. There was nothing I could do."

As high-strung as Nancy was, Susan believed his story. She must have gotten turned around when she went to pee and then accidentally ran into Jerrod.

"That's awful. It's all so horrible." Her eyes filled with tears, and she was too tired to pretend she wasn't terrified anymore. Susan hugged her knees to her chest and dissolved into tears.

Jerrod's massive hand patted her tenderly on the back and slid around her shoulder. He pulled her into his chest and hummed a baby's lullaby into her hair. Goose flesh spread across every inch of her skin.

She released her knees and moved away slowly. "I'm okay. I'm just sad. They were my friends." She glanced at Jerrod's face. He looked stricken.

"I'm sorry you're sad. I'll make it up to you." He lifted his chin towards Kiera. "I'll let you keep her."

His words sent shards of ice through her core. Sometimes he seemed caring and gentle, but then he would snap into a mode as if he had no real feelings at all.

"Will you please let me give her some water, then?"

He sighed and thrust the water at her. Susan clutched it and wiped grease from the mouth of the opening. She held it to Kiera.

"Please, Keira. Drink. I need you." Susan tilted the water till it trickled into Keira's mouth. Once the cool liquid touched her lips, Keira tilted her head back and drank lustily.

When Kiera turned away, Susan drank a few swallows and handed the flask back to Jerrod. "Thank you."

He nodded and reached to wipe a drip from her chin.

"Will you tell me about Prue? She was tall and had short dark hair. Brown like yours."

Jerrod stood. He tugged once on Kiera's tether, and she stood too. He held his hand out to Susan. "I don't want to talk about this anymore. It makes you sad." He grabbed her hand and they set off once again.

Chapter Nineteen

❦

By late afternoon, Burke had stopped caring if Clay had asked Susan out or even if the two of them had dated and fallen in love. All he cared about at this point was saving Susan's life. The pace they kept as they followed Annie was brutal and reminded him of boot camp, except this hike was fear induced and never ending.

Thankfully, Kendra was diligent about giving Annie regular rest and water breaks, which gave them the same.

"I'm starved. Even after eating that entire MRE this morning. Want an energy bar?" Kendra slid her pack to the ground. She poured water for Annie, and then dumped an electrolyte packet into her own water. She tossed a pack to Burke and then shook her bottle to mix in the powder.

"This trek is ruthless. I wish I had the kind of energy that Annie has."

Kendra chuckled, "Yeah. Baxter would have been much easier on us. But, with her pace, we should be finding the women soon. I can't imagine they were moving at this fast of a clip."

"Bax didn't move as fast?"

"Well, he's a bloodhound. His favorite command besides *seek* is *lehne*—to lay. He was far more methodical than Annie, but great at his job nonetheless." Melancholy cast a painful shadow across Kendra's expression, and Burke figured she was remembering how her first K9 partner lost his leg trying to save her life. Now, the dog was living in peaceful retirement.

"I'm sure you miss him."

"I do." She peered up at him. "But, I'm glad to have Annie on this hunt." She reached over and patted his knee. "We'll find her, Burke. Susan's a survivor—obviously."

Burke tried to smile at his friend. "Thanks. Your confidence helps."

After their rest, Kendra sent Annie back on the trail, and they did their best to keep up. Her dog stopped more often, indicating more intense scents.

"Burke, look. There's an overturned stone. If I wasn't already sure of Annie, I'd know someone had come by here recently. See, the dirt where the rock was dislodged is still moist. With as dry as the climate is here, I'd say this means we're close."

They followed Annie to a spring. The dog lapped at the cold mountain water, and then sat down, barking excitedly. Burke and Kendra studied the spot her dog indicated.

"I don't see anything." Burke knelt by Annie and studied the muddy area around the spring.

"Wait." Kendra stared at the ground. "Look, there." She clipped Annie's lead on her collar and led her away from the potential tracks. "*Zustan*," she ordered. Annie sat down and waited patiently. "I wish Rick were here. He's an expert tracker. Something he learned in the Marines and perfected while working with his old partner, Jack."

Burke didn't see what Kendra saw until she pointed out

a perfect curve pushed into the mud. "I think this is a boot heel impression."

Burke leaned closer. "It looks like a hoof print, too though, doesn't it?"

"Maybe, but there's no cleft, which you usually see with a hoof." She squinted for better focus. "Do these brush marks look odd to you? I mean, what would cause those naturally?"

Burke shrugged. Following signs in the wilderness was not his strong suit. Give him some computer code and a string of IP addresses, and it was a whole other story.

"It looks to me like someone covered up these tracks. Susan wouldn't do that. I think it's highly likely that they've been kidnapped." She glanced up at Burke.

A heavy stone dropped into his gut. It was hard to breathe. "You think the killer kidnapped her?"

"It's possible. Presumably, Susan and the other woman. At least that's the premise I'm going to go on until we find evidence that suggests otherwise."

Burke ran his hand over his grizzled chin and tried to breathe through his desperation. "Where would he be taking them."

"I don't' know, but Burke, think of it this way. In one sense, this could be good news."

"How?" His voice broke.

Kendra stood and walked toward him. "If he's taking them with him, they're still alive. He *wants* them alive."

Burke's analytical mind immediately set off to give him reasons the killer might want Susan alive, and the answers made him sick with helplessness. "Oh, God. Kendra, we have to find them."

"I know. We are. We will." Kendra stepped aside and clicked on her radio. "Headquarters, this is Dean."

"Go ahead, Agent Dean."

"Any news?"

"Nothing since Jennings called in this morning."

"Okay. We're still hot on the trail. Will you call Agent Sanchez and tell him we could use his help tracking? Tomorrow's Saturday, isn't it?"

"Roger, Agent Dean. Will do."

"Thanks. Dean out." She looked up and met Burke's eye. "Rick is the best I know."

Burke nodded. "I can't believe tomorrow is Saturday already. It was just a week ago..." He bent forward and braced his hands on his knees and attempted to slow his breathing.

Kendra rubbed her hand up and down his back. "I know. Susan really cares about you too, you know. I'm sorry you got called into work on your last night together."

"Me too."

"Listen, Susan is smart and resourceful. She's in great shape too. All of those things will come in useful to her now. She's going to survive, and we're going to find her. Let's go." Kendra gave Burke a final firm pat. "*Kemne.*" Annie rushed to her side. She unclipped the lead and sent her dog off.

They moved through the greener area surrounding the spring and the small stream it created before angling back down the slope of the mountain. At the bottom of the hill they found a small, shallow creek. Annie ran up the bank, turned back and ran back down before she returned to the very edge of the water. She barked and sat down.

"Looks like they may have crossed the creek here." Kendra entered the creek and crossed to the other side with Annie. The dog sprang out of the water, searching for the scent she'd been following but after running up and down the water's edge, she returned to Kendra and cocked her head.

"Did she lose the trail?" Burke widened his eyes in fear and followed Kendra through the cold mountain water.

"They may have walked in the water for a while. If that boot heel was brushed away in an attempt to hide it, the kidnapper might be trying to make it hard to track them." Kendra sent Annie back off in search of the scent. "We'll see if we can find where they came out of the water."

Annie scampered along and then began barking. "Looks like she found something."

By the time Burke and Kendra caught up to Annie, the dog was sitting at the edge of the water again in the midst of several boot marks, but she barked at a branch overhead.

Burke pointed to a clutch of hair caught in the tree. "Look, Kendra. This is hair. Blonde hair."

"Nice work, Annie." Kendra carefully pulled the hair from the bark into a plastic evidence bag. "There are three sets of prints here." She pointed to a large boot print with a stick. "Presumably a man, and two smaller boots—Susan and the other woman. At this point they are both still alive."

"Thank God." Hope surged warm through Burke's chest. "Compared to the others, these tracks look intentional to me. Why would the kidnapper leave such an obvious sign?'

"I think we should assume that he's trying to mislead us." Kendra pointed upstream. "Seek, Annie." The dog took off, happily following the scent.

"Why do you say that?"

"Because the tracks at the spring were covered up.

These were left, deep and obvious, making it look like they came out of the water and walked upstream."

Burke and Kendra followed Annie as she tracked the scent in and out of the water. She finally circled an area on the bank and sat down, whining.

Kendra met up with her dog and pulled out a treat for her. "She's lost the trail. They probably re-entered the creek and walked a long distance to lose us." She looked upstream for several minutes before turning and gazing downstream.

Burke rested his hands on his hips. "You said the kidnapper might be trying to trick us, right?"

"Yeah?"

"I wonder if he was trying to make it look like they were headed upstream, when in fact they went downstream instead?"

"Could be. Let me send Annie upstream on both sides first, since we're here, and if she doesn't find anything, we'll head down."

Annie wandered in a zigzag pattern on both banks, but found nothing, so after an hour of lost time, they tried her in the other direction. A little over a mile downstream from the initial entry point, Annie caught the scent and bolted straight up the mountainside.

Exhausted from the chase, the small search team stopped for a rest at the top of the ridge. Burke wolfed down a chewy, peanut flavored Power Bar while Kendra tended to her dog. After their break, Annie found Susan's track and scampered along, with her nose to the ground, wagging her tail.

Hours and miles later, Annie barked like she'd found a cat shaped chew toy covered in dog treats. She yelped and sprang up and down, spinning in circles. Kendra called her off the spot. "*Lehne*." Annie laid down, panting in the shade of a tall pine.

Burke ran to the area that had Annie so excited. He fell to his knees and reached his hand out.

"Don't touch anything, Burke."

"Right." He sat back on his heels. "What is this?"

Kendra caught up to him and squatted down. She didn't answer.

"It's blood, isn't it?" He stared at the red brown stain on the side of a jagged rock where Annie led them. "But it might not be Susan's. It could have come from anything—an animal." He cringed at the desperate plea in his voice.

Kendra bit down. Her jaw flexed and she clasped his forearm. "No, Burke. With Annie's strong reaction, I believe this is Susan's blood. But—,"

"Oh, God. Do you think he killed her? Do you think she's dead?" He leapt up and turned in circles, blindly searching the area surrounding them. Panic chased away his professionalism.

"Burke!" Kendra barked at him. "Listen to me. I do not believe she's dead."

"How do you know?"

"Because, first of all this isn't a lot of blood, and second, this guy doesn't bother to hide bodies. If he killed someone, we'd find them."

Burke clung to what Kendra told him. He sucked in a calming breath and forced his mind to think clearly. Annie barked several times, wagging her tail.

"Go on then, girl. Seek!"

Annie was off again, following her impeccable nose. Burke followed Kendra, jogging to keep up while wondering with a certain dread what they'd find around the next corner.

What they found was a camp. The spot where the fire was had been brushed, but not with as much care as they'd seen before. Perhaps the killer was getting complacent as he got farther away from the scene of his crimes.

Annie happily showed Kendra all the spots where she smelled Susan's scent. There were small bones buried in the ash left from the fire. "They must have roasted some kind of small game. Our killer is definitely feeling more relaxed. That's a good sign. He may be letting down his guard."

"If so, Susan could escape."

"That's my thought, too." Kendra swung her pack off her back and stretched. Let's camp here tonight. Annie has to rest, and frankly, so do I."

Burke nodded, though he didn't want to stop. He had to admit his body would quit on him if he didn't get rest too.

They lay in their bags on the ground under the stars, both silent with their thoughts. Kendra finally spoke. "We're close, Burke. I can feel it."

Burke closed his eyes and tried to stretch his thoughts out to Susan. He hoped somehow she knew he was coming.

Chapter Twenty

❧❦❧

Dusk wrapped her cool arms around the small band as they plodded on. Gradually, Susan noticed that her feet were treading down a worn, dirt path, and she looked up at her surroundings with new interest.

"Where are we?" Susan stared at a large meadow that lay ahead, nestled in the middle of the thick pine forest, its trees standing sentinel all around. In the center of the grassy flat, stood a rugged log cabin. A split-rail fence surrounded a barn and several nearby lean-to outbuildings. It would have made a quaint scene if Susan didn't recognize it as her new prison.

Three feral looking puppies cavorted up to them, and Jerrod bent down to stroke each head. He glanced up at Susan, his beard stretching wide over his smile. He stood tall and swept his hand across the view of the meadow. "We're home."

"You have dogs?" Susan's exhausted mind struggled to shove the pieces of this scenario together.

Keira stopped behind them, dead in her tracks. "No, no, no," she moaned.

Jerrod tugged her tether, but she pulled back, trying to turn away. "No!" she screamed.

In one long stride, Jerrod grabbed her around the waist and slung her up over his shoulder. She kicked and hit him, but he marched forward as though he felt nothing more than a mosquito pestering him.

He held his hand out to Susan. "Welcome to your new home. The puppies aren't mine. Their mama's here some-where. They just like to visit."

Susan stared at the giant man who held a fighting Keira in one arm as he bent down to greet the little coyote pups with the other, and her knees buckled.

Jerrod reached to steady her. "You're tired. Let's get you to bed."

Her eyelids fluttered closed as she collapsed the rest of the way to the ground, her final thought was of Burke's brilliant smile.

THAT WAS THE LAST THING SHE REMEMBERED BEFORE waking in a small room on a cot. A candle burned inside a lantern sitting on a small bedside table. There were no windows in the room. She bolted upright. With her heart slamming against her ribs, Susan ran to the door, but found it locked.

Susan called out, "Kiera? Jerrod? Let me out of here!" She pounded her fists against the solid wood. She railed against her cell door until, worn out, she slid to the floor. Susan crawled to the cot and pulled a musty, thread-bare quilt from it and drew it to her chest. She wanted nothing more than to weep into its faded fabric. Afraid that if she allowed herself to cry, she wouldn't be able to quit. She wiped her eyes, took a big breath, and forced herself up from the floor.

Susan tossed the blanket onto the cot and began pacing. He'd locked her up for the time being, but Jerrod would come, and Susan wanted to have a plan for when he did. Her eyes darted around the room for something, anything she could use as a weapon. Now that her hands were free, she had to at least try to defend herself.

The cot was too heavy, too bulky, but she might be able to hit him over the head with the side table. If she didn't knock him out with a single blow, however, that plan could prove to be deadly. Her gaze focused on the candle flame. Two new options came to mind. One, she could light the cabin on fire, but Jerrod could simply leave her inside to die. Or she could break the glass in the lantern, hide a shard in her pocket, and wait for the perfect moment to cut him. Perhaps slice a major artery like his carotid.

The plan gave her a sense of power and the possibility of hope. If she could incapacitate Jerrod, she would have time to find and rescue Kiera and make their escape. She sat on the edge of the cot and went through each step in her mind. She could quietly break the glass inside the quilt, but Jerrod would surely notice the lantern was missing around the candle when he showed up. She'd have to knock it off as though by accident and then grab her weapon before he came in to see what caused the crash. *He better come in or all I will have accomplished is being locked in here in complete darkness.*

A piercing shriek cut through the silence. Susan bolted to her feet and ran to the door. "Kiera? Kiera, answer me!" Another scream and a crashing sound had Susan trying to pry the barrier open. She banged on the wood again.

"Kiera!" Susan's fingernails spilt and tore as she frantically dug at the seam of the entryway. She called through the crack. Kiera was shrieking unintelligible words, and Susan could hear the tenor of Jerrod's deep voice responding. She pounded on the door with both fists and fell to her knees in utter helplessness.

"Kiera." She whispered. "I'm so sorry." Susan pressed her forehead to the wood and wept in frustration and fear. If they managed to survive this, Kiera would never be the same happy yogi she once was. The poor young woman she met that first day had already died on this trip.

The screaming stopped and for a long while, Susan listened to Kiera crying. Eventually, the whimpering ended, and a terrifying silence hovered around her. Susan knew her turn was coming, and she was prepared to fight back.

Trembling, she strode to the side table and slapped the lantern off the top. The candle blew out before the glass shattered, and Susan groped in the dark to find a suitable size shard.

"Susan?" Jerrod's deep voice sounded on the other side of the door.

She felt her way to the cot and sat down, pulling the quilt up to her chin. The raw glass cut into her hand underneath the cover. A rattling sounded at the entrance and a thin line of light seeped through the crack as Jerrod opened it. The air caught in her lungs.

"What happened?" He flung the door wide, and sunshine spilled across the floor, temporarily blinding Susan with its brilliance.

"I accidentally knocked the lantern over." She took a stuttering breath and forced herself to look at him. "I'm sorry I broke it."

Jerrod studied the room, and his gaze finally landed on her. He held his hand out to her. "Come."

She was sure she would vomit. Her legs refused to comply with his request. "Where is Keira? I heard her screaming."

He shrugged. "Come," he said again.

When Susan didn't move, he walked toward her and pulled the quilt away. She hid the glass under her leg before he saw she had it, but she couldn't hide the blood in her palm.

His brows knit together, and he reached for her injured hand. "You cut yourself." He unfolded her hand so he could see the damage, then lifted her bloody palm to his lips and kissed it.

Susan snatched her hand away from him reflexively, repulsed by him and the blood on his mouth and beard.

"We need to sew that up."

"No!" Susan's nostrils flared as her breathing kicked into panic mode. "It's not deep enough for stitches. I'm fine."

"Are you hungry?"

Susan stared at him. He seemed detached from the present. "Where is Kiera? I heard her screaming."

Jerrod grasped her wrist and pulled her to her feet so fast, she left the glass shard on the cot behind her. "Come." He led her out through the door into the main room of the cabin. It was functional but held nothing extra. No decoration of any kind. He pulled her to a table and nudged her into a chair.

"Please, tell me where Kiera is."

He stared into her eyes before he answered. "She ran away." He stepped over to an old-fashioned cast-iron stove and stirred something cooking in a pot. With the spoon, he dipped out what looked like oatmeal into a bowl and set it on the table in front of her. "Eat."

"What do you mean she ran away? I heard her screaming." Rage built a fortress inside her belly.

"She screamed and then she ran off. But she won't get far."

"Why? What do you mean?" Panic speared through her anger. "Where is she, Jerrod?"

A muscle jumped in his jaw, and Susan registered the warning. "I told you, she ran away." He stomped out the front door and slammed it behind him.

Susan scoured the room for something more she could use to defend herself against him. She knew it was only a matter of time before he came for her. There were no drawers holding utensils. Jerrod hung the few cooking items he had from nails driven into the wall. She considered the cast-iron frying pan. She'd never get it up fast enough to hit him with it while he was awake, but once he was asleep, she'd have a chance. If he didn't lock her in the room again. If he didn't... *Oh, God. Help me escape. Please!*

The porridge was thick and pasty and boasted little flavor. It didn't matter. Susan understood she needed the fuel. The cereal would give her the energy she required to fight. It was her only hope. After she finished it, she tried the front door. It swung open with ease. She didn't know why he trusted her, but she was glad of it. His trust was her opportunity.

Susan stepped out onto a wooden porch. Jerrod was in the yard, chopping wood. He'd taken off his shirt and Susan saw scrapes that looked like fresh, raw claw marks on his back and shoulders. She swallowed back the breakfast that threatened to return, and she closed her eyes against images of Keira desperately trying to fight him off.

His muscles rippled in his work, their bulk raising pure terror in Susan's soul.

"Jerrod?" Her voice quavered. "I want to go look for Keira. She needs me right now."

He let the axe swing to his side as he stood with his back to her. He glanced at her over his shoulder, his hair dripping with the sweat of his exertion. "No."

Chapter Twenty-One

B urke slept fitfully, constantly woken by images of Susan laying hurt somewhere and him unable to get to her. His neck had a crick, and every muscle in his body complained when he pushed himself off the cold, bumpy ground.

"Good morning." Kendra was already up and looked fresh and ready to go.

He gave her a nod. "How come you're so chipper? Every muscle in my body is screaming."

"I'm used to this. This is what my work day looks like a lot of times."

Annie trotted to him and licked his hand. "Hey, girl." He scratched her ears.

"Get some breakfast."

"I don't want to take the time. I can eat something on the trail. Let's just go." Honestly, Burke didn't know if he could hold down any food right now. His intestines had twisted up like a sailor's knot.

Kendra shook her head. "You have to be smart about how you treat your body on these searches, Burke. If you run yourself into the ground, what are you going to do when we find Susan and she needs help?"

That convinced him. Burke sat next to Kendra and cut into the MRE she handed him. He opened a packet and reconstituted a salty, pork sausage-patty with gravy, not bothering to heat it with the flameless rations heater. He ate all the extras and drank the carb and electrolyte dense drink. He would need all the protein and extra calories on the mountain even if his stomach balked at the rich food.

He rolled up the packaging and stuffed it into his pack. "We're going to find her today. I can feel it." He truly felt it, but what he didn't say was that he hoped with every cell in his body that when they found her she'd still be alive.

"That's right." Kendra smiled at him encouragingly. She finished her meal and packed her few items while Burke did the same. Within minutes they were back on Susan's trail.

Annie happily scampered along a path obvious only to her. Occasionally she would hesitate and sniff the ground in a spot and search in a circle, but then the scent would catch her nose again and she'd bolt forward. They stopped for water every couple of miles and by lunchtime, Burke estimated they'd covered about ten.

Kendra's radio sputtered, and she squeezed the button. "This is Dean. Go ahead."

"Dean, message from Agent Sanchez. He's got your GPS coordinates and will be helo-dropping in to join you. There's a small accessible clearing about three klicks to the south of your location. Meet him there."

"Roger that. Out." The smile that brightened her face left Burke with a painful yearning. He had to find Susan alive or die trying. "Let's go. If anyone can locate Susan, besides Annie, it's Rick."

"I'm glad for the back-up."

Kendra called Annie off the trail. She snapped on her lead and they headed south to meet Rick at the drop zone. They barely got there themselves before they heard the clip-clip-clip of the chopper blades. A streamline, black helicopter hovered above the tree line and minutes later, a man rappelled down a rope to the ground. He ran, crouching away from the jet-fuel exhaust blowing in the wind caused by the rotors and approached them.

"Hey, beautiful." Rick lifted Kendra off her feet and kissed her before he set her back down. He held out his hand to Burke. "How you holding up?"

"Good. Thanks for coming."

"Not a problem. I brought some supplies and more water."

Kendra took a bottle and kneeling down, poured some for Annie. "Let's grab a quick bite and then head out. Annie's tracking, but personally I haven't seen any signs of anyone in a while."

Rick handed Burke a bottle of water. "Well, let's trust Annie then. It's a good sign that there's still a trail to follow. Let's keep that in mind."

Kendra looked up. "I agree, but we've been moving at a brisk pace. Honestly, I'm surprised we haven't overtaken them by now."

"Then we must be close." Rick slapped Burke on the back. "Don't worry, man. We'll find her."

Burke nodded and gulped down the rest of his power bar.

WITH EACH SWING OF JERROD'S AXE, SUSAN FLINCHED. He was so strong she knew she'd have to outsmart him rather than fight him off physically. Her stomach seized at thoughts of Kiera and what the poor woman must have gone through.

"Why do you think Kiera will come back here?"

Jerrod slung the axe into the chopping block with a loud crack. He stood and wiped his brow with his arm and turned to face her. "Because she can't survive out there on her own."

"No, but she might get killed trying to. Please, can we go find her?" Susan struggled to keep the tears and fear from her voice. She knew weakness made Jerrod angry.

His eyes softened as he regarded her. "Why do you want her so much? She is worthless."

"Worthless?" His statement stunned Susan. "She's a person. She's... my friend."

He cocked his head to the side, and his mouth quirked into a one-sided grin. "Friend, huh?"

At moments like these, Susan could almost believe that Jerrod was a kind man. If he cleaned up, he'd might even pass for handsome. It was as though he were two different people. One side of his personality was wild and unfeeling —a being that took what he wanted and discarded everything else. Then he'd look at her with tenderness and treat her with kindness or empathy. It was difficult to reconcile his moods, and it was becoming hard to keep her thoughts about him straight.

He reached for his shirt which looked like it was made from homespun fabric. His leather pants hugged his legs and the power she saw in them caused her to tremble. Susan wondered where his clothes came from. There were no modern products or conveniences on this little homestead, at least none that she had seen. It was as though someone had dropped her into a different century.

"If she doesn't come back before lunch, I'll go find her."

"But she could be in danger out there by herself. Can't we go now?"

His brows bunched together. "No." He hopped up on the porch and grasped Susan's hand. "I have something for you." Jerrod pulled her into the cabin with him. "Sit."

She did as she was told, and Jerrod tugged a wooden chest out from under the table by the window. He brushed the top with his hand, and dust motes filled the air. Undoing the clasps, he opened the creaking lid. Jerrod reached inside and lifted out a parcel wrapped in brown paper and tied with twine. He brought the package with him and knelt in front of her. His eyes were those of a hopeful child as he handed her his offering.

Susan didn't know what to do. Why did he have a gift for her? How could he have known she'd be here? Her heart dropped, and her limbs shivered. He had gone out to get a wife. This present was for whatever bride he happened to bring home. She shook her head.

"Yes." He pushed the package further into her lap. "Open it."

She drew in a shaky shallow breath and pulled the twine bow. Fold by fold she opened the paper and stared at the contents. On her knees lay a folded dress made with white lace. Her fingers brushed over the delicate home-made tatting which had yellowed over the years to a dingy ivory. Something had nibbled away at the edge of the collar. Susan's gaze flew up to meet his.

"It was my ma's." He said in a reverent tone.

She tried to nod, but her head and neck seemed frozen

in place. "Jerrod, I can't marry you." Her words sifted out on a breath.

He jumped to his feet so fast she let out a shriek. "You *will* marry me. Tonight." He strode to the stove and back. "Try it on."

Susan thought quickly. "It's bad luck for a groom to see a bride in her dress before the wedding."

He frowned. "Why?"

Her reason flowed smooth from her lips. "Plus, there's no minister to marry us, so..."

"When I married my first wife, my pa said some words. I'll say them this time since he's gone." He rested his hands on his hips, and Susan was face to face with his bare chest and lean belly.

She scooted her chair back. "This dress needs washing." Susan raised her chin at him. "And so do you."

"Yes, ma'am. I'll get the tub." He turned and left a fully shocked Susan staring after him.

Jerrod responded to her when she showed him strength. Maybe that's why he had no interest or respect for Kiera. He took what he wanted from her and offered her only disdain in return. Perhaps she could use this insight to her advantage. Susan looked out the window and watched as Jerrod filled a bucket with water from an outdoor pump. He poured it over his head. The water sluiced down over his muscled torso and soaked his breeches. She turned away and shook out the old dress.

The gown was meant for a woman much smaller and shorter than Susan. She wasn't sure she could squeeze into it at all. A loud bang and scrape sounded on the porch, and the door flew open. Jerrod pulled a huge metal tub into the room. Two of the wild coyote puppies followed him inside, wrestling and tumbling together on the floor. He went back out and filled a large pot with water. Spilling only a little, he set it over a fire on the stove.

"When that heats up, you can wash the dress and then have a bath yourself." He looked down at his hands. "If you want." Color seeped into his cheeks above his beard.

If Susan didn't know better, she'd have thought he was feeling bashful. This giant of a man, this killer. Susan pushed some hair behind her ear. Maybe she had it wrong. Perhaps he *didn't* murder the other women. He said he didn't mean to hurt them. Was he telling the truth? Could Nora and Audrey's deaths truly have been accidental? He told her Nancy ran and fell off the cliff on her own. Susan could see that happening.

"Thank you, Jerrod."

He tilted his gaze and smiled at her.

But what about Prue? Part of her brain refused to buy into this conciliatory side of Jerrod's personality.

He sat at a chair by the table and lifted one of the puppies to his lap. It licked and chewed on his beard, and he laughed. When the water boiled, he poured it into the tub and then made several trips to the pump for more. He brought her a pail from the corner of the kitchen. He tilted it so she could see a cream-colored lump at the bottom. "Soap, if you want. My ma liked it."

Susan nodded and pressed the old gown into the water, lathering it up with lye-scented suds. While keeping one eye on Jerrod, she washed the fragile fabric. She wrung it out and handed it to him. "Go hang this out to dry and give me my privacy." His eyes narrowed briefly, but he took the wet dress and left to do as she asked.

As soon as Jerrod closed the door behind him, Susan looked for a way to lock him out. There had to be some means to bolt the entrance from the inside. There was a latch attached to a long leather strap that he fed through a small slit in the door. She pulled on it, and the end of the strap slid through the slit into her hand. She realized she'd found the lock. When the strap hung out the front of the door, he could pull it to lift the latch. Locking the entrance involved simply pulling the strap inside. Now, there was no way to unlatch the door from the outside.

Susan was giddy with her discovery. She washed her face and hands, the rustic soap stinging the cut on her palm. Rushing with the luxury, Susan dipped her hair into the warm water to rinse some of the dirt away. She used a hand-embroidered cloth she found in the kitchen to dab at the scabbed-over scrape on her leg. Jerrod had only been outside for a few minutes, but the clock in her head ticked loudly.

She remembered the shard of glass on the bed and ran into the room where she left it—but it wasn't there. A cold apprehension filled her belly and spread tendrils of icy fear through her limbs.

He knew.

A knock sounded on the front door, and she spun around to face it, but did not move to open it.

"Susan, open this door." His voice was rough and low, devoid of the kind tone he often used with her.

She stood frozen. There was no second ask. No warning. With a loud crack the door flew open, the latch shattered and sent splintered wood flying across the floor. Susan stared at Jerrod. Was it her turn to die now?

"Never lock a door against me again." He stared into her, reaching the core of her fear. "A wife has no right to keep her husband away. Ever." Jerrod turned then and left her on her own in a prison with no bars. Susan knew now that she could never keep him away, and she doubted she could escape. She'd never survive out in the wilderness on her own—besides, Jerrod would catch her in two strides.

Unless…

Susan had one hope left. If she could crack his head with the cast-iron pan while he slept, she could get away. It was her last hope, and she held it fiercely inside her heart.

Once, Susan scoffed at Burke's gun collection and him teaching her to shoot, but now she'd give anything for a firearm and the skill to hit what she aimed at. Picturing Burke's handsome face and his vivid blue eyes, stabbed at her emotions. Why did they think their silly differences mattered? She wondered why she thought it was so important that Burke like the same things she did. It all seemed so petty now, and she yearned to be wrapped in the safety of his arms.

Tears flowed down her face, and she leaned against the door frame, sliding to the floor. She sobbed into her hands until a frantic laugh bubbled out of her chest. Burke taught her how to fish, so maybe she could survive after all. All she needed was a hook and a string. If she ever saw him again, she would never let him go. Never.

JUST BEFORE DUSK, JERROD RETURNED. HE PULLED AN old quilt off a set of shelves and stalked back outside. He didn't look at Susan once. She heard him working on something out by the barn. As dusk descended, Susan found a flint and caught some dry wood shavings on fire inside the stove. When the flames grew, Susan took a candle from the table, lit it and from it, lit several others.

When Jerrod finally came back in, he wore a stricken expression and couldn't meet her eye.

"What's the matter?"

He shrugged, trying to appear indifferent but couldn't pull it off. "I told you, you could keep her, but she ran away."

"Kiera?" Susan's pulse spiked. "Did you find her?"

He nodded once but still refused to look at her.

"Where is she?" Dread thickened in her throat.

Jerrod shook his head. "She got caught in a trap." He looked at her then, and his eyes appeared haunted. "I have traps set for bears and cougars." He approached her and fell to his knees. "She'd have been fine if she stayed on the path. Why didn't she stay on the path?" His taut expression held agony.

"Is she going to be okay?" Fresh tears washed across her cheeks.

He shook his head, his eyes pleading with her—for what, she didn't know. "She's dead."

"No!" Susan ran toward the door, but Jerrod intercepted her, blocking her exit with one thick arm.

"Don't go out there yet."

"She might still be alive. I can try to—"

"She's dead."

Susan collapsed, and Jerrod caught her before she hit the floor. He pulled her tight to his chest and absorbed her sobs and her pounding fists. When she spent all her sorrow and fury, he sat in the rocking chair and held her in his lap and rocked. He hummed the same lullaby he had before, and her skin stiffened.

"Let me up." She pushed away from him. "This wouldn't have happened if you went after her when I asked you to." Susan glared at her captor.

"You're right. I'm sorry. I didn't think about the traps. They're all around the farm, but I forgot."

"You forgot." She retorted.

"I have no call to think on them unless a beast gets caught in the spikes. Then I hear their roars and I go put them out of their pain." He rested his forehead in his hand. "She should have stayed on the path."

Susan spun around to face him, her venom boiling up. "Why was Keira screaming this morning when you had me locked in that room?"

Jerrod's gaze rose to hers, and he blinked lazily. His other personality stared out of his eyes. The one she needed to be careful of, if she valued her life.

"She refused to carry my seed." He stood. "She learned she didn't have a choice. Now, she's wasted it by being a fool."

The cold finger of death trailed up Susan's spine. She stepped backward.

"I've dug her grave. If you want to say some words over her, you can come out." He turned on his heel and left the door open behind him.

Chapter Twenty-Two

B urke, Kendra and Rick followed Annie for another fifteen miles before the team called it quits for the evening. Burke was hopeful, though. True to Kendra's assessment of Rick's tracking skills, he identified several marks of a group of people traveling together through the woods. Throughout the day, he showed Burke how to tell the difference between two slight boot marks left in the dust at the base of a tree. Nothing passed his notice—flattened grass, trees with chunks of bark peeled off, or scuffed moss missing from a carpet growing on a rock. At times, they found parallel signs that were too far apart for one person alone to make.

Rick started a small campfire by lighting pine needles. "It's safe to assume Susan and the other woman..."

"Keira." Kendra supplied.

"Right. That they are being taken somewhere." His gaze sought Burke's and bore into him. "That's a good sign."

Burke let out a heavy sigh. "I know you're right. He's keeping them alive for some reason. I just hope we can get there before he changes his mind." He sat down next to Annie and dug his fingers into her fur, massaging her shoulders. Annie licked his hand and his face then rolled over so Burke could rub her belly. The contact soothed some of Burke's tension.

Kendra dumped a bundle of kindling she'd collected, by the fire Rick was working on. "We've got to be close. We probably traveled twenty miles today. That's a brutal pace to keep with kidnap victims."

Burke scouted out some larger fallen branches and stacked them next to the other wood. "I just want to get enough sleep to keep going and start off again first thing. Susan's life depends on us."

Rick's dark eyes met his. "We will find her, Burke."

"Tomorrow?"

"I think our chances are good. Their tracks are fresh."

Burke slept close to the fire. His body was depleted, and though he needed sleep to heal his muscles, horrible dreams tormented his mind.

A COLD BLACK NOSE WOKE HIM, AND HE SHOVED IT away. The nose returned, and the pointy muzzle insulted further with a sharp bark. Burke bolted upright. The dog staring him in the face—barking—was not Annie. *What the hell?*

Clay Jennings stood across the fire ring from him snickering. "*Knoze*," he commanded, and Ranger immediately scampered to Clay's left side. "Time to wake up, Sleeping Beauty."

Burke rubbed fists in his eyes and glowered at Jennings. "Where the hell did you come from?" The last person he wanted to see right now was Clay Jennings. But on the other hand, if he and his K9 partner could help them find Susan any faster, he'd welcome him with a red carpet and a band.

Rick handed Burke a tin cup. He hadn't had coffee since Thursday morning, at the retreat center. He practically gulped the searing, bitter liquid down his throat.

"We lost radio-com with your team. When I heard Sanchez flew up here, I had them drop me and Ranger in too. We tracked you from the drop site. Fortunately for me, you guys hadn't gone too far."

Clay tossed both Kendra and Burke their morning MREs. Burke nodded his thanks. "I had some crazy dreams. I must have finally drifted off hard. Why didn't you wake me before now?"

Kendra swallowed. "Obviously you needed the rest, but now we're just about ready to go."

Burke didn't have time to sleep in, and it irritated him. They had to find Susan. He wolfed down his food without heating or tasting it and chased his meal with a long drink of water. Tightening the laces on his boots, he stretched and said, "Let's move."

The group set off, both dogs hot on a trail that seemed clear to them. Every mile or so, Rick pointed out something that confirmed they were trailing a small group of people.

"You truly do have an amazing eye for tracking." Kendra smiled at her fiancé.

Rick winked at her. "To be honest, if we didn't have the dogs, I would have lost the trail a long way back. The marks are too far apart. The guy who has the two women knows what he's doing, and I think he's trying to cover any tracks they leave."

Kendra nodded. "Yeah, I thought the same thing.

Burke and I came across a spring and it definitely looked like there were footprints that had been brushed over in the mud."

Rick raised his brows in thought. "Unfortunately, that makes him more unpredictable. When we get close, we must be extra cautious. We don't want to let him know we're on to him. He clearly knows these mountains, and there's no telling what he might do."

Clay whistled and Ranger stopped in his tracks and looked at him. "*Kemne*." Ranger jogged back to Clay. "Let's give the dogs a break." Kendra patted her leg, and Annie followed.

Kendra poured the K9 contingent some water before drinking some herself. "I'm guessing we've gone about five miles already."

Rick nodded while he chugged his drink, spilling some over his head and down his neck.

Clouds moved across the sky in the early afternoon which provided a nice coolness to their pressed hike. The dogs trotted about twenty feet ahead. Rick led the human section, followed by Kendra. Burke was on her heels, and Clay brought up the tail.

Kendra's head snapped up at the same time as Rick stopped in his tracks and held his fist in the air. Both she and Clay breathed out soft whistles, and the K9s returned to their sides. Kendra clipped Annie's lead to her vest. Ranger remained inches from Clay's left leg until he was commanded otherwise. All four humans crouched down and stared at the bloody sight before them.

SUSAN WOKE IN THE DARK ROOM, WITH NO IDEA WHAT time it was and no light to gauge from. She made her way to the door and found it unlocked. It opened with ease, and she stepped out to the main area of the cabin. Susan peeked into Jerrod's bedroom. His bed was made and he was no longer inside the cabin. Creeping on her bare feet across the cold plank floor, she peered out the kitchen window. Chickens chased each other in the side yard and pecked at strands of green grass.

The cast-iron skillet was no longer hanging in its place on the wall, and Susan felt its loss like a missing limb. She counted on that particular weapon as her only true way out of this insanity. The front door burst open, and Jerrod filled the doorway.

"You're up."

Susan startled and gaped at him.

He smiled and the kind glint she'd come to recognize and think of as *the good Jerrod* hovered in his gaze. "Good morning. Today's our special day."

She shivered violently.

"You're cold." In two strides he'd plucked a quilt from the back of the rocking chair and brought it to her. He draped it over her shoulders. "Get dressed. Breakfast is almost ready."

She rushed to her room and left the door open only enough so she could see to find her boots and jacket. She ran her fingers through her hair and pulled it back and banded it with an elastic. Susan pulled the quilt tight around herself again, and stepped out onto the porch.

The tantalizing smell of bacon frying over the open flame had her stomach crawling over itself in excitement. She resolutely turned away from the shed on the far side of the barn where two pigs grunted in the mud. Funny, no matter how horrible the situation, the human body still responded to the scent of food cooking. Susan approached the fire and saw that there were also eggs and some kind of golden skillet bread.

Jerrod grinned up at her, proud of his offering.

"It smells good." She sat on one of the five logs he had positioned around the fire pit.

He scooped up a plate mounded with breakfast. She didn't think she could eat that much, but she surprised herself with a ravenous appetite. After her first serving, she took two more slices of bacon and another serving of the sweet corn bread.

Jerrod even had coffee percolating in an old-fashioned pot. The scene was so homey, Susan had to dig her fingernails into her wrist to keep her mind in the true present. She could not afford to slip into Jerrod's make-believe world. Though, if she hoped to survive, she would have to pretend to.

"Today, you should rest, because we will marry at sundown tonight. Then I will take you as my wife." His eyes sparked with excitement.

"What about love? Don't you think a man and woman should fall in love before they get married?"

Jerrod smiled at her like she was a small child and patted her knee. "Don't be nervous. I'll be gentle with you, and love will come. It just takes a little time."

She bit her lip, stretching her mind to create a way to postpone his twisted idea of a wedding and worse—the wedding night.

"Don't worry. You'll love me when our first baby is growing in your belly."

Her intestines roiled like oily snakes slithering through her body. She gagged on her coffee and turned it into a false cough. She wouldn't be here long enough for that to happen. Even if she had to die trying to get away.

Jerrod didn't seem to notice her revulsion. He cleaned up the breakfast things and started on his daily wood chopping chore. Between strokes, he spoke to her about their future.

"Starting tomorrow, you will do the woman's duties."

Her eyebrow arched mightily, but the man before her was far too primitive to realize his insult. "What do you mean by the *woman's* duties?"

"Cooking, cleaning, collecting the eggs. Sewing too. I need a new shirt."

"I don't know how to collect eggs or sew."

Jerrod shook his head and laughed. "Of course you do. It's what women do."

"Is that so? What else do women do?" She regretted the question as soon as the words passed her lips.

The lusty glimmer in his eye frightened her. "If you don't know, I'll teach you tonight."

She stood abruptly and practically ran into the cabin.

He called after her. "It's normal for a bride to feel scared."

Maybe, she thought, but it wasn't normal for her be terrified to the depths of her soul.

After Jerrod stacked the wood he'd been chopping, he boiled water in the skillets and scraped them clean. Bringing them inside with him, he hung them on their specific nails over the stove and Susan breathed easier knowing her primary weapon was once again, close at hand.

"I'm going to take a nap. You should too. We'll be up all night." He leered at her, causing her skin to itch. If her plan went as she hoped, Jerrod would fall asleep and never wake again. At least not until she was miles away. Jerrod locked the front door with his newly fashioned latch so she couldn't leave.

"That's fine. I'm just going to rock in the rocker." She peered out the window. "Where are the puppies?"

"Probably with their mama. They'll show up again, looking for scraps when they're hungry." Jerrod pulled off his shirt and tossed it in the corner of his bedroom. Susan watched his muscles ripple, and a dark fear coiled in her belly. She turned away.

As soon as Jerrod's breathing evened out, Susan searched the cabin's cupboards and drawers looking for anything she might use as a weapon. Jerrod either used only the one knife he had tethered to his leg, or he hid all the others. At the bottom of a chest in the main room, Susan discovered stacks of old, children's schoolbooks. There was a book on shapes and colors and several early readers. She ran her fingers over their worn covers. Jerrod's mother must have taught him from those books when he was a boy. Beside them was an old-fashioned slate-board harking again back to the nineteenth century. It was odd to picture Jerrod as an innocent young child running about this mountain farm.

Susan waited for over an hour. When she heard him snoring, she crept to his door to be sure he was sound asleep before she garnered her iron weapon. She peeked in his room and simultaneously his eyes popped open. Susan stifled a scream.

Jerrod snickered. "Can't wait for tonight?"

She spun out of the doorway and pressed her back against the wall so he couldn't see her. Her hand held to her chest to settle her clamoring heart.

"Come on in. Lay next to me. I promise I won't touch you before we're rightly married."

Susan's head swung back and forth in a silent no. She drew in a steadying breath and said. "Sounds like you're the one who can't wait, but you have to. Those are the rules."

He chuckled and drifted off to sleep once more. Susan didn't dare attempt to sneak up on him again. He had the survival instincts of a wild animal. She'd have to find another way.

Jerrod woke an hour later. Donned his crumpled shirt and came out into the main room. "I've got to go outside for a few minutes, but I'll be right back. Won't be long now." He grinned at her and left.

Chapter Twenty-Three

B urke strained to see what brought them to a sudden, silent halt.

"Do you see that?" Rick whispered to Kendra.

"Yes, but what the hell is it?" She swung an uneasy, questioning gaze to Rick.

Clay edged up next to Burke's side. "What's going on?"

Rick turned back. "I'm not certain, but there is some sort of trap built out of spikes. Looks to be set on a tension wire. Could be for large animals, like bears. I don't know, but it's manmade, that's for damn sure, and there's blood on all the spikes."

Burke rose on his knees to see the device causing the alarm and instantly wished he hadn't. The blood was still red, meaning that whatever, or whomever, had been impaled on the skewers had been a recent victim. His head swam, and his stomach threatened to upend at the thought of Susan crushed in the large jaws of the trap.

Rick pressed him back down and left his hand on Burke's shoulder. "Don't jump to conclusions. All this tells us is we're close to where this guy lives. That trap is not a temporary structure."

Kendra pointed forward. "There's a trail worn through the underbrush up ahead."

"Everyone remain on the path and stay together. Keep the dogs on leads." Clay clipped Ranger in. "We'll advance slowly from here."

The group hunched down low so as not to be seen, and they moved toward the trail. When their feet hit the worn earth, they got their first glimpse of a small farm in the center of a clearing. It was rustic and showed no signs of modern equipment or technology of any sort. There were no cables or dishes on the cabin, no cars or tractors. Smoke puffed from the chimney and the scent of fire was on the breeze, but other than that, there was no sign of life.

"We found her." Burke's rough whisper was met with a wary glance from Clay.

"EMCON from here on out. We'll settle in while it's daylight and stake out the situation. Spread out, but watch each inch for boobytraps. I don't like the look of that bear trap back there. By nightfall, we'll have a plan. Hand signals only for the time being." Clay took over command of the team and Burke fell in as naturally as if Clay was Burke's captain back in Afghanistan.

Carefully, the unit dispersed, studying each step before they set a foot down. Clay and Kendra stayed closest to the path, to keep their dogs out of harm's way. Burke found a spot where he could lean against a rock and watch the homestead through binoculars. It was hard to control his arms and legs with the overload of fresh adrenaline pumping through his system. He searched the homestead for a glimpse of Susan. He had to know if she was still alive.

The afternoon drew out. Little bee-looking flies took stinging bites out of his arms and neck. When dusk came, so did the mosquitos. Through it all, Burke's eyes never wavered from the farm. Finally, the door of the cabin opened and Goliath stepped out onto the porch. Burke swallowed hard. The man leapt off the landing and strode to an open field next to the home. It looked like he was digging. Maybe he was gardening, but it was difficult to see anything clearly beyond the wooden fence.

After about ten minutes of the huge back bobbing up and down, the bear of a man stood. He held a fist full of wild flowers in his hand. He ran his fingers through his long scraggly hair and over his beard before he went back to the cabin. Burke looked over at Kendra to see her reaction. She grimaced at him and shrugged.

Burke returned to his spying position. It was full on dark by the time the door opened again, and a warm yellow light spilled out onto the porch. The man backed out of the entrance and held his hand out to someone inside. Burke's heart mule-kicked his sternum, and he sat up. He rubbed his eyes and peered hard into the magnified lenses.

SUSAN GLANCED AT THE WEDDING DRESS JERROD SPREAD across the table. It was pretty after the washing—in an old-world way. Her heart wrenched. She longed for the wedding of her dreams. A big southern event at her father's country club, no expense spared. Susan closed her eyes and pictured the elegant gown she'd created in her imagination since she was a little girl. She saw herself walking down the green lawn strewn with pink and white rose petals, holding her father's arm and looking at her future husband. Her mind's eye stretched forward, and she imagined Burke, breathtakingly handsome in a black tuxedo watching her walk toward him with immeasurable love in his gaze.

Mourning a day that would never come, Susan collapsed onto the table in a fit of sobs. The door opened behind her, and Jerrod entered. She cried harder, and he came to her.

"Don't cry." He stroked her hair and touched her chin with incredible tenderness. He drew her face up to look at him. "Please, don't cry. I'll take good care of you. I promise I will." He held up a bouquet of wild flowers and handed them to her.

The blossoms were a bit crumpled in his huge fist, but the gesture was sweet. Susan accepted his offering, and his smile showed true delight. In another world, if this man had grown up civilized, he might truly have made someone a wonderful husband. *Except that he is a murderer!* Susan's conscience screamed at her. She shook her head hard to clear her emotions away and think clearly.

"You can get dressed in the bedroom. I'll wait for you. We'll go out at sundown." Jerrod lifted the dress and spread it across his bed. The bed he planned to make theirs in a few short hours.

"I don't expect the gown will fit me, Jerrod. It's too short and well, your mother must have been a tiny woman." She considered the man before her and wondered at the physical possibility of his mother being so slight.

Then it dawned on her. "This wasn't your mother's dress, was it?" She choked on her sudden understanding. The dress he wanted her to wear belonged to an abducted thirteen-year-old girl.

"No. It wasn't. But it is all I have." He said the words in such humility it stunned her. "I hope it will do." Then, as quick as a whip, the other Jerrod appeared. "If you can't make it work, I will." He closed the door on the end of his threat, and Susan took up the gown and threw it on the floor.

The sky darkened faster than she hoped. Susan could hear Jerrod pacing outside the bedroom door. He wouldn't be patient, and she believed he'd force her into the dress himself if she didn't comply. Quickly, she peeled off her t-shirt and shorts and pulled on the yellowed lace. The length hung at mid -calf. The arms were too tight, so Susan tore the seams to make more room. There was no way she could button the gown in the back. She rummaged through a chest of drawers and found a soft knit blanket, which she wrapped around her shoulders like a shawl.

Jerrod knocked and then opened the door. He stared at Susan. His eyes roamed over her and stilled at the knit cover she wore across her back. "That blanket was for the baby." She hardly heard his words he spoke them so softly.

"I'm sorry, I'll take it off. It's just that I can't close the dress in back."

"No." His eyes were shiny but held no malice. "It's fitting, I think. Let's go."

Jerrod opened the front door and backed out holding his hand out to his bride. She stepped forward and with trembling fingers, took his hand, determined to play this out until she got her first opportunity to escape from this warped reality. Susan tried to imagine that it was Burkes' hand that held hers—that he was the man she was pretending to marry. It was the only way she could force her feet to move.

Chapter Twenty-Four

B urke's sharp intake of breath caused his team to shush him with their hands. Though all three of them appeared equally shocked at what they were seeing. Susan, whom they had been tracking desperately, stood on the porch, dressed as a bride, taking the hand of the man they thought was her captor.

Kendra made her way to his side. "I don't know what's going on, Burke, but I'm certain it isn't what it looks like. It can't be."

Too stunned to speak, Burke sat back on his heels and shook his head.

Clay gestured that they meet on the central path. His plan of attack and clipped orders snapped Burke into focus. He drew his idea in the dirt with a hunting knife, lining out the route each one of them would take. Kendra and Clay kept their dogs on lead. They would follow Rick and Burke, each agent skirting an opposite side of the meadow, hopefully remaining unseen until the last moment.

Burke and Rick low crawled through the undergrowth.

When they were on the outskirts of the farm, on opposing sides of the cabin, Kendra and Clay made their move. Burke wished he could call in an air strike. If only it were possible, as soon as he had Susan safe in his arms, he'd order a rain of fire down on this farm.

That is, if Susan wanted to be in his arms. Burke could not understand what was going on. It appeared that she was acting out a wedding with the stranger. A murderer and a kidnapper. Maybe he'd brainwashed her? It made no sense, but none of it mattered because she was alive. He was in time to save her if she wanted saving.

Susan looked tiny next to the giant beside her. The way he held her hand made Burke think of the Beauty and the Beast. He ground his teeth together and searched the edge of the forest on the far side of the farm, watching for Rick's signal to breech. He couldn't see the K9 units but knew they were getting into position.

There was no sign of the second woman that had been with Susan. She was probably in the main cabin, or possibly an outbuilding.

A light flashed twice across the meadow, and Burke took the cue. He crept toward the cabin, his SIG drawn and ready. He used a short fence that ran up to the back of the barn for cover as he made his way forward. He glanced over the pickets and saw that he was skirting what looked like a family grave yard—with a lot of graves.

Freshly dug dirt was piled into a long narrow mound. A stone sat on top of the mound holding down a handful of long colorful strands of hair that furled in the night breeze. Burke closed his eyes. He'd likely found Kiera. Swallowing the bile that filled his throat, he continued to the front of the barn. His gun held level at the head of the man walking toward an arbor with the love of Burke's life on his arm.

Rick should be equally close to the couple, but on the other side. Burke ran forward and shouted, "Freeze! FBI!"

The hulking man spun around, and with one arm, thrust Susan behind him, giving Burke the perfect shot. He steadied his hand to fire, but Susan screamed and darted out in front of her groom.

"No! Don't kill him!"

She may as well have stabbed Burke's heart clean through with a combat knife. He stood up and lowered his gun. In that second, the giant grabbed Susan around her chest from behind and pulled a long blade from a sheath strapped to his leg. He held it against her neck.

"Who are you?" The wild man bellowed.

Burke found his voice. "Drop the knife. You're surrounded."

"Toss your gun away, or I'll slit her throat."

Susan whimpered and pressed both her hands against her captor's arm, pushing against his threat.

Burke re-aimed his SIG, sighting in on the man's huge head. He had a clear shot and the confidence to make it. His only hesitation was he wasn't sure where Rick was. He needed to buy some time, so he played along. "What exactly am I interrupting? This looks like a wedding."

"That's right, and you're not invited," the bear growled.

"Why would you want to kill the woman you're marrying?"

A wicked grin spread within the man's beard. "Because, obviously you want her too, and I'm not the kind of husband who's willing to share."

A warning tremor shot through Burke's body. "Okay,

neither am I. But, I can see she's here with you willingly," he lied, hoping to appease the killer.

Susan's eyes flared with terror. Hot resolve oozed inside Burke's chest. Susan didn't want to be with this man. Burke couldn't imagine what they'd stumbled upon, but he prayed Susan wouldn't say anything to contradict him and make her kidnapper angry. Rick dashed behind the scene and took cover at the back of the cabin. Burke now knew his position, but still couldn't be certain where Kendra and Clay were. He wouldn't fire into the dark without being positive of their locations.

Burke pulled his finger from the trigger housing and held the weapon up above his head in a non-threatening manner. "Let's calm things down. If Susan has agreed to marry you, I won't do anything to stop it. What's your name?"

Though he didn't answer, the man's blade hand relaxed a little, and Burke took that as a good sign. "Susan, introduce me to your groom."

Her eyes spilled over and Burke's heart wrenched into a tight fist. He didn't want to put her through this charade but didn't know a better way to de-escalate the situation.

Susan stared at Burke, and he nodded at her encouragingly. She drew in a staggered breath. "Burke," her voice broke, and she struggled for control. "This is Jerrod."

Jerrod's hand moved away from her throat by a few inches, and he eased the tightness of his grip on her body.

"It's good to meet you, Jerrod." Burke edged one step forward. "Looks like I got here just in time to be a witness to your marriage. You need a witness, don't you?"

Jerrod narrowed his eyes as if considering Burke's question. "You could say the words."

"What words, Jerrod?"

"The ones like my pa said when he married me to Lorilee. To make it true."

Susan took Jerrod's hand and pushed away from his tight hold. He allowed it but kept her hand in his. "Lorilee was Jerrod's first wife." A sob escaped as Susan explained, settling into her role in the macabre farce.

"Where's Kiera? Isn't she a bride's maid?" Burke saw right away that was the wrong question to ask and thought again of the fresh-dug grave he had seen in the lot behind the barn. Jerrod's grip tightened, and the blade flew back to Susan's throat.

"She ran away." Jerrod answered, glaring at Burke. Susan's eyes glazed over, and she looked like she might pass out.

"It's too bad she won't get to see the wedding." Burke wished he could lend Susan his strength, though fury alone was keeping him on his feet.

Out of the corner of his eye, Burke saw two flashes of light to his left. He received an all clear to shoot when the opportunity opened.

"Where do you want me to stand to say the words, Jerrod?" He took another step forward.

"You need to put your pistol down first."

"No problem." Burke bent down to set his gun on the ground, and Jerrod relaxed his grip on Susan. The instant before he touched the metal to the dirt, Burke re-gripped his firearm, dropped to the dirt, rolled up to one knee, and fired.

Two consecutive blasts echoed between the mountain sides, and burnt gunpowder singed Burke's nostrils. His pulse hammered at his temples.

Susan screamed as Jerrod spun away from her, his shoulder a pulverized, bloody mess. Jerrod roared. He dropped his knife, and clutched his wound. Burke kept his aim, ready to fire again, but Susan cried out.

"Burke, don't kill him! Please!"

Confused, he wavered for just a moment, long enough for Jerrod to reach for Susan. Burke ordered the man to freeze. His heart shattered over the fact that Susan chose a killer over him. Yet no matter how much it stung, he couldn't go against her wishes. If Susan wanted Jerrod alive, Burke couldn't kill him.

"But, Susan, he's a murderer." The pain in his voice echoed back to him on the night's breeze.

Jerrod went for his knife with his good arm and in that second, Clay released Ranger to attack. Out of the darkness, a command that sounded like "dursh" was ordered. White fangs flashed in the firelight. Like a specter, Clay's all black Belgian Malinois speared through the night. With a blood chilling growl, Ranger lunged at Jerrod's injured arm. Razor sharp teeth sunk into flesh. Ranger viciously locked his jaw and pulled back. The Malinois twisted and shook his head and body back and forth causing Jerrod to scream out. The giant man fell to his knees and reached for Ranger with his other hand, but Ranger tugged on him hard enough to keep him off balance. Clay and Rick raced to back up their K9 partner. They apprehended the man, cuffing his wrists. Jerrod roared in agony. His eyes were wild, rolling back in his head like a rabid beast. Within seconds, he passed out from the pain of his shattered shoulder bones and torn skin. All the while, Ranger stood by growling and poised to attack again if the situation went sideways.

Susan scrambled to her hands and knees and tripped on the dress as she lunged toward Burke. He caught her in his arms, and they fell to the ground.

"I've got you. You're safe."

Susan sobbed into his shoulder, clutching him as if her survival depended on it. Burke pulled her onto his lap and cradled her there. He kissed her hair and held her tight. Susan's body shuddered violently as her emotions took over.

Kendra and Annie sprinted toward them, snatching up the blanket Susan had worn on her shoulders. She wrapped it around her friend and spoke to Burke. "She's in shock. Take her inside. We need to warm her up."

Burke lifted Susan in his arms. Rick ran ahead to check the cabin. "Clear," he yelled and returned to assist Clay.

Burke laid Susan down on a quilt Kendra had spread on the floor in front of the fireplace. "Get her a pillow and any other blankets you can find." He yanked a utility knife from his belt and carefully cut the too-small dress away where it was cutting off Susan's circulation. Kendra returned with a pillow and two quilts. Burke covered Susan with the blankets and tucked the cushion under her feet to elevate them.

Annie sat where she'd been told to stay, but she whined until Kendra allowed her to come. As if she knew Susan needed warmth and comfort, Annie curled up next to her and laid her head across her belly.

"Hello, Annie girl. You found me, didn't you?" Susan whispered. "Good, girl." Susan lifted her gaze to Burke.

He hovered over her. "You're safe, now." He reached out to touch her cheek, but suddenly uncertain if the gesture would be welcome, he dropped his hand down.

"Is he dead? Did you kill him?" Worry filled her eyes.

Burke rocked back to his heels. His chest crushed under the pressure of all his hopes and dreams. Somehow, Susan had fallen in love with a murderer. He shook his head once and then stared at Kendra who frowned and shrugged.

The ache behind his sternum forced him to take shallow breaths, and Burke stood to leave. He could not stay inside with Susan any longer. Kendra would tend to her. He closed his eyes and lost his balance. Steadying himself on a rocking chair, he turned to go. He couldn't get out of the cabin fast enough.

RICK SPOKE INTO HIS RADIO IN THE MEADOW'S clearing, and Burke heard him call for a medical evacuation team. The voice on the other end said the helicopter was fifteen minutes out. Clay and Ranger stood guard over the subdued giant, so Burke sat on a log by the fire and buried his face in his hands.

A short time later, Kendra called to him from the cabin door. "Burke, can you come in here?"

"I can't do this right now, Ken. Tell her it's okay, I get it —but I don't want to hear her explanations." What he wanted was to crawl into a hole somewhere and sleep until this nightmare went away. His body had given everything, emotionally, and physically, and his exhaustion was complete. Burke needed to be alone with his wrecked heart.

Kendra said something to Annie over her shoulder and then closed the cabin door behind her as she walked down the steps toward Burke. "Hey, I think you're jumping to conclusions. I know what it looks like, but Susan has been through a harrowing experience. She's messed up, and what she needs is love and understanding. Now isn't the time to abandon her."

"Abandon her? We've spent the last four days tracking

her down, trying to save her from what now appears like someone she wanted to be with."

"This is a case trauma connection."

Burke stared at her, realizing the truth of Kendra's assessment.

Kendra crouched down in front of him and rested her hand on his knee. "It's similar to Stockholm syndrome. I think Susan may suffer from it. She knows we saved her life, and she's beyond grateful that we're here, but she's concerned about Jerrod too. Not because she wants to be with him, but because she's confused and has misplaced empathy for him. She needs you to be strong for her a little longer Burke. Can you do that?"

The ache in his chest intensified, but he swallowed to press down the cannon ball rammed inside his throat and nodded that he could. "You're right, I didn't consider that. Thanks, Ken. She's gonna need all of our support."

Kendra stood and held out her hand to help him up. "Your problem is that you're too close to all of this."

Burke nodded and followed her back into the cabin.

The heat from the fire had eased Susan's trembling, but tears flowed down her cheeks. Kendra knelt down and stroked her face, pushing hair out of her eyes. "You're safe now, Susan. You're going to be okay. Burke's here."

He knelt by Susan's side but didn't touch her.

She reached for his hand. "I knew you'd find me. I never gave up hope..." Susan whispered. She clutched his fingers tighter and stared up at him. "I knew you'd come. I had to believe it."

"I will always come for you, Susan." His voice broke. "Always." She pulled him toward her, and Burke nuzzled her hair, pressing her head to his heart.

Kendra leaned in. "I'm sorry to bring this up right now, but Susan, where is Kiera?"

Susan's tears flowed again, and she cried with silent jerks. "She was killed in a bear trap in the woods. Jerrod buried her in his family cemetery."

Burke nodded. "I saw what appeared to be a new grave when I came in that way. There are a lot of gravestones out there."

Kendra looked up at Rick as he entered the cabin. He'd heard them and said, "I'll go check it out."

"Susan, are you injured anywhere?" Kendra returned to her first aid assessment.

"No, I'm okay." She stared at Kendra. "At some point, Jerrod decided he wanted me to be his wife. Once he came to that decision, he took good care of me. Kiera—wasn't so lucky." More tears, silent ones, streaked through the dried tracks of those that flowed earlier. "I tried to help her, but it was as if her mind had left her body." Pain and confusion poured from Susan's eyes. "It was like she just wasn't in there anymore."

Kendra reheated some coffee for Susan to sip on. "That's a self-defense mechanism. It was her way of dealing with the horror of your situation."

Burke stroked Susan's forehead. "You're so strong. It's likely you saved your life by staying present and playing along." Burke wiped fresh tears away and pressed a kiss to her cheek, tasting the salt of her sorrow.

THE MEDIVAC HELICOPTER ARRIVED, FOLLOWED CLOSELY by a chopper carrying a crime scene investigation team. Within twenty minutes, they air-lifted Jerrod off to the hospital. Clay and Ranger went with him to stand guard.

Burke took the next flight with Susan in a second heli-copter that took them to a different hospital for a complete checkup and trauma assistance. Rick, Kendra, and Annie stayed behind with the crime investigation squad. The worst of it was over, and Burke had Susan back in his arms. But the hard road to Susan's recovery was only just beginning.

Chapter Twenty-Five

❧❧❧

Susan leaned back against her pillows and smiled at her dear friends and the man who was the love of her life. It had only been a little over two months ago that Susan met Burke when he interviewed her about her near miss with Abbot Lee. Through him, she'd become close friends with Kendra and Rick.

"What has you looking so happy?" Sitting in the chair next to her hospital bed, Burke lifted Susan's fingers and pressed them to his lips. He'd been at the hospital with her since they brought her in two nights ago. She'd received a complete examination, and the doctors found she suffered from dehydration, several cuts and contusions, and minor complications due to exposure. A nurse set Susan up with IV fluids, and they expected her to heal physically in no time. However, the ER doctor scheduled an appointment for her to meet with a psychologist who specialized in Post Traumatic Relationship Syndrome to help Susan cope with the mental and emotional injuries that weren't so readily visible.

"I'm just happy. Happy that you are all here and that...

well, that I'm alive." She squeezed Burke's hand, and sudden tears dripped from her eyes.

Burke stood and kissed her forehead. "What is it? You were just smiling..."

Susan clutched his arms. "I can't avoid thinking, sure, I survived, but what about the others?" She blinked up at Burke and whispered, "Why me? Why did I get to live?"

Kendra brought Annie in with her to see Susan. Kendra's K9 partner and friend hit it off from the very beginning and then, Susan became Annie's first rescue. The incident bonded them, and now they shared a unique connection. Susan patted the mattress for Annie to jump up.

"*Zustan,*" Kendra overrode the request, and Annie sat back down. "Susan. She's not a pet." Kendra chuckled with mock indignation. "I keep trying to tell you that. Annie's a working dog. No way am I letting her hop up on your bed. Besides, we'd all get tossed out of here if she did."

Susan spoke to Annie. "You know you always have a place to run away to when you want to sneak away from your drill sergeant."

Annie gave her a Labrador smile and happily draped her tongue out the side of her mouth, but she stayed where her partner had commanded.

Rick, who pulled a chair up to the end of the bed, propped one foot on the edge of the frame. "So you're outta' here tomorrow?"

Susan nodded. "Yes, thank heavens. I just want to go home and get on with my life."

"When do you start therapy?"

"I'm meeting with the therapist the ER doctor recommended tomorrow afternoon. I think I'm doing all right though."

Kendra shared a quick glance with Burke before patting Susan's knee. "It can't hurt to talk to someone, anyway. You've been through a trauma, and most times people have lingering issues to deal with after something like that. It's all very normal."

Burke sat back and ran a hand over his scruffy chin. "I'm just glad we've got the killer behind bars."

Susan bit her lower lip and dropped her gaze to her lap. "I still don't think Jerrod willfully murdered all those women."

Three pairs of eyes stared at her. Burke rose from his chair and walked to the window. "How you can say that? After all he put you through."

Susan braced against his tension and the sudden distance between them, both physical and emotional. She shivered and pulled up her blanket. "Burke, please. I know he killed them. All I'm saying is that I don't believe he meant to—that it wasn't his intention."

Burke turned and looked at her with narrowed eyes and drawn brows.

"I'm not defending him."

His jaw flexed. "Aren't you? Because that's what it sounds like to me." There was an underlying furor in his tone that Susan couldn't make sense of.

"No, I'm not. I know that he killed those women. I'm only saying that it wasn't with a murderer's heart."

Kendra sighed. "It'd make an interesting psychological study, *after* he's settled into his prison cell."

Hot anger flashed behind Susan's eyes. "None of you understand. He was only doing what his parents had raised him to do. Jerrod didn't have any influences in his life besides them. They were the ones who taught him it was fine to take what he wanted. His father kidnapped an adolescent girl and presented her to Jerrod as a bride. It's how he thought things were done."

"See, you *are* defending him." Burke's eyes flashed.

"I am *not*. I just understand how he saw the world, that's all."

Rick sat up in his chair and cleared his throat. "Speaking of Jerrod's first wife. They did DNA tests on the bones from the graves on the farm. They found a match and finally closed the missing persons cold case for Jenny Manning. She'd disappeared from her family's campsite in the Gunnison National Forest over seven years ago. Jenny was thirteen years old when her family last saw her."

Susan noticed Rick and Kendra share a look. She felt ganged up on, and tired of trying to explain herself to these three federal agents. Only a moment ago, she was pleased to have them there. Now she wished they'd leave.

Kendra sat on the side of her bed and picked up her hand. "I think I understand what you're saying, Suz, but there's some information you should know." She glanced at Rick, and he nodded, so she continued. "When the ME finished her examination on Prue Wilkens's body, he determined that multiple brain contusions and ultimately strangulation caused her death."

Susan closed her eyes, remembering how Jerrod had avoided talking about what happened to Prue. As her mind filtered back, Susan heard the echoes of Kiera's screams when Jerrod kept her locked inside the windowless room in the cabin. She knew Jerrod was raping her friend, but somehow she'd since blocked that out. How could she have forgotten that? Susan's shoulders shook as tears seeped from her closed lids.

Burke was by her side in a flash. His powerful arms

encircled her, and she leaned into their security and comfort.

"Poor Prue... and Keira. Oh, God." Susan cried into Burke's solid shoulder. "I wanted to believe Jerrod when he told me he didn't mean to hurt the others. At times he showed such tenderness." She looked up hoping for understanding. "I can't make sense out of it."

Kendra touched her cheek. "Of course. You needed to believe him, Susan. That's the only way your mind could cope with the terrible situation you were in. Sort of like Kiera, only she went to a distant place in her mind in order to survive. It will be good for you to talk with your therapist about these things. She'll be able to help you reconcile all of it."

Rick stood and moved to stand behind Kendra, resting his hands on her shoulders. "Just remember, no matter what, we're all here for you. Okay?"

Chapter Twenty-Six

Burke swallowed his fiery rage. His fury wasn't aimed at Susan, but he secretly wished he had ten minutes alone with the bastard who had scarred her innocent heart and mind. He stroked her hair and murmured what he hoped were comforting words.

Kendra leaned back into Rick's chest. "We'll head out and let you rest, but I'll see you tomorrow." She glanced over at Burke. "Are you staying?"

"I'll wait until Susan's mom gets here. She'll probably want to stay here at the hospital with Susan, and I need a shower and a shave." He kissed Susan's cheek. "I'll be right back. I'm going to walk these guys to the elevator. Okay?"

"Sure." Her voice sounded tired and hollow. "Thank you both for being here for me."

Kendra reached forward and hugged her. "Always."

Rick squeezed her shoulder. "Let us know if you need anything."

They left the room, and Burke followed. Once he was certain they were out of earshot, he asked. "Any more information?"

Rick nodded. "They exhumed Keira's remains from her grave at the homestead and flew them down here to the ME's lab. Apparently her body was a grizzly sight. From what the doc could tell, she had been brutally raped and beaten before she got speared through by that home-made bear trap. Her official cause of death was a punctured heart and subsequent bleed out, but she suffered from a whole lot more than that."

"My God." Burke covered his eyes with his hand for a second before dragging it the rest of the way down his face. "That man is a monster. I can hardly stomach thinking about Susan being with him for so many days, being touched by him—what might have happened to her." His muscles shuddered.

Kendra rested her hand on his forearm. "You can't think like that, Burke. Susan is safe now. You saved her. We all need to focus on that, and on how we can help her from here on out. She definitely has some PTSD from this."

"I know you're right, but it's difficult not to go there in my mind."

"I get you, man." Rick gripped Burke's shoulder. "Kendra was only missing for a couple of hours when Abbot Lee drugged her, and it was insanely hard for me to deal with and then get past it. Sometimes, I still feel an uncontrollable rage toward that man. That's when I go for a long run or exhaust myself with a good workout. You'll find a way to cope."

Burke listened, knowing they were right. "But I can't help fantasizing tearing that sick bastard apart limb from limb."

"Stay away from those kinds of thoughts." Kendra

reached up and kissed his cheek. "You're a better man than that. Way better."

"Thanks. I'll try to remember that." Burke gave her a lopsided smile. "My gut twists when Susan insists that Jerrod wasn't so bad. A tiny part of me wants her to know exactly what he did to Kiera, but I realize that'd be too much for her to handle."

"Don't worry. She'll be seeing a therapist who is skilled at working with trauma-connection and PTSD. They'll get there, but it will be on Susan's psychological timeline, and only when she's ready to deal with it."

The elevator bell dinged, and the doors opened. Burke hugged Kendra and shook Rick's hand. "Thanks for being here guys. Your support means everything."

Burke returned to sit with Susan and wait for her mother.

Susan ran her fingers down his arm. "Hey, are you okay?"

"Me? I'm not the one in the hospital." He tried to joke, but it fell flat.

"Talk to me. What's going on inside that handsome head of yours?"

Burke shrugged and, bracing his arms on his knees, he looked at the floor. "I'm just thankful you're alive and safe. That's all."

"And I am, Burke. I will get through this and be fine."

"When did you say you see the therapist?"

Susan studied him before she answered. "You're worried about me emotionally. Is that it?"

He shrugged again. "There's no possible way you could go through all that you did without incurring some emotional wounds."

"That's true, and I'm scheduled to meet with a therapist starting tomorrow. But I'm stronger than you think. It may be difficult, but I will deal with this and put it behind me."

Burke smiled then and gazed up at her. "You're the strongest woman I know." He barked a laugh. "And one of my best friends is Kendra Dean who is a bad-ass."

Susan laughed. "I don't think I'm as strong as Kendra, but I can do this. Especially because I have you, Kendra, and Rick to lean on." She leaned toward him and pulled his chin close, kissing him sweetly. "Okay?"

The door swung open and an elegant blonde woman in her mid-fifties rushed in. "Susan—oh thank God!"

Burke stood as Susan's mother hurried to the bedside and placed her hands on either side of her daughter's face.

"I'm okay, Mom."

Mrs. Bell pulled her daughter's head into her breast and crooned. Susan rolled her eyes from inside the all-consuming embrace and smirked up at Burke.

He waited for Mrs. Bell to realize he was there, and after more fussing and checking Susan over to appease her own concerns, she did.

"Burke. You saved Susan's life."

"Not just me, ma'am. There was an entire team."

"But I called you, and you made it happen. We have *you* to thank for rescuing our baby girl."

Susan smoothed her ruffled hair. "Who is this 'we' you're talking about, Mom?"

"Me and your father, of course."

"My father? You haven't talked to him, or about him, in years."

Mrs. Bell slid out of her light overcoat, and Burke moved to help her. "Well, all of that changes when your little girl gets lost in the Colorado wilderness." She smoothed her dress with her hands. "In fact, your father flew out here with me in his firm's private jet. He's downstairs dealing with the driver and confirming hotel arrangements. He'll be up in a few minutes."

"He, what?"

Burke noted the shocked look on Susan's face and the reluctance of her mother to meet her daughter's eyes. He stepped toward Susan and took her hand in his.

"Daddy's here? With you? Seriously?"

Mrs. Bell finally lifted her chin and met Susan's challenging gaze. "Of course he's here, darling. Admittedly, he's been distracted with building his law firm over the years. He's not been present to either one of us. But it's also true, that neither you, nor I, have ever wanted for anything, and when it came to the possibility of losing you, he dropped everything."

Susan's mouth fell open. "Never wanted for anything? I wanted his attention and his love, and frankly so did you. I can't believe you are brushing all of that aside."

Her mother sat on the opposite edge of the bed and took Susan's other hand. "Of course I'm not brushing it aside. I don't forgive him for any of it, but I'm grateful that *this* time he dropped everything and brought me to you."

Susan blinked at her mother, clearly stunned. Her father, a tall and stately man, entered the hospital room. His impeccably groomed hair was a faded blond. The man's fine-boned features were reminiscent of old-world aristocracy. His sharp gaze assessed each person in the room, pausing for a time on Burke before settling finally upon his daughter.

"Susan." Mr. Bell's gentrified southern accent soothed. "You don't know how good it is to see you safe and well."

He approached the bed and reached out a hand to cup her face. His other hand he placed on his ex-wife's shoulder blade.

Burke cleared his throat. "If you'll excuse me, I'm just gonna step outside and give you all some privacy."

"No need." Mr. Bell crossed the room and held out his hand. "You must be Agent Cameron. The man responsible for saving our daughter's life."

"Yes, sir." Burke gave him a firm handshake. "I'm Burke Cameron, that is. But I'm not the only one responsible for saving Susan's life. Most of the credit should go to the two FBI K9 teams that tracked her across almost sixty miles of wilderness."

"Yes, well. Margaret told me she called *you* when the retreat center informed her that Susan was missing, and now our precious girl is here, safe and sound. That's all I need to know."

Burke's face heated, and he tugged on his collar. Susan's rescue was much more than her parents imagined, but maybe it was better if they never knew the extent of Susan's experience. He gave the older man a brief nod and turned to Susan.

"I'm going to head out and let you catch up with your parents. I'll be back first thing tomorrow." The kiss he desperately wanted to give her would have to wait. It wouldn't be appropriate under her parent's scrutiny.

Susan's vivid blue eyes saddened. "I thought you would stay here with me overnight?"

"Well, your parents are here now, and I'm sure they want to be with you."

Mrs. Bell let out a small pfft of air. "Don't leave on our account, Burke. We're staying at a hotel tonight."

Susan's brows crunched together. "What? What is going on with you two?"

Mr. Bell stepped behind Susan's mother and rested his hands on her delicate shoulders. "We spent the week with each other, worrying and waiting to hear some word of you, and well, we had a lot of time to talk."

"And remember." A soft smile brightened Mrs. Bell's face as she gazed up at her ex-husband.

Susan stared at them shaking her head. "Mom. I don't want you to get hurt again," she pleaded.

Her father squeezed her mom's shoulders. "Sugar," his southern drawl stretched his words out long and sweet like taffy. "I'm looking forward to retiring. Our lives are in a different place now. Your mother and I realized over this past week that we never stopped loving each other. With you safe and sound, we're looking ahead to a much happier future."

"I..." Susan stopped.

Her mother leaned forward and kissed her cheek. "Don't fret, now, darling. Be happy for us and focus on getting your strength back."

"Now that we've seen that you're safe and sound," Mr. Bell leveled his gaze on Burke, "And in good hands, we'll go get settled in the hotel. We'll see you both tomorrow morning. First thing." Susan's father held his hand out to her, and she grasped it. He pulled her into an embrace and kissed the top of her head. "I love you, baby doll. I'm so thankful that you're all right."

"I love you too, Daddy." Burke smiled at the slight drawl sneaking in and softening Susan's words as she spoke with her parents. "I'll see you in the morning." She sat up. "And Daddy?"

"Yes, sweet pea?"

"Don't you dare hurt Mama again. I mean it."

His severe features softened. "Oh darlin', I'll be spendin' the rest of my years making up for the pain I caused you both. I hope you'll be able to forgive me one day, but even if you can't, I want to see as much of you both as I can from now on."

Tears sparkled in Susan's eyes and she bit her lower lip. When her parents left, she allowed the tears to spill. "Was that real?"

"Looked real to me." Burke shoved his hands in his pants pockets. "It's kind of crazy how coming close to losing someone you love can change your perspective."

Susan gazed up at him. "What do you mean?"

Chapter Twenty-Seven

The next morning, Susan's doctor released her from the hospital. He prescribed an anti-biotic for the cut on her palm, suggested over-the-counter pain relievers for her other various cuts and scrapes, and gave her a list of names of therapists he recommended if she wasn't happy with the one she was scheduled to see. Susan thanked him and moved from her bed to the wheelchair they required her to ride in until she got outside. Burke walked alongside as the nurse pushed her to the front doors.

"Ready to go home?" Burke opened the door of his truck for her. He and the nurse helped her get in and settled before the nurse said goodbye and took the chair back inside.

"I'm readier than you can imagine."

Burke reached across her and snapped her belt in, then kissed the tip of her nose. "Good, let's get out of here."

They drove for a while in relaxed silence before Susan spoke. "You know, I'm weirdly angry that I had to miss that conference."

"Really?" Burke gave her a quizzical glance.

She knew she sounded crazy. "Yes. It's like Jerrod stole that from me too. He robbed people's futures, their hopes and dreams. I'm super pissed off at him about that right now."

"It's true, you missed out on the conference, but you can still make whatever you want out of your future." Burke rested his hand on her knee and gave her a gentle squeeze. "Do you still want to build your online business?"

Susan turned her gaze out the window and was quiet for several miles on their way to her apartment. Burke didn't press for an answer. Later, Susan asked, "What will happen to Jerrod?"

She glanced at Burke and noticed his grip tighten on the steering wheel, but his voice was calm. "He'll go through psychological testing and stand trial." He reached for her hand. "You will be called to testify, but I don't want you to worry about that right now."

Cold dread gripped her chest, and Susan's mind tried to block the memories that flooded in. She squeezed her eyelids to keep the sudden tears in.

"I'll be with you. You won't have to go alone."

Susan pulled Burke's hand into her lap and held onto him tightly with both hands, clinging to his strength.

When they got to her place, he helped her inside. "Want to lie down? Are you hungry? Maybe you'd like to take a bath?"

Susan laughed. "You're very sweet. Why don't you sit down and I'll make us some lunch?"

"No way. I'll do it. You either go to bed or sit on the couch. I'm taking care of you, like it or not."

Susan kissed his cheek and crossed the carpet to her

small sofa. "What do you make of my parent's reconciliation?"

"I think it's great. Don't you?"

"That's because you're a romantic." She gave him a sideways glance.

Burke laughed. "Perhaps."

"I thought about you the whole time when I was up in the mountains." Her eyes sought his. "I knew you'd come, or at least try to. Honestly, I wasn't sure if you could ever find me."

Burke crossed the room and knelt at her side, holding her hands. "I wouldn't have stopped searching until we found you, Susan. Never."

She leaned against his chest and sighed. "I've become absolutely certain about one thing during all of this."

"Hm?" He nuzzled the top of her head with his cheek.

Susan pulled back and looked him in the eye. "I love you, Burke Cameron."

His eyes moistened, and he slid his hands up to the sides of her face. "I realized the same thing. I love you too, Susan. I even love all the things about you that make me crazy." He kissed the tip of her nose. "I promised God, that if He'd let me find you, I'd do whatever you want. Even go to Tai Chi in the park and wear hippy beads and burn incense. Whatever crazy thing you want." He pressed his lips against hers, soft and reverently. He spoke against them. "I love you so much."

Susan caught his lip between her teeth, and pulling him closer, encouraged his kiss. Emotions flooded through her. Love was the most overwhelming feeling, and passion, but rage and anguish were mixed in too. She pushed her body against Burke's solid and safe frame, partly inviting him and partly railing against what she'd gone through.

Burke drew back a few inches and stared into her eyes. "I want you to know, I love you more than anything. But, let's take our time. You've been through an incredible trauma. You need time to heal."

Susan closed her eyes. She knew he was right, though she wanted to lose herself for a while in mindless passion, but she didn't want to sully the beautiful thing growing between them with anything that happened in the mountains.

"Let's have lunch and then maybe you can take a nap."

"Burke?"

He raised his brows.

"Thank you."

He smiled and kissed her fingers, turning her hand to kiss her palm.

As Burke cleaned up their lunch dishes, a knock sounded on the door. He crossed the room to open it, and Susan's parents swept in.

"You look even better today, sweet angel," Mrs. Bell crooned.

"Thanks, mama." Susan slid over on the couch to make room. "I'm tired though."

Mr. Bell nodded to Burke. "Cameron."

"Nice to see you, sir. Did you two have lunch? We just ate, but I can make you something."

"No, thank you. We won't stay long. Suzie needs her rest." He sat across from his wife and daughter.

"So, what are your plans? I'm still having a hard time believing the two of you are back together." Susan tucked her legs underneath her.

Mrs. Bell's cheeks glowed an attractive pink. "I'm moving back to the estate."

"I've no doubt your mother will spend the first several weeks redecorating." Mr. Bell gazed lovingly at his wife.

Susan tilted her head. "That's it? You're just going to move in together again and act like nothing is different after twenty years?"

"Of course not, silly." Susan's mother reached for her hand. "We're planning to renew our vows and take a long European honeymoon." She glanced at her husband. "Then we will start life over. It's a do-over."

"But—"

"The problems we had all stemmed from my working too much. Now, I'll be retired." Mr. Bell laughed. "Your mama will probably tire of having me around all the time."

"I wish you'd consider moving back home too. I could take care of you." Susan's mother held her hand with both of her own.

"No way. You two can relive your glory days all you want, but you'll have to do it without me. Besides," Susan glanced at Burke. "I have plans of my own."

Mr. Bell's eyes hardened slightly as his gaze followed his daughter's to Burke.

Susan's mom remained unaware of the silent conversation happening in the room. "I thought you said you quit your job. What are your plans?"

"Mother, I told you I was starting my own business."

Mrs. Bell waved her fingers in the air. "Yes, sure, but you can do that anywhere."

Susan sighed.

Burke finished putting the plates away and entered the sitting area. "Susan should probably take a nap before meeting with her therapist."

Mr. Bell stood. "Of course." He held a hand to his wife. "Margaret?"

She leaned forward and kissed Susan's cheek. "All right, you get some rest. Call me later. I want to know how your session goes."

"I will." Susan pulled her mother into an embrace. "I love you."

"I love you too, my precious girl." Margaret reached her hand out to Burke. "Thank you, again, Burke. I knew we could rely on you."

He walked Susan's parents to the door, and her mother stepped out. Mr. Bell paused. "I expect I'll be having a conversation with you in the very near future."

Burke grinned and shook the man's hand. "Yes, sir. You will."

Chapter Twenty-Eight

The following month, on a beautiful July morning, Burke drove Susan to Kendra's home in Sedalia. It was the day Kendra and Rick were becoming man and wife. Kendra asked Susan to be her maid of honor. Rick's old partner from his time in Chicago, flew in to stand with Rick. Susan wore a simple periwinkle summer dress similar in style to Kendra's white gown.

The closer Burke's car got to the foothills, the tighter Susan's stomach muscles became. She picked at the pearl beads on her purse and fidgeted in her seat.

"Are you okay?" Burke glanced at her. "You seem nervous."

"I'm fine." As soon as the word crossed her lips, she heard her therapist's admonition to be honest about her feelings and to face them. "Actually... I'm not fine."

"What is it?" The concern in Burke's eyes warmed her heart and helped to ease her tension.

"I'm uncomfortable being so close to the mountains. I

just need to breathe through it. I'll be all right in a few minutes."

Burke reached for her hand. "Okay, but if at any point you need to leave. We leave. Deal? Kendra will understand."

Susan pressed his knuckles to her lips and kissed them. "Thanks, but I have to work through this. And I will."

It was the perfect day for an outdoor wedding, and since it was a small ceremony with just a few friends and family, if the inevitable Colorado afternoon rain shower came, the wedding party could all duck inside. As soon as they arrived, Susan left Burke with some of his FBI coworkers and went into the house to find Kendra.

She opened the door to Kendra's bedroom and found a stunning bride gazing at herself in the mirror with her mother crying softly next to her. It was the perfect bridal scene.

Kendra noticed Susan in the reflection. "Come on in Suz." She turned. Her gown was an elegant, strapless sheath with a train flaring from her knee. Simple and graceful, just like the bride. "Mom, this is my friend Susan." Kendra introduced them and Mrs. Dean embraced her.

"It's nice to meet you. Kendra told me a little of your story. I'm so sorry for what you went through."

"Mom!" Kendra clutched her mom's hand. "Please."

Susan smiled and did her best to ignore the shiver that slid through her body. "It's okay. It was awful, but it's over now. Today is Kendra's day. Let's focus on that." She held out her arms. "Kendra, look at you. You are beyond gorgeous. Rick will pass out when he sees you."

Kendra turned to look at herself in the mirror once again. "Do you really think so?" She gazed down at the sparkling ring on her finger. "I don't believe I've ever been so happy."

Susan and Mrs. Dean helped Kendra attach her veil to her loosely curled updo, tucking stems of baby's breath into a few places. They toasted Kendra with champagne and touched up their own hair and makeup. With bouquets in hand, the women left the bedroom.

A young man waited for them at the end of the hallway. He held his elbow out to Kendra's mom.

"Susan, this is my brother, Michael."

They nodded and smiled at each other before Michael walked with his mother to the back door of Kendra's house. He escorted her to the front row of white chairs lined up across the lawn. Susan stepped toward a ridiculously handsome man with dark, almost-black hair, and startling blue eyes.

"You must be Jack Stone?"

"Guilty. And you're Susan?" He held his arm out.

She nodded and slipped her hand in the crook of his elbow. "Nice to meet you."

"Glad you're safe. Cameron's a lucky man."

Susan's cheeks flushed at the sudden wash of terror her memories brought. *Will I ever be free from these reactions?* Susan swallowed hard and together, she and Jack stepped out the door and walked side by side up the aisle, parting at the end. Jack moved to Rick's side and clapped him on the shoulder.

The music changed, and everyone in the small congregation rose. Susan had already seen how beautiful Kendra was—now she wanted to watch Rick's face when he caught his first glimpse of his bride. She wasn't disappointed. Rick, usually cool and in control, swallowed hard, his Adam's apple ducking up and down. His black eyes glimmered with tears of joy, and then he smiled. His teeth bright against his tan skin. Susan hoped the photographer got a photo of his expression for Kendra to keep forever.

Kendra walked up the aisle on her dad's arm. They'd traveled a rocky path before today, but Kendra's family had come through her tragedy, loving each other better and growing closer. Susan recognized the same tendencies in her own parents. Her mother and father had reconciled, and now they both doted on her. She and Burke too, were closer. It was as though they all came face to face with losing people they loved and realized that life and relationships were too precious to take for granted.

Kendra handed Susan her bouquet and kissed her dad's cheek. She turned and took Rick's arm. Their love was palpable. Susan glanced at Burke standing in the back next to Clay and the contingent of dogs. Clay brought both of his, Gunner and Ranger. Burke stood with Baxter, who sported a bowtie, and Annie who wore a bow that matched the color of Susan's dress. Burke's gaze was on her and filled to the brim with deep emotion.

When the pastor asked for the rings, Burke sent Baxter and Annie down the aisle together. They each had a ring tied to their collar. The crowd laughed, and Baxter barked once with what Susan believed was his approval.

After the ceremony, everyone enjoyed a catered dinner and dancing. The party went into the night. Susan relaxed and had more fun than she'd had since before the incident. Her heart filled with a sense of growth and sure hope of complete healing. Rick and Kendra made a beautiful couple, and Susan couldn't keep from watching them. She leaned against Burke's arm. "They're so in love," she said, dreamily.

As the night went on, the only people left were Rick

and Kendra's close friends. Susan met Jack's fiancée, Laurel, who enchanted everyone with her lovely Scottish accent. That couple also embodied love, and the emotion flooded through Susan's heart. It was a magical night.

A slow beat drifted through the night stars, and the lead singer crooned over the speakers singing *Unchained Melody*. Burke held out his hand to Susan. "Dance?"

She smiled, happy to slide into the place that had become her own in his arms. He held her head to his chest as they swayed to the rhythm of the love song. Susan closed her eyes and lost herself in Burke's strength, breathing in his cologne, and listening to his pulse speed up. His grip tightened on her, and she tilted her face up to see if he was okay.

His eyes misted, and Susan brushed her fingers across his cheek. "What is it?"

"I was thinking about how much I've come to love you and how close I came to losing you forever. It's overwhelming sometimes."

Susan slid her arms around his waist and pulled him in tight. Her cheek nestled against his chest, and she listened to his heart beating life and love. Overwhelmed was exactly how Susan had felt many times over the past few weeks. Amazed that she'd survived. Grateful that Burke and Kendra found her and never gave up. Stunned at the skill of the K9s without whom, she'd still either be living the existence of a slave or be dead. Her feelings for Burke flowed richer and deeper than they had before, back when she only saw him as hot and fun to be with.

Susan smiled to herself. "It's funny, I thought I loved you before, but love is a different color now. Isn't it?"

His hand pressed her head closer. "I can't find language that's descriptive enough to express how I feel."

She tilted her chin up and kissed his jaw and then reached for his lips.

He murmured against her mouth. "Ready to go?"

The vibration of his words hummed throughout her body making promises. "Take me home."

Chapter Twenty-Nine

After they said their goodbyes, Burke and Susan rushed to his car, impatient to be alone. Before opening her door, Burke pulled Susan into his arms. She seemed delicate, fragile even, though he knew that certainly wasn't the case. Still a sense of protectiveness surged through him that stole his breath. She pressed against him, kissing him with a glimmer of passion to come, and his senses swirled. He wished they didn't have to make the thirty-minute drive back to her place.

"Hurry." She whispered into his mouth as she turned her head and deepened their kiss.

Burke reached for the door handle, but it remained locked. The tangible world bumped into his lust-addled brain, making him deal with the fact that his key fob hadn't automatically unlocked the truck when he approached. Burke pulled away and patted his pockets. The key was missing. Irritation pinched the back of his neck. His jaw hardened, and he steadied his breath.

"I don't have my keys."

"Where did you leave them?"

"I don't know." A frustrated growl pushed through his throat. "I'll go look in the house." He kissed her once again, sliding his hands up into her hair, loosening the flower pinned on the side. "Don't move, I'll be right back."

He ran inside, feeling like a complete idiot. Burke scanned the counter-tops and the table. His jaw flexed with impatience.

"Hey, I thought you left?" Rick came in through the back door to the kitchen.

"I'm trying to, but I can't find my car keys."

Rick chuckled. "Smooth."

"Right? Why now?"

Rick lifted a key fob hanging from a row of hooks by the door and tossed it to Burke. "Here, take my Explorer. We can switch vehicles back on Monday."

Burke snatched the keyring from mid-air. "You're coming in to work on Monday? Aren't you guys going on a honeymoon, or something?"

"Yeah, but we're not leaving until next weekend, so this works. Besides, I want to be there on Wednesday for our first joint task force meeting on human trafficking."

"Right, but how does your new wife feel about you choosing work over your wedding trip?"

Rick laughed. "She'd make the same choice, and you know it."

"True." Burke shook his head in mock dismay, then grinned. "Thanks for the car loan, man. I owe you."

"I'll collect." Rick smirked. "Now get out of here."

"See you, Monday." Burke jogged outside and clicked the unlock button. Lights flashed on Rick's Explorer, and Susan met him at the passenger door. "A loan."

"Whatever gets us home." Susan smiled.

Burke's pulse did a hop-skip. *Home. Yeah, that sounds right.*

They didn't speak more than a few words on the way to Susan's apartment, and the tension caused by their mutual desire sparked between them. Burke parked the car and ran to open Susan's door. When she slipped her hand into his, a snap of electrical current jolted up his arm and shot throughout his body. Every nerve ending stood tall at attention.

They rushed up the stairs, and Susan removed her keys from the tiny purse she carried. She trembled when she tried to insert her key into the lock. Burke covered her hand with his to help, but the curve of Susan's neck distracted him, and he ran a few small kisses along the graceful arc before they turned to nibbles. She released a soft moan and leaned back into him. Hot, demanding blood surged through him, and his breath came fast.

Susan turned to face him, and leaving the key dangling from the door handle she slid her arms around his neck and pulled his mouth to hers. Burke ran his hands down her back, cupping her perfect ass in his palms. They needed to get inside before he tore her dress off outside in front of anyone who happened to come by. He inhaled the fragrance of her skin kissed with a spicy musk and fumbled with the lock. The door swung open, and they almost fell. Burke held her up to keep from tripping, and she wrapped a long leg around his waist. He slammed the door closed.

Burke's mind dismissed anything that was not sensory or Susan. He pushed her against the wall and poured the extent of his wonder into his kiss.

SUSAN GRIPPED BURKE'S BROAD SHOULDERS AND HELD fast. He lifted her, and she circled him with her leg. It seemed like she couldn't get close enough. Burke suspended her between his chest and the wall, steadying them with one hand. His kiss reached the depth of her soul. For a second, she opened her eyes and gazed at his chiseled features to reassure herself that this was real and not a fantasy. She'd dreamt about him before, but never had she felt his solidness and the demand of his body. The sensation ignited a blue-fiery flame low in her abdomen, and her head rolled back.

Burke feasted on her neck and trailed feverish kisses down to the neckline of her dress. His free hand moved from her face to her side and slid up the silky fabric. He cupped her breast, and she gasped. Clear, bright-blue eyes flashed open and stared into hers. Susan searched their depth and glimpsed forever. Her own eyes filled with warm tears.

His brow dipped, and his head tilted slightly. Over panting breaths he whispered. "Are you okay? Do you want me to stop?"

"I'm incredibly happy, that's all. Absolutely. Do. Not. Stop."

He grinned, and she felt his pleasure clear down to her curling toes. "Your wish, is my..." He never finished, instead he showed her he had a perfect understanding of her desire. Burke swept his arm under her knees and carried her to her bed. He laid her down as if she was made of spun glass and gazed at her with such tenderness her heart ached.

"You're the most beautiful woman in all creation." He whispered as though to himself. Burke ran his fingers under the spaghetti straps on her shoulders and pulled her dress away. His eyes filled with adoration.

A sudden pressure weighed down on Susan's chest. She felt incapable of living up to the purity of his expression, but Burke quickly quieted her concern.

"You're stunning." Burke tore his tie from his collar and undid a few buttons before getting frustrated and yanking his shirt off over his head. He kicked off his shoes and lowered himself to the bed. Propping himself above her on his forearm, he found her mouth with his once again.

Susan skimmed her fingers over his flexed biceps, and a delicious inner tremor demanded more. She pulled him closer and reached for his belt. The heat of their passion flared. All she was aware of was Burke—his eyes, his mouth, and every solid inch of his body. Nothing else in the universe existed.

Merging with him was like the righting of all things wrong, the relief of an out-of-tune symphony coming together. Their separate beings gliding from dissonance into a pristine harmony that hummed through their souls intertwining them so beautifully she cried.

Burke traced the track of her tear with soft, warm kisses. "You—We—This, was worth waiting for, but I never want to be apart from you again."

He made love to her again slowly and with an unbearable reverence Susan wanted to spend the rest of her life earning. He took her to heights she'd never known were possible, as if he knew her body better than she did.

At some point they slept. Or perhaps she had died in bliss and now floated across the heavens, a whispered echo of purity and love.

Chapter Thirty

Was it the coffee or the delectable scent of bacon sizzling that woke her? Susan rolled over in the tangle of sheets and comforter. She pulled one pillow from over her face and kicked at others bunched at the foot of the bed. Memories of her night with Burke filtered through her groggy mind and lit a satisfied smile across her face. Susan sat up, stacking pillows behind her, tugging the covers up over her chest.

"Good morning, beautiful." Burke entered her room carrying a mug of steaming coffee and wearing only a towel wrapped around his hips.

Susan's smile jumped in voltage. "Hello." Her gaze dipped from his smile to his tantalizing chest, dusted with golden blond curls.

"Hungry?"

Her smile changed to a naughty grin. "Yes, as a matter of fact. I may never be full again."

He chuckled. "That sounds like a challenge." He handed her the mug. "One I'll be happy to address after we re-energize. I'm starving." He kissed the tip of her nose. "Be right back."

Burke left, and Susan enjoyed watching the terry cloth cling to his backside as he walked. She sipped from her cup, resigning herself to becoming a coffee drinker.

THEY SAT TOGETHER ON THE BED WITH A TRAY OF bacon, eggs, toast, and mimosas between them. After eating, Burke gazed at her for a long while saying nothing.

"What's going on in that brilliant mind of yours?" Susan reached for his hand.

Burke removed the tray and sat on his knees next to her. He ran his fingers down her arms until he held her hands in his. The look in his eyes gave her a slight alarm. He looked happy—almost drunk, though she knew he wasn't—not on one mimosa. She cocked her head to the side and was about to speak when he slid his hand under his pillow and pulled out a small blue box.

Susan's eyes flew open, and she covered her mouth.

"Susan Tabitha Bell, I love you more than my life and more than anything in it. When I thought I'd lost you forever, I couldn't imagine going on. A life without you in it wouldn't be worth living. Susan, will you do me the honor of becoming my wife?"

Tears sprang from her eyes, and a sob escaped her throat. She gave a trembling giggle. "Are you asking me to marry you and stay home and have your babies?"

He grinned in his self-deprecating way. "Or, you can build a career and become the CEO of a major corporation. I don't care. I've learned that all I want is for you to have whatever your heart desires. I'm just hoping that includes marrying me."

Susan held out her left hand to him. "Yes, Burke. Yes. I want to marry you more than anything." She laughed. "And be a CEO... *and* have your babies."

Burke slid a beautiful emerald-cut diamond solitaire onto her finger and rose on his knees, pulling her up to join him. He enveloped her in a spine-dissolving kiss.

"I had something more elegant in mind for the proposal," he murmured into her ear, his breath sending sparks skittering across her skin. "But I couldn't wait."

"I'm so happy you didn't."

AFTER SPENDING THE REST OF THE MORNING AND EARLY afternoon in bed, they finally emerged from their cocoon.

"I want to tell everyone that we're engaged." Susan held her hand out away from her and stared at the elegant diamond gracing her finger. She had to share their news, or she'd burst. "First, let's call Rick and Kendra. Then we can call our parents."

Susan clicked her phone to FaceTime. Before Kendra even said hello, Susan thrust her left hand in front of the camera to show off her new engagement ring. "We're engaged!"

Kendra grasped her cell close and peered at the screen. "That's gorgeous! Wow! Congratulations!" She bounced back into her spot on the couch beside Rick. "This is so wonderful!"

Annie's black nose appeared on the screen, and Susan clapped. "Did you hear, girl? I'm getting married!"

Annie barked and offered the newly engaged couple her warmest Labrador smile.

"Sorry, Kendra, but I think I will have to ask Annie to be my maid of honor."

Kendra laughed. "I'll back her up."

A grin flashed across Rick's face. "Congratulations, you two. We couldn't be happier for you."

"Neither could we." Burke snuggled Susan into his side. "I can't imagine life ever gets better than this."

- The End -

THANK YOU SO MUCH FOR READING *BODY COUNT*. I HOPE you enjoyed it!

It would absolutely make my day if you would take a minute to leave a review on Amazon. Thank you!

- Jodi

Review Body Count

Order Book 3 Now! - Concealed Cargo
The next book in the FBI-K9 Series Now!

Concealed Cargo

WHEN SPECIAL AGENT CLAY JENNINGS AND HIS K9 partner, Ranger, take to the streets of Denver to fight human trafficking, he is shocked by the inordinate number of stolen innocents who've been forced into the sex trade. With each new face, his resolve to help these children escape their personal horror grows stronger.

El Clark, a social worker who dedicates her life to rescuing exploited kids from the streets, works valiantly to locate their families or find them a safe place to live while they recuperate. She understands the plight of these young victims more than anyone knows.

When these two champions of enslaved children team up, they discover a web of deviant corruption that reaches into the upper echelons of US politics and society. Adding to the nightmare, a vicious serial killer focused on murdering female prostitutes threatens to pull Clay and El away from unearthing the man behind the treacherous, Colorado-based, child prostitution ring.

For Clay, working to solve these crimes is like taking one step forward and three back until El shares her story with him. Inspired by her bravery and fortitude, he is re-committed to the fight for justice. Clay and El battle against a mountain of power and money the height of which they'd never conceived, and end up building a powerful bond with one another along the way. El teaches Clay that every life they change matters—that they must do what they can, even when it's only one child at a time.

Stay up-to-date on all my new releases and other news.
Join my mailing list!
or
Visit my website at Jodi-Burnett.com

Acknowledgments

Thank you to all the many people who help me put *Body Count* out into the world. My Beta Readers and everyone on my Advanced Reader Team are invaluable to the process of writing a book. I couldn't do it without you all. Thanks especially to my husband, Chris, who has to live each day with my imagination, questions, and self-doubt. His encouragement helps me get to the end of each book. And thanks, of course, to the good Lord who continues to pave my way.

About the Author

Jodi Burnett is a Colorado native. She loves writing Romantic Thrillers from her small ranch southeast of Denver where she also enjoys her horses, complains about her cows, and writes to create a home for her imaginings. Inspired by life in the country, Jodi fosters her creative side by writing, watercolor painting, quilting, and crafting stained-glass. She is a member of Sisters In Crime, Rocky Mountain Fiction Writers, and Novelists, Inc.

Jodi-Burnett.com

Also by Jodi Burnett

Flint River Series

Run For The Hills - Book 1

Hidden In The Hills - Book 2

Danger In The Hills - Book 3

A Flint River Christmas - Free Series Epilogue

FBI-K9 Series

Avenging Adam - Book 1